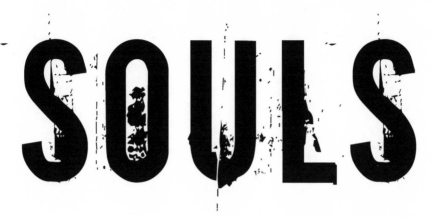SOULS

BOOK ONE

THE BATTLE FOR OUR ETERNAL DESTINY

HOPE HOLLINSWORTH COAXUM
BOB TODARO

DIVINE WISDOM PRESS

I truly thank God for the inspiration to write this book and for the blessing of co-authoring it with Hope Hollinsworth Coaxum. I dedicate my efforts to all those, who in spite of the difficulties and struggles of this life, strive to live each day by the guiding principles of love, kindness, compassion and empathy for others. "Whatever you do for the least of these my brothers, you do unto me." (Matthew 25:40.)

—Bob Todaro

TO MY BELOVED FAMILY

…you know who you are. For always loving me and supporting me. You have given me the priceless gift of affection embraced in a safe space where no one can touch, in such measure that will bring me happiness and comfort for the rest of my existence. I Love You

TO MY FRIENDS

…you know who you are. For our untold stories, for your abundance of laughter, your overwhelming support, for always being there in good times and bad. I adore You

TO MY CHILDREN AND GRANDCHILD

Thank you for letting me truly understand the kind of love that will last beyond the moon and the skies above. You are my everything.

Read this book with the Assurance of everlasting life!

—Hope Hollinsworth Coaxum

CONTENTS

Preface by Bob Todaro ix

Preface by Hope Holinsworth Coaxum xii

Prologue 1

1. Text Styles Inc. 17
2. The Takeover 25
3. Impulse Reaction 32
4. Escape 45
5. The Element and Cost of Corruption 51
6. Victor's Reality 68
7. Critical Situations 76
8. Casualties of War and Life 90
9. The Power of a Mother's Love 97
10. The Angels are Watching 108
11. In the Blink of an Eye 121
12. Distractions and New Beginnings 128
13. Old Acquaintances and New Faces 134
14. The Books Tell the Stories 138
15. Protocols, Probes and Progress 145
16. Wheels in Motion 158
17. A Deadly Night 173
18. Actions Have Consequences 179
19. What Happens in the Dark Comes to Light 184
20. Evil Versus Good 191

21. The Police Investigation and the Truth 197

22. Clean Slate 211

23. Liberation 216

24. Afterlife 225

Epilogue 234

About the Authors 240

"THE BATTLE LINE BETWEEN GOOD AND EVIL RUNS THROUGH THE HEART OF EVERY MAN."

—Aleksandr Solzhenitsyn

PREFACE

BY BOB TODARO

My purpose in writing SOULS is to take a closer look at some fundamental principles in life we sometimes take for granted. Our lives are a constant series of choices. All of our choices, and subsequent actions, do have consequences. Some are inconsequential while others can be life altering. Our decisions not only impact us but those around us as well, yet we don't always pay attention to all the factors and forces influencing our decisions.

The world has shown us there are both good and evil forces at play in our lives. Through God, we are all created with a pre-disposition for goodness, kindness, compassion and love. After all, we are created in His image. In God's infinite wisdom, He gave us free will. Free will gives us the ability to make our own choices and determinations. It is why love and compassion are truly meaningful when they are given and received unconditionally. They are not robotic responses, but a conscious choice we make for ourselves. That is the true beauty of what God created us to be. We all have the innate ability to choose our path in life and this is what makes us fully human.

Yet, just as there are forces of light and love all around us leading us to make good decisions, there are also forces of darkness. These forces seek to destroy our souls, obliterating the goodness that God created in us.

The demonic are the fallen angels of heaven who, out of hatred for God, want to destroy us. Many people choose to ignore this and many deny their existence by treating them as purely mythical characters. Convincing us they do not exist is the first victory against us for the underworld. Yet there is evil all around us, never ceasing to influence our behavior and choices. It's undeniable. Hatred, discrimination, racism, abuse, violence, murder and destruction are the trademarks of evil. The absence of God's light is the darkness of the demonic and it is real.

Mankind is constantly tempted to want more from the secular world. Whether its power, possessions, lust or fame, the inclination to want these things often comes from dark places. Anywhere there is an absence of love, evil can flourish if it's fed. Darkness looks to exploit weakness, playing on personal pride and pushing its victims to a selfish mindset, making them feel a greater sense of entitlement. The demonic focuses on convincing us to be 'me' centered instead of 'we' centered.

But how can they succeed if we are made in God's image? Shouldn't we be immune to the temptations and deceptions of evil? Yes, it's true we are made in His image, but the same gift of free will that enlightens us is also used by the demonic against us. They use our own humanness to exploit our weaknesses. Through lies, deception and deceit, they work to convince us we are being taken advantage of by others. They utilize greed, pride, envy and jealousy as ways to pit us against each other. They stoke the flames of resentment, anger and personal pride to get us to become self-righteous. If you don't think evil exists, just take a closer look at the world around you.

So how can we withstand this silent onslaught of the demonic? The only way is by putting on the full armor of God each day...

"Finally, be strong in the Lord and in his mighty power. Put on the full armor of God, so that you can take your stand against the devil's schemes. For our struggle is not against flesh and blood, but against the rulers, against the authorities, against the powers of this dark world and against the spiritual forces of evil in the heavenly realms. Therefore put on the full armor of God, so that when the day of evil comes, you may be able to stand your ground, and after you have done everything, to stand firm.

Stand firm then, with the belt of truth buckled around your waist, with the breastplate of righteousness in place, and with your feet fitted with the readiness that comes from the gospel of peace. In addition to all this, take up the shield of faith, with which you can extinguish all the flaming arrows of the evil one. Take the helmet of salvation and the sword of the Spirit, which is the word of God. And pray in the Spirit on all occasions with all kinds of prayers and requests. With this in mind, be alert and always keep on praying for all the Lord's people."

Ephesians 6:10-18 NIV

My hope is that as you read this book, you will realize there truly is a battle raging all around you and you are right in the middle of it. If you need a reminder, turn on the news media. The good news is that we do have a choice in our eternal destiny...

PREFACE

BY HOPE HOLINSWORTH COAXUM

I was in search of a way to tell a story that was encouraging and appealing but also, in some way, a life lesson. We all have life lessons, purpose and choices that are part of our very being. I, you, we have an opportunity set forth in front of us, to choose, to be honest with one's self and in making decisions that form our lives and how we live them. Although this novel/book is fiction, our actions are dictated and executed in everyday life, which is reality. We are given free will to decide, determining how those decisions will not only influence our lives but all those we interact with. Having free will is one of the most independent choices that we take full responsibility for. I'm sure you've heard the term, "I do this of my own free will", therefore giving you the capacity to act at one's own preference. Free will defines your moral responsibility, your behavior and your reaction to whatever life has in store for you. You choose, we choose and I choose as we all are distinctive.

My motivation within this novel is to show not only the goodness and the beauty of God's kindness, love, joy, peace, patience and favor, but His mercy, His humanity and forgiveness. He is all of those precious things and so much more. And as we embrace what He offers us as humans, there are dark forces that are constantly pulling us in the opposite direction, forces that are preying upon us and tugging at our "free will", our choice, and our decisions. There is a constant battle within us that is taking place. It is comparable to the term good and evil, asking the questions of how you will live and what choices will you make.

In search of what this book would entail and how the story would be told was easy in one sense, as it focused on a portion of the good within humanity. The portion manifested as strength and the wisdom and the gestures of thoughtfulness. Yet the story wouldn't be valid if the propensity of evil wasn't explored. When we speak of the unseen, the angels and the goodness of heaven, we also must speak of the fallen angels of hell and the evil that threatens us, exposing deception, worry, greed, pride and envy and the shallowness of where we are most vulnerable to the forces around us. It channels hate and unrest filled with glorified self-righteousness that is no longer hidden, but visualized in the world around us, eyes wide open.

So the battle rages on, the conflict between good and evil at the surface, creation pushing forward, busting at the seams and you have a decision, a choice to examine within yourself as to what your fate will be. What will you choose?

PROLOGUE

It's a typical busy weekday morning in New York City. The sun is up and shining brightly without a cloud in the sky. The streets are lively with people scurrying about to work, school or wherever the day has planned before them. Some stop at the nearby coffee shop, grabbing their morning latte, while others hail a cab at a busy street corner. Buses and cars fill the air with the noise of their horns and engines. A siren of a passing ambulance rushing by adds to the everyday sounds of a busy city. It all seems normal, with nothing out of place in the streets of New York.

Suddenly, the sky fills with an ominous bank of dark clouds, seemingly threatening as if a storm is fast approaching, declaring the nature of a future event, good or evil. The dark clouds swirl and shift quickly, depriving the sky of the sun, continually turning the day into night and night into day. In an instant, the sky is overcome with large, dark and menacing figures, the demonic angels of hell. You can feel the evil just by glancing at them. Their faces transform repeatedly from a human likeness into ghoulish distortions. Their large dark wings spread six feet wide across their backs as they appear and disappear repeatedly.

A few become hundreds, then thousands, swiftly darting back and forth through the sky, narrowly missing one another. There are so many they outnumber all the people on the busy streets. The demons are all around the people, circling above them, watching them closely. The people in the streets have no knowledge they are being watched. The demons are undetectable to the mere human. Their menacing presence cannot be seen nor heard.

In that same moment, angelic figures appear. These figures are a unique combination of strength and beauty. They have an aura and glow about them that is righteous and good. After all, they are the angels of God. Undetected, like their demonic counterparts, they are there to fight the demons and protect the humans as best they can.

As people scurry about the city, banter takes place in the sky as the angels and demons engage each other. Each knows the intimate details of the people's lives, distinguishing who are the sinners and who are the saints. The demons know which of their prey are rooted in sin, making them opportune targets for destruction. The angels know those with a loving heart, working to keep them in the light of God. Both the angels and the demons are restricted by the actions of the humans. They merely observe them, looking for influential opportunities to lead them further down a path of sin or righteousness. Each human possesses free will and the ability to choose their own actions. The angels and demons are there to either assist or exploit them.

The backchat between the angels and demons becomes loud and expressive in the sky above, amongst the clouds. The demons start to follow certain people, trying to attack their souls. The angels thwart them at every opportunity. Some people seem well protected by the angels, while others present themselves as easy victims for the demons. The rest seem vulnerable to either side. This immense battle between the angels and demons rages all around, indiscernible to the people below. Abruptly, within an instant, all the angels and demons vanish as the humans continue about their ordinary day.

In the bowels of hell, there is a dark and gloomy room. You can feel the intense heat as the horrible smell of burning sulphur fills the air. There is nothing pleasant about this place. The walls are dark stone, with steamy, stench-filled slime clinging to them. The room is claustrophobic, with a thick, choking feel to it. The atmosphere is riddled with fear and hate. Its darkness and despair would be more than anyone could stand, even for a moment.

Dante is giving instructions in his lair. He stands in the front of the room, drilling his minions. He is a large, imposing figure, strong and arrogant in his swagger. His look and demeanor are both menacing and intimidating. His face is humanlike, but his body is a cross between human and spirit. His body looks semi-transparent, but still like a real human. He is dressed in all black. His facial expression is one of pure terror and anger. His piercing glance strikes fear in anyone caught in his line of sight. Everything about him is pure evil, a complete absence of anything remotely good. He is the demonic leader of Satan's angels, the general, so to speak. He is the supreme commander in charge of wreaking havoc on earth with the express purpose of pulling souls into hell.

The plan to destroy souls has been detailed and carefully orchestrated throughout time. For Dante, it's all about execution and numbers. But this is not a democracy. It's a "demon-ocracy." His orders are demands and the constant message is one of strict obedience, couched in deep fear. All demons under his rule are strictly subordinate to him. They do not dare step out of line or ever question his authority.

Dante looks out at his demons sitting before him in disgust. Whatever they do, it's never good enough for him. Evil is never satisfied. It can't be. It simply thirsts for more and more evil and destruction. His demon subordinates, although knowing he is far superior to them in stature, are just as evil nonetheless. In fact, the more they absorb Dante's wrath and impatience, the more they will project their own evil onto their human targets. They listen to his instructions carefully, in hopes of gaining insight into how to impress and please him. The only reward for them is to please Dante in such a manner that he might report their efforts up the chain of command. Their hope is to one day be revered by Satan himself for their cunning and ability to destroy souls and possibly earn for themselves a higher position in the demonic hierarchy. But make no mistake, there is no one, other than Satan himself, more powerful than Dante.

Dante impatiently paces back and forth in front of the room. Suddenly, he turns abruptly to his demon subordinates and starts his verbal tirade.

3

"I am not pleased with our current progress. In fact, it's pathetic. Our supreme ruler is angry. Must you tempt his wrath...and mine? Must I remind you our enemy is doing all He can to save these worthless humans? Your job is simple. Destroy them by any means possible and make them lose their souls to us. There is no excuse for ever letting up on your prey.

"Be relentless," Dante continues. "Use every available weapon at your disposal: pride, envy, greed, lust, gluttony, wrath, sloth. They're not called the seven deadly sins for nothing. Disguise your deceit and lie in half truths. They are too stupid to realize the difference. Don't let up on these weak, wretched beings. They are more vulnerable than their pathetic minds realize. They think they're intelligent, yet some of them are more easily manipulated than a mere child."

His eyes suddenly become balls of flames as his voice vibrates down below.

"You need to be relentless. Sharpen your attacks. It's easy to outwit these creatures. They succumb so easily it's laughable. They all possess free will, that so-called wonderful gift from their creator that leads them right to us. These putrid, gullible creatures are easily conned and swayed in our direction. Dangle temptations in front of their greedy little eyes and they can't help themselves. They are so full of their own self-worth they think they're entitled to everything. Even the ones who claim personal pride. Toss in opportunities to use their weak counterparts to piss them off and cause resentment and anger. They'll tumble right to us if you push them hard enough.

"Lead them into sin! Strengthen what is evil in your prey, multiply occasions of sin and help benumb their souls till it sinks them into a state of lethargy and apathy. Good is bad, bad is good. That is the road which is fatal to them. Especially the ones who think they're 'spiritual.' What an undefined crock of crap that is. The ambiguity of how they view what 'spirituality' actually means gives them the audacity to define it on their own terms, not their creator's terms. They are so vulnerable through their own self-righteous stupidity you should be scooping them up with a shovel. They conveniently toss out the principles and teachings of our enemy and create their own values. They pick and choose what to believe in, what makes them personally feel good. What morons. Add in the droves of them who don't believe in 'organized religion.' We don't either—we hate everything from our enemy—but these pathetic individuals use it to justify their own egos. This is a special bunch.

"Seduce the ones who convince themselves that they are 'good people' because they didn't commit murder or other extreme acts. Yet they redefine everything in the world to fit their way of thinking. How convenient. They are too ignorant to realize they are making themselves into their own personal deities, with their own personal belief systems. They are ripe for the picking. As long as it's good for them, they do it. They don't want to be told what to believe. This is truly an army of new recruits we can count on, if we are relentless in pushing them down the road to their own destruction. How pathetic these creatures are! If it wasn't for the damn enemy and His angels assisting them, we'd have them all.

"Beware of our enemy," Dante continues, focused and determined, his body now floating across the fiery hot room. "As much as we despise them, they are nonetheless cunning. They'll play on emotions and those 'heavenly' traits of love, forgiveness and mercy. What a farce! They look to infuse principles of kindness, love and compassion, whatever those are. Yet if we are not diligent, these weak humans will succumb to it. The more opportunities the enemy gives them to be teary-eyed and emotional, the greater the risk of them slipping away from us. Pride 'drives the bus' to all their sins. It opens the door to self-centered thinking. Push them down that road...hard! Don't let them fall into the trap of our enemy of wanting to be forgiven for their past indiscretions and wanting to be helpful and kind to each other. Convince them there is nothing to be forgiven for.

"The enemy has this grandiose concept of sin, as if some actions have no justification and merit and need to be avoided, requiring their repentance if committed. What a joke. It's laughable. It's just

His way of telling them what they can't do or shouldn't do. Make them stay focused on doing whatever they want if it feels good. Make them understand there are no inappropriate pleasures, just pleasures they are denying themselves based on the enemy's rules. The most vulnerable to us are the ones who convince themselves it's just the enemy's attempt at controlling them. The more we can lead them down this road, the more we can make them eventually doubt the enemy even exists. This is the ultimate opportunity to snatch THEIR SOULS. As soon as we can get them to abandon the enemy and His assistance, they are ours. They are too stupid and weak to realize that by themselves. They become defenseless.

"We have most of them already convinced there is no hell and that our supreme leader doesn't even exist. They think he is a simple character in a book who tempted one of them to bite an apple. Purely fictional. Ignorant fools. They have convinced themselves of their own personal righteousness. I especially love when one of them dies. They all hold some memorial service and speak glowingly of their dearly departed. They always assume the deceased are looking down on them from up above and smiling, content in some wonderful afterlife. They are too ignorant to realize the hordes of them who are here with us! Imagine if they only knew how many of their beloved deceased are looking up at them from their torturous eternity with us in hell! They think they all go to heaven regardless of how they lived. What fools!

"That's enough for now. You have too much work to do for me to keep you here any longer. Don't let up. Don't let souls escape us! Get after your assignments and bring me souls. Now go!!!"

As the demons fly away, Dante stands in front of the room in his agitated state. He paces back and forth. He knows the supreme ruler is relentless in his expectations. He is never satisfied. There is never any letup, never enough souls until every last one is dragged from the enemy.

Pondering briefly, Dante says aloud, "O supreme ruler, I will not fail you," before flying upward into a cloud of flames and vanishing.

Far away from the depths of hell is the heavenly realm, a place of indescribable beauty. Anything beautiful the mind can imagine, from flowers of every kind to lush greens and rolling hills, is everywhere. The most beautiful thoughts and memories that come to mind are instantly visible. The feeling is pure love, calmness and tranquility.

Matthias is the head of a group of good angels assigned to do battle with the demons. They work to assist souls in their earthly journey, with the goal of leading them to heaven. Matthias is under the leadership of Michael the Archangel, who is assigned by God to be the protector of all men and women against the wickedness and snares of the devil. God's angels are there to rebuke Satan and all his evil spirits who travel throughout the world, seeking the ruin of souls. At the prompting of all who pray for assistance, Matthias and his angels intervene wherever they can. Through the mercy of Almighty God, they assist everyone, even those that have fallen away from God's light. After all, they are all created in His divine image and likeness. Through God's endless mercy and inexhaustible compassion, divine assistance is always there for all. For those who have fallen away, the angels work harder to fight the efforts of Satan and his minions to lead them deeper into sin.

Matthias addresses his team of angels. Although angels are spiritual beings, they take on human form from time to time. In certain situations, they appear to humans as other people to take advantage of fitting moments to console, encourage and assist. Angels can also appear as a light, as a feeling or as a sound. Here, in front of his team of angels, Matthias is in human form. He is strikingly handsome, dressed in all white. His angels look like both male and female humans but have an aura around them that makes them look both angelic and human at the same time.

There are a multitude of angels gathered around Matthias for instruction. The atmosphere here is calm and loving, quite the opposite of Dante's in his demon lair.

"Michael our Archangel is pleased with our progress thus far. He obviously knows what we are up against. You all know our job is to continually help every soul in need of a greater love of God. God gave them free will, so the choice is ultimately theirs. Free will allows them to choose between accepting God's love or, unfortunately, rejecting it. Some are caught in the middle, as the events of their lives make them inconsistent in their decisions. Pride sometimes gets in the way and they lose focus. The influences of the world and the underworld are quite powerful. The underworld has been successful in creating a growing secular culture, one which celebrates the individual and celebrates tolerance at the expense of truth and love. The forces of evil constantly look to eradicate God from everyday life and get people to center their focus on individuality. Sadly, this is happening more and more, and our task is becoming more challenging. If they only knew the depths of God's love for them, there would be no battle with the demons of hell.

"The good news is they were all created to love God, so it's embedded within them. They are all predisposed to goodness, love, compassion and kindness. We need to help them move always toward the light and protect them from Satan and his demons. Satan knows he has an opening for a time in this world to destroy souls. Free will works both ways. He and his demons are relentless, and the power of their deceit is very strong. It's often well disguised. Never underestimate the 'father of all lies.' We need to assist in situations where adoration, kindness and forgiveness can change hearts. Seek opportunities to uplift those in need, especially those in pain, those in despair and those that are losing hope. The power of God's love is so much stronger than anything evil can throw at them; they just need our assistance to see beyond the wicked. Stay focused on those who are especially vulnerable. The demons prey on the lonely, the disconnected, the abandoned and afraid. They seize opportunities to exploit those who are having difficulties by feeding them lies. They will stop at nothing to turn those in need further away from God's truth and forgiveness. It is imperative we encourage and increase moments of hope and love whenever we can.

"So off we go into battle, with the power of God with us. Praise be to our Lord, now and forever."

The angels and demons have both left their instructional sessions, flying off from heaven and hell en route to their current endeavors. It's as if they are racing each other, acutely aware of their adversary's determination to seek immediate openings to impact souls.

In the city of Chicago, angels and demons swoop through the sky, past the downtown buildings and skyscrapers, racing towards an old apartment building on the south side. They arrive just outside a window on the fifth floor, anticipating something happening.

A slender woman named Susan awakens from a restless night's sleep. Her face is drawn and pale as she shuffles from the bedroom into the living room of her apartment. She is dressed in an old blue cotton bathrobe, which covers her worn-out pink flannel pajamas. As her bare feet hit the cold floor, she pauses, turns and steps into her pair of ragged faux leather slippers. Her hair is unkempt and messy, as she didn't bother to brush it after she awoke. Her expression is blank, as if she is completely tuned out from her surroundings. There is obviously something heavy weighing on her mind. As she sits in her drab apartment, she sips coffee from a worn white coffee mug. The words "Rise and Shine" printed on the mug are faded to the point you can hardly read them. Susan turns on the TV but barely pays attention to it. She appears worried, as something is deeply troubling her. She glances down at the coffee table and repeatedly stares at an unopened envelope, seemingly afraid to open it. She instinctively knows what it is, but she can't bring herself to tear it open. The name on the envelope reads "Thomas H. Driscoll, Esq." With a nervous look on her face, she finally musters up enough courage to tear it open.

Susan speaks the words on the page out loud in a whisper. As tears well up in her eyes, she begins to sob. A look of complete despair engulfs her face. "He's filing for a divorce," she says over and over in a low whisper. A single teardrop starts to trickle down her

9

left cheek and falls onto the paper as she reads the words *is suing for full custody of their two children*. Susan is no longer able to control her silent cry and bursts into tears of pure sorrow. Each falling tear lands on the paper, smearing the ink of the words. She then hides her face in her palms and sobs. All at once, she is overcome with a flood of emotions. First, in anger, she curses her husband's name. "Screw you, John. You asshole." Quickly, though, her anger turns to dread and fear, consuming her. She slumps back on the couch and sits in silence, looking down at the floor while holding the letter, completely lost in deep thought.

After about ten minutes of sitting there listlessly, she rises slowly from her slumped position and walks out of her apartment in a complete daze. She walks out into the hallway and solemnly climbs up the staircase that leads to the roof. As she takes a few steps up the stairs, she lets the letter slip from her hand. It falls behind her. When she gets to the top of the stairs, she pushes open the door. The morning breeze hits her face as it rustles her hair. She steps out onto the roof and walks to the edge of the building. Without looking down, she pauses for a final moment, wiping the lingering tears from her face. The full reality hits her and she knows she can't go on. She takes a step up on the concrete ledge. She briefly looks up towards the sky and then steps off the edge of the building, and her body plunges to the street below. A driver in a passing car sees her body violently crash into the ground. In sheer horror, the driver slams on his brakes, but he can't stop the car before it rams into a parked delivery van. The car's airbag deploys, saving the driver from hitting the windshield.

Shrieks of shock fill the street as an ordinary morning becomes a tragic death scene. Her lifeless, broken body lies bleeding on the sidewalk. Suddenly, a bright white unbroken cloud gently cascades from the sky above. Angels disperse from it, one by one, and settle about her lifeless body. A few seconds later, dark shadowy figures emerge from deep beneath the street below. The demons are on the scene, but they are met by the protective wall of angels surrounding Susan. The demons, seeing their adversary encamped around her, realize this soul is protected. They retreat and slip beneath the surface of the street in disgust, hurling insults at the angels. The demons' job is to be there as instructed, but they don't always know who the soul belongs to until the moment it passes from life to death. This was not their soul to claim, so they must submit to defeat for now.

IN THE MOUNTAINS OF NEW HAMPSHIRE, DENNIS BARNWELL, A bearded, husky man in his late fifties, is driving his hunter-green Ford Bronco along his usual route to work. It's a crisp but cloudy Tuesday morning along the scenic Kancamagus Highway, a beautiful road that runs through the majestic White Mountains of the Granite State. Out of nowhere, a confused deer runs across the road. Dennis catches the darting dear out of the corner of his eye. He swerves to avoid it, but it hits the hood of his Bronco with tremendous force, bouncing off it and smashing into his windshield. He loses control of the truck as he tries to steer it. The truck crashes violently through the guardrail and down a steep embankment. The Bronco flips over five times and smashes into rocks below, coming to rest on its side on the bank of a large stream. All the windows are shattered and there is broken glass and mangled metal all around. The roof of the truck is collapsed around Dennis. He is badly injured. This stretch of road is remote, and unless another vehicle was close by or heard the crash, he knows he may not be found. It's apparent that his legs are broken as they are pinned beneath the steering column. He is bleeding heavily from a deep gash on his head. His left shoulder is dislocated. His severe injuries cause Dennis to go in and out of consciousness. He knows he's in trouble. He struggles to see if he can find his phone, but with the wreck, it's nowhere in sight. Thoughts of his wife and children flood his head. He quietly hopes and prays someone saw or heard the crash. He softly starts to pray the Lord's Prayer:

"Our Father, who art in heaven …"

His breathing becomes heavy and labored. He closes his eyes as he slowly and quietly slips away into unconsciousness. At just that moment, there's a burst of sunlight that pierces the clouds and it shines ever so brightly on his face. A sense of peace overtakes him. His labored breathing is no more, yet his prayer fills and quivers in the air. The heavenly angels appear in an instant, flying down the embankment and into Dennis's truck, surrounded by bright light. Then a beam of light ascends in a flash toward the sky as the angels take Dennis's soul to heaven. There are no demons to be seen near him, for Dennis was a truly blessed man.

———

IN A SMALL SUBURBAN TOWN IN NEW JERSEY, AN UNASSUMING two-family home on Fairfield Street is bathed in the warm sun of a beautiful day. At 17 Fairfield Street, there sits a quaint old brick center-hall colonial home. In the backyard, just down the driveway, sits a garage made of the same weathered brick. It's a typical garage inside, but the owner keeps it fairly organized with not too much clutter. Adjacent to the garage is a small yard with a rusted sliding pond and swing set. A round glass patio table and four lawn chairs sit atop an older brick patio. The surrounding grass is worn and sprinkled about, telling that young children once lived and played there. The main door to the garage is closed, as is a side entrance.

Inside the garage is a young girl in her late teens. Her name is Peggy Mulvey. She lives in the downstairs apartment of this home with her mother and brother. The homeowners are at work, as is her mother. Her younger brother is at band practice at the high school. Peggy is a plain-looking girl with long, stringy dirty-blond hair. She is rather skinny and awkward, dressed in ordinary jeans, a dark blue T-shirt and some old worn sneakers. She's sitting alone in a chair in the center of the garage, anxious and in deep thought. Her eyes are red from crying. In her hand is a letter in an envelope that simply says "Mom." She has a Bible in her lap. She reads a verse or two and then closes her eyes and mouths a prayer. After a few moments, she puts the letter down and the Bible on the ground. As she stands up, she says in a low voice, "I'm sorry, Mom…I love you."

She glances up at a rope tied to a beam onto the garage ceiling, which she placed there earlier with a ladder. She stands on the chair, wobbling a little, while putting the loop of the rope around her neck. She mouths the words without sound: "Forgive me."

Without much hesitation, she quickly kicks the chair away from underneath her and hangs herself. The rope pulls tight and shakes the beam. It begins to crack under the weight of her body. As the rope tightens around her neck, Peggy's entire body struggles. The rope begins to choke her to death. Her legs and arms flail about violently. It continues for a few minutes, until suddenly, there is no movement at all. A complete stillness fills the garage. Peggy is dead. Demons swoop down and fly through the closed garage door and through the closed windows as their demonic spirit bodies allow them to do. Angels appear simultaneously. The demons try to approach Peggy, but the more powerful angels swoop in front of them and push them back with great force. They battle back and forth as the angels form a barrier around Peggy. The demons lash out at the angels.

"She killed herself. She committed suicide. Her soul is ours."

The angels multiply and crush the demons. The main angel says, "Have you not learned that judgment belongs to God alone? Begone, you wretched demons!"

The demons are enraged and depart in disgust. As the mortal life leaves Peggy's body, her soul is lifted into the angels' arms and they vanish straight up through the garage roof into the sky.

ELSEWHERE, IN A DARK ALLEY IN A RUN-DOWN PART OF DETROIT, demons descend out of the dark night sky, diving into the street and below it, out of sight. The alley at night is a place of deep gloom, a breeding ground for violence and evil—a place where the demons seem at home. A young male in his twenties, named Jesse, is out of breath. He's a scrawny-looking young adult, dressed in ripped jeans, a torn T-shirt and a dirty jean jacket. Jesse stands behind one of the buildings, counting bloodstained money. He just robbed a convenience store an hour ago, severely stabbing the clerk who tried to tackle him. He ran about six blocks, cutting between some buildings and up a small walkway to Montague Street to elude police. He looks out to make sure the police are nowhere in sight, stuffing the bloody money into the back pocket of his worn jeans.

At the corner, Jesse spots the usual drug dealers and approaches them to buy some heroin. The oldest one, named Sketch, looks at him up and down. "Well, if it isn't Messy Jesse. Did you bring some damn money this time?"

"Eff you," Jesse replies as he pulls the money from the robbery from his back pocket. "Here's your money." He shoves it into Sketch's hand.

"Wait, is that blood?" Sketch examines.

"I cut my finger on a piece of glass. It's money, ain't it? What do you care?" Jesse responds angrily.

Sketch hands him a small bag with heroin. "Pleasure doing business with you."

Jesse takes the heroin and turns and flees across the street. Sketch looks at the money once again, hunching his shoulders as if he doesn't care where the money came from.

"That boy is in a damn hurry to get high," cackles Sketch to his cohorts, stashing the money in his pocket as he watches Jesse run away.

Jesse runs back to the dark, secluded alley and cops a squat on a couple of broken milk crates next to a dumpster filled with garbage. Rats run past his feet and scurry away. They don't faze Jesse at all. He wipes the sweat from his brow and licks his lips in anticipation of a score. He quickly digs into his jacket pocket and pulls out a tarnished spoon. Nervous and anxious, he tries to steady his hand from shaking while scattering the heroin from the small wax bag onto the spoon. He secures himself on the crate, trying not to spill anything. He dips the tip of his tongue into the wax bag before tossing it, making sure not to leave one speck behind, then slowly rises from the crate, placing the spoon on top of it. Kneeling beside the crate, he pulls a needle and syringe from inside his jacket. He licks his lips again as sweat covers his forehead, yearning for a hit of the heroin. Carefully he cooks the heroin in the spoon while the flickers from the flame glow in his eyes.

The heroin liquifies, and Jesse cautiously fills the needle, biting his lip with eagerness. He briefly places the needle in his teeth while he ties off his arm with an elastic strap, right above his elbow. He then sticks the needle in his arm, ever so slowly. The drug starts to take effect, and he suddenly feels a deep sense of fear, sensing an evil presence around him. After a moment, his eyes roll back and he falls over unconscious.

In the corner of the alley, a small but visible light appears; it's his guardian angel. The angel looks at him in deep sadness, and as the bright light dims, the angel vanishes. A dark manifestation appears, then another. The demons have arrived. Multiple entities come up through the ground as an unpleasant stench overwhelms the air. Jesse lifts his head for a moment and takes his last breath. The demons move in. They tug at Jesse's limp body and pull a dark mist from his chest as they pull his soul from his body. They flee in haste to hell with Jesse's soul, down through the pavement. His lifeless body lies dead on the cold ground of the alleyway. Another young life wasted.

Back by the convenience store Jesse robbed, the police and an ambulance are on the scene. The clerk is lying on an ambulance transport stretcher. His name was Ayaan Bakshi. Ayaan had come to America from India with his family, seeking a better life. He was enrolled at the University of Michigan and he was studying medicine. He was working part-time at the store to help pay for his education. He loved being in America. He was a kind and gentle soul.

The internal bleeding from the stab wound was just too much. Ayaan gradually lost consciousness. An EMT yells, "We're losing him. We need to get him out of here."

Suddenly, there are bright beams of light all around the scene, though not visible to the people standing by. A multitude of angels appear, surrounding Ayaan as he takes his final breath. The EMTs check his pulse and they look at each other dejectedly.

"Damn, it's too late. We lost him."

The angels escort his soul to heaven as his body is loaded into the ambulance and they close the door behind him. Another senseless death from the consequences of the deadly power of drugs.

Angels and demons continue to go about their daily business across the earth, moving from situation to situation, from opportunity to opportunity, looking to save or steal souls.

"If all the demons that are here on earth were to take bodily form, they would blot out the light of the sun."
　　　　　　　　　　　　　　　　　　—Saint Padre Pio

"For what shall it profit a man, if he shall gain the whole world, and lose his own soul?" (Mark 8:36)

CHAPTER ONE

Text Styles Inc.

I t's a typical hot, sunny day in Southern California. The freeways in downtown LA are snarled with their usual congestion. It seems as if there's never any relief from the traffic, no matter the day or the weather.

In nearby Malibu, the ocean breeze makes the temperature a little bit more bearable. Just off the Pacific Coast Highway in Malibu Hills, a beautiful four-story glass-enclosed building overlooks the ocean. The glass has a deep blue tint, which cleanly reflects the warm California sun. The architecture is not only breathtaking but award-winning. The building is the home of the esteemed Text Styles Inc., one of the top textile design firms in the world. The building features beautiful terraces that wrap around the ocean side of the building, providing stunning views of the deep blue ocean. It's the appropriate place for this company. The architecture speaks to the talented design work that goes on inside.

Text Styles Inc. is the brainchild and creation of Maggie Hargrove. Maggie is an attractive brunette woman in her late forties. She's tall and slender, with striking features. She is smart, with a great personality and a somewhat sarcastic wit. She has a personable, sensitive and caring demeanor, although she can be tough as nails when the situation calls for it. She really doesn't like confrontation, but it sometimes comes with the territory. She's more about finding solutions than complaining.

Maggie is a founder and senior partner of the company. She is well known throughout the fashion and textile industries for her designs, which have garnered her and her firm multiple accolades and industry awards. She's known for her creativity and her keen sense of creating the right designs for her clients. Like any true artist, her gift allows her to see things through a different prism, making her work fresh, original and inspiring.

Maggie grew up in Elgin, Illinois, west of Chicago. Elgin was a predominantly blue-collar town back in those days, not exactly the kind of place a young girl's dreams are made of. Maggie was raised by Jane and Bill Hargrove—simple, hardworking parents who came from humble beginnings. Both were only educated as far as high school and were raised with a strong family and work ethic. Bill worked multiple jobs. By day he worked as a factory worker driving a forklift. By night, he drove a delivery truck for the Chicago Tribune. The hours were long and hard, and at times, it took a toll on Bill physically. As Bill liked to say, "I ain't got much, but it's mine and I worked for it."

Jane Hargrove worked as a classroom assistant at the local public school. She used to dream of being a teacher, but her family could never afford the tuition to pay for her teaching degree. The assistant's position was the next best thing to being an actual teacher. Money was always tight and the bills kept on coming, but like many others, the Hargroves always tried to do the best for their girls, Maggie and her younger sister, Kate. They raised their girls to appreciate what they had and consider anything beyond that a blessing.

Maggie was always good at drawing and painting. From a young age, she would spend hours drawing all kinds of pictures, with a meticulous bent for detail. Not only was Maggie the type to color inside the lines, but it had to look as good as it did neat. At Elgin High, she worked on every opportunity to do some type of art. She volunteered to work on scenery backdrops for the drama club. In fact, she was so good at it, teachers and faculty members sought her out to do everything from posters and flyers for school clubs to designing covers for award presentations. She just had a gift for bringing even a mundane project to life. A taller, skinny girl from a humble home, she defined herself by her artistic ability, dreaming of one day being a designer and having a career that utilized all her talent and flair for creativity with colors and patterns. When she got to her senior year at Elgin High, she dreamed of going to one of the better design schools in the country. She begged her parents to let her go to New York to study at the Fashion Institute of Technology. For her to escape the everyday, humdrum life of Elgin and study in one of the fashion design capitals of the world would be a dream come true.

Her parents knew they couldn't afford to send her there, not with two daughters to support and Bill struggling to make ends meet. They hated to dampen her enthusiasm, but they told her they just couldn't afford it. They encouraged her to set her sights on something local and told her to apply at a local community college and maybe find a job doing some graphic design in Chicago. Maggie was crushed. Once again, a dream had to be put on hold and she needed to make the best of it.

Maggie approached her guidance counselor, Mrs. Petrocelli, and told her the news about leaving the idea of attending FIT behind. Mrs. Petrocelli was especially fond of Maggie, as she was both a teacher and a mentor to her, so Maggie knew she would help her come up with another option.

"Maggie," Mrs. P said in a convincing tone, "I sent your transcript to FIT. Not only did they accept you, you're getting a full scholarship in their elite design program. They were so impressed with your portfolio, they called me personally. Maggie…you're going to FIT, even if I have to drive you there myself."

Maggie stared at Mrs. P with a shocked look on her face.

"A scholarship, to FIT?" Maggie said again in quizzical astonishment.

"Yes," Mrs. P said with joyful tears in her eyes, "you're going to FIT. Let's go call your mom."

Maggie hugged Mrs. P tightly, the kind of hug where you just don't want to let go. They walked down the hall towards Mrs. P's office as smiles brightened their faces. Suddenly, for Maggie, the drab hallways of Elgin High felt cleaner, wider and a little brighter. In that moment, Maggie saw a light of optimism and possibilities shine through the gray cloud of her little small-town world. That moment was one of the best in her life.

On this typically beautiful Malibu late afternoon, Maggie pulls up to work in a silver Mercedes SL convertible, pulling into her reserved executive parking spot. Today is Friday, the day of the annual Text Styles Inc.'s Founders party, celebrating their tenth year in business. Maggie started the firm after years of working her way through the ranks of notable design agencies. Her hard work is paying off as Text Styles Inc. is one of the most sought-after firms in the industry.

Maggie enters the lobby of their beautiful Malibu headquarters and takes the elevator to their penthouse offices. As she gets off the elevator, she sees that the party has already started, with colleagues and team members mingling about, sharing casual conversation and cocktails. From across the room, Maggie spots her ex-husband, Brad Collins. Brad is a venture capitalist by trade who invested in Text Styles Inc. when he and Maggie first met. Brad is tall, athletic, charismatic and handsome. Maggie was intoxicated by his good looks and charm, only to find out, over time, that behind the good-looking façade, she had married a manipulative, opportunistic egomaniac. His huge ego is only surpassed by his ability to flirt with every woman in the room. They divorced a year earlier, yet Brad owns a piece of the firm and helped it grow through many shrewd business deals, something his influence was good for.

Brad is sharing a cocktail with an attractive young intern. Maggie observes them for a few moments before making her way over to them.

"Why are you here?" asks Maggie, trying not to cause a scene. "I don't need you intruding on our staff party. This isn't the Amazing Brad show."

Brad smiles, trying to avoid eye contact with Maggie as if he didn't hear what she said. Realizing she's not going away, Brad gives Maggie his signature sly look. "Nothing wrong with a little networking, is there? I'm an investor in this firm. Kara invited me. Besides, these people love me."

Maggie quips, "No, you think these people love you. You're just tossing around your phony charm as usual."

"Now, now," says Brad. "Why the hostility? Can't we be civil for a change? After all, this is your company. You don't want to make a scene now, do you?"

The woman who Brad was conversing with realizes by their tone and gestures that Maggie and Brad are about to have an argument. She excuses herself and quickly walks away, not wanting to be caught in the crossfire.

Maggie looks him point-blank in the eye and whispers so only he can hear her, "Why don't you just get lost, Brad? I'm tired of watching you try to sweet-talk every intern in the company."

Brad, sensing her anger, softens his tone. "Look, I'm just here to network. Can I help it if they find me engaging? I'll be more than happy to avoid you."

Maggie walks away, disgusted. She stops by the bar and grabs a cocktail and then walks out to the terrace to speak with some colleagues. The view from the terrace is spectacular, as is the scent from the ocean breeze. Brad walks to the other end of the room, away from Maggie. He hugs Kara Kline, Maggie's partner. Kara is also an attractive woman in her late forties. She is statuesque, with long blond hair. She has a tougher demeanor than Maggie, with a keen, demanding business sense, but she lacks the creative intuition Maggie is gifted with. For Maggie, it's all about designing. For Kara, it's all about fame and wealth.

As Brad approaches Kara, she looks around to see if anyone is watching, then gives Brad a romantic peck on the cheek. Brad looks at her approvingly. She turns away quickly so as not to be obvious. There is something coy and deceiving about the two of them. It's evident that these two are up to something. Their personalities are a match as both are cunning, sharp and self-centered. They make a deadly combination.

Maggie, now on the terrace overlooking the ocean, notices that across the balcony is Don Phillips. Don is in his early fifties. He's an athletic-looking man with salt-and-pepper hair. Don is vice president of sales. He handles their largest domestic customers, along with all the firm's emerging international business. He is smart, well-spoken and likeable. He knows Maggie is highly creative and innovative, which gives him an edge over his competitors with his customers.

Don is sipping a Dewar's on the rocks, chatting with staff, when he sees Maggie coming towards him. He always makes time for her. He politely excuses himself from his other conversation and walks towards Maggie.

"So, it looks like we're close to landing the Argent Design account. It's about ten million dollars annually. They loved your designs for their new Fall line."

"Great news, Don. Let me know the next steps so we can start planning for their production timeline. Where are they producing?"

"At their Indonesia plant. It's got its issues, but their technical people run a first-rate facility. The target is to launch the line early next year."

Maggie is obviously pleased with the news. Text Styles was in heavy competition with their main rival, Stuart Industries.

"That's all great news. Nice job, Don! You keep this up, we might not be able to afford you," she jokes.

"Your designs are what sold the account. The sales pitch was the easy part. They absolutely loved them."

Maggie looks at Don approvingly and continues, "It was a complete team effort; we couldn't have pulled it off without you, Don."

"I appreciate that, Maggie, thank you," Don replies proudly.

Maggie smiles and walks back into the main room. She goes over to the bar and gets another drink.

"Maker's, neat," she tells the bartender.

Maggie takes her drink and walks across the main room towards the area that leads to her office. As she walks past Kara's office, the door is not fully closed. She glances in and sees Brad, out of the corner of her eye, grabbing Kara's rear. Kara returns the gesture by seductively stroking his crotch.

Maggie, seeing this, is suddenly enraged. She pushes the door open, walks in and slams it behind her. People at the party hear the door slam and wonder what just happened. In a violent motion, Maggie tosses her drink in Brad's face.

As the drink runs down onto his designer suit, Brad blurts out with a phony, shocked look on his face, "What the hell? What's your damn problem, Maggie?" Maggie completely ignores Brad and focuses her rage directly at Kara, who takes a step back, realizing this situation could get ugly.

"You're screwing him?" Maggie screams at Kara in complete disgust. "I can't believe you're screwing him. Of all the guys in LA you had to choose him?" Maggie is furious.

Kara, looking like the kid caught with her hand in the cookie jar, responds defensively, "It's not what you think."

"Really?" Maggie fires back in anger. "Then why are his hand-prints all over your butt?"

Kara repeats her insincere defense: "It's not what you think."

"Save it, Kara. I'm done with the two of you. I want you both out of my company."

"Our company," Kara says softly.

"Really, Kara? You couldn't design paper bag logos for a grocery store. Without me, there is no company." Before Kara can respond, Maggie storms out of the door. As she passes Brad, she throws him a piercing look. "Asshole!"

She heads out of Kara's office for the elevator. Brad follows her.

"Maggie, it's not what you think. We're just playing around." Trying to switch the tone, he coldly adds, "Besides, last time I checked, we're divorced. Even if we were fooling around, what business is it of yours?"

Maggie sternly replies, "If it's not my business, then what is it? This is my company. Kara's my partner. You're an asshole. It's bad enough you own a piece of my company. Wasn't screwing the interns good enough for you? You must screw Kara too? We've been divorced a year now. It's time for you to get completely out of my life."

Maggie gets on the elevator. When the doors close, she pounds the walls and screams. The elevator goes down to the main floor; the doors open. She leaves in haste, heading for her car. Suddenly, Kara emerges from the next elevator and follows Maggie outside.

"Maggie, wait. I'm sorry you had to—"

Maggie stops and looks Kara straight in the face.

"Of all the guys in LA, you need to screw Brad. Give me a break, you selfish bitch. How could you do that to me? How could you betray me like this, Kara? You know I want him out of this company. I've got nothing left to say to you. Name your price. I'll buy you and lover boy out now."

Kara stands there speechless while Maggie gets in her car and quickly drives off. She bangs the steering wheel repeatedly as she drives away. Kara walks back inside. Brad is now standing just outside the elevator.

"She was going to find out sooner or later." Kara now looks aggravated and annoyed.

"Now she'll be unbearable. We need to get her out of the way. She says she wants to buy us out. She couldn't run the business end of this place without me. She gets all the credit with her designs and I'm doing the dirty work around here. I'm sick of carrying her lunch bag. We need to make a move."

Brad, listening, is still patting down the liquor all over his suit with his handkerchief.

"It's already in the works. Leave it to me."

"The sooner the better. I'm done with her," says Kara.

They both get back on the elevator and head back up to the party.

CHAPTER 2

The Takeover

Maggie is speeding down the Pacific Coast Highway, still visibly upset. She pulls off to the Windjammer restaurant and bar, which overlooks the ocean. This is a favorite spot for the locals and tourists alike. Their patio is a spectacular place to view a beautiful sunset. She heads inside and takes a seat at the bar, where a large glass mirror shows her reflection. A strikingly handsome bartender steps in front of it, blocking her view, and greets her.

"Good evening. What can I get you?"

"A shot of Tullamore Dew Irish whiskey," Maggie replies quickly.

The bartender puts down a sparkling clean shot glass and pours the whiskey.

"One Tullamore Dew."

No sooner does he fill the glass than Maggie downs the shot.

"Another?" he questions. Looking up, he sees Maggie is agitated and anxious. "Tough day?"

"No, just my ex-husband is having an affair with my business partner," Maggie says sarcastically.

"Ouch. Sorry about that. Should I leave the bottle?"

Maggie doesn't reply. She points to the shot glass with her finger and he pours her another. She downs that shot as well. She looks at her iPhone and thumbs through some e-mails and missed messages. She now asks for a Tito's vodka on the rocks and the bartender pours it. She picks up the glass and walks outside to the patio overlooking the ocean. She leans up against the railing and stares out at the water. With a tear in her eye, she downs the drink.

She knows she needs to act. Will the board agree to buy out Kara? Brad? Or is she stuck in this situation? These questions and many others race through her mind. The thought of it makes her more upset, there is no easy solution. She walks back through the bar and leaves one hundred dollars in cash for her tab and a generous tip.

"Anything else I can get you? You need a cab?" the bartender queries.

"I'm fine, thanks," Maggie replies, not really paying attention.

The bartender offers some brief words of encouragement.

"Sorry about your situation. I've seen a lot of that from this side of the bar, especially in this town. Don't let them beat you. Trust in the person you know you are. The truth has a way of making things work out for the better. Life is not always easy, but you'll rise above it. Have faith."

Seeming preoccupied, Maggie keeps walking but then pauses. There was something about the gentle way this total stranger offered her some encouragement. She pauses, turns and says, "Thank you for being kind. I needed that."

"You're welcome. You get home safely now."

Maggie turns and heads out the door, gets into her car and drives away. As the bartender turns around, we realize he's Matthias, the head angel, only he's in human form. Another man dressed as a waiter comes over to him.

"Keep watch over her all the way home," Matthias instructs.

As the waiter walks out the door, he transforms from a human into an angelic being and takes off into the sky.

IT'S MONDAY MORNING AND MAGGIE SETS OUT FOR THE OFFICE. She's had the whole weekend to digest the events of Friday's office party debacle. She seems to be calmer but still edgy, as the events really angered her. As she is driving, she calls her attorney, Bill Smithburg. Bill has been Maggie's personal attorney for the last ten years. They met when she was first creating Text Styles Inc.

"Hey, Bill, it's Maggie."

"Hey, Mag, what's up?" replies Bill.

"I need you to pull up the partnership agreements with myself and Kara, and I need to know what exit strategy there may be to buy out Brad. Let me know my options."

"Wow, what's going on?"

Maggie, not wanting to reveal too much, simply states, "It might be time to review all options and change some of the people in this organization. I can't talk now, but I'll fill you in later."

"Okay. You got it. I'll review the details and get back to you."

"Thanks, Bill." Maggie disconnects the call and speeds along the highway. After the episode Friday, she seems determined to put her own plan in motion to move on from Kara and Brad. Being pragmatic, she'll do it fairly and professionally. To her, that'll be best for everyone involved.

Maggie comes into the lobby of Text Styles Inc. building and takes the elevator to her office. Her administrative assistant, Crystal Bowers, an attractive but proper-looking young woman in her mid-thirties, stands up to greet her.

"Good morning, Maggie. Kara and the board members want to see you in the conference room as soon as you got in."

Taken by surprise, Maggie replies, "Really? We have nothing scheduled. What's it about?"

"They didn't say, just for you to come to the boardroom when you got in."

Maggie knows this is odd and can't figure out what it could be about. The board doesn't call meetings without all the partners knowing in advance. Something is up, but she doesn't know what it is. She walks to the boardroom with a puzzled look on her face. As she steps inside, she sees Kara and the other board members.

Inquisitively, Maggie asks, "What's this about?"

Mark Reinsdorf, a senior partner and CFO of the company, stands up. Mark is an older gentleman in his late sixties, with a full head of wavy gray hair. He is the consummate professional with a strong financial pedigree.

"Take a seat, Maggie. I apologize for this impromptu meeting, but we felt it was necessary under the circumstances."

Maggie, still bewildered, walks to the corner of the conference table and sits close to Mark, but away from Kara.

"What circumstances?"

Mark continues, "As you know, we are looking at outside investors to bolster our growing European business. While our accounting firm has been handling the due diligence with the investors, they have found some improprieties that need immediate attention."

"Really? What did they find?" says Maggie.

Mark starts with a quick summation of the issue.

"Well, in a nutshell, money from client account receivables was transferred to private offshore accounts. It didn't make much sense, so we've been digging into it for a while."

"How can that be? We run a tight operation. Nothing of that magnitude could possibly get done without board approval or authorization from a senior partner. It doesn't make any sense. Who would possibly do that?"

"Agreed. As we dug into it, we found a paper trail that was cleverly disguised. But it did lead to someone," Mark says.

"Who?" says Maggie.

Calmly and carefully, Mark says, "You."

"Me? That's insane," Maggie protests. "I built this company from scratch. I am the face of this company. I don't need to steal from it."

Mark maintains a professional demeanor, not wanting to give in to emotion.

"I was shocked at the allegation, but it's your signature on the transfer documents and this is a serious matter." He shows her the document. She looks at it in stunned disbelief. Maggie is dumbfounded.

"It looks like my signature, but I have no idea what this is. I did not send company funds to a private account."

Mark replies, "The offshore account is in your name. Are you telling us you have no knowledge of this account or of these transactions?"

Maggie becomes agitated and defensive. "Yes, that's exactly what I'm telling you. This is complete BS. I assure you, Mark, that I had nothing to do with this."

Maggie glances around the room at the rest of the board members. She looks at Kara, who is looking away. Maggie stares at her and suddenly becomes enraged. She stands up and looks intensely in Kara's direction.

"You did this, you bitch!"

Kara looks at Maggie in complete shock.

"You're sleeping with Brad and now you want to set me up? You evil bitch! I won't stand for this BS and have my credibility questioned."

Mark, looking surprised, inquires, "What are you talking about? Brad and Kara? Brad Collins, our minority equity partner? What does he have to do with this?"

Maggie, now further enraged, blurts out, "Kara's sleeping with Brad. They're trying to set me up because I told them I want them out of the company."

Mark, now getting upset, looks at everyone. "I don't know what's going on between you two in your personal lives, but this is a serious matter. It is our job as a board to investigate this fully. You can sit with the legal team and discuss it, but until we get to the bottom of this, the board has no choice but to temporarily suspend you, pending a full investigation. I'm sorry, but we have no choice."

Maggie is getting angrier by the minute. "Suspend me? Are you serious? This is total nonsense. I founded this company! I do not need to steal from it." She looks directly at Kara. "You won't get away with this little stunt of yours. I promise you that. When I'm done with you, they'll take you out of here in handcuffs."

Turning back to the board, Maggie further says, "My attorney will contact our corporate legal team immediately. Whoever did this to me is going to pay. I'll get to the bottom of this."

Maggie turns to leave. As she starts to storm out of the room, she stops, picks up a glass of water from the table and throws it in Kara's face. Kara pushes back hard on her chair as the water drenches her face and suit. Other board members scramble to assist her by giving her linen napkins to wipe up some of the water.

Mark, looking shocked, says, "That was uncalled for, Maggie. Have a little more respect for this board in the way you conduct yourself."

Maggie, now furious, turns to Mark. "With all due respect, Mark, you blindside me with an unscheduled board meeting, accuse me of embezzling funds from the company I created and then suspend me on some unproven nonsense without investigation. No, that's uncalled for."

Maggie heads for the door. As she passes Kara, she quips, "I thought witches melted when they got wet?"

Maggie storms out the door. She heads to her office, grabs her valise and heads for the elevator.

Crystal, seeing Maggie is furious, says, "Is everything okay, Maggie?"

"Yeah, just dandy! I'll fill you in later. Right now, I need to get out of here."

Mark turns to Kara. With a stern look, he says to her, "I don't know what's going on with you two or about your little affair with Brad, but I'll get to the bottom of this and there better not be any nonsense in this matter."

Kara shoots back, "Whatever is going on between us personally has nothing to do with anything else. The evidence shows she set up the account and transferred the funds. Her signature is clearly on the document. I run this company and I'm tired of her acting like she built this company alone. Now she's stealing from us. She's pathetic."

Mark says sternly, "I don't want to hear any more opinions and accusations. This company will investigate this the proper way. Meeting adjourned."

Mark picks up his papers and hastily leaves the conference room. Kara gets up quickly and heads out the door in the back of the room and disappears down the hallway.

Maggie gets in her car and dials her attorney. Bill answers, "Hey, I didn't think you'd call back so soon. I'm still reviewing the contracts."

"Forget that for the moment. I need you to get in touch with our corporate attorneys immediately. Kara and Brad are trying to set me up for embezzling money."

"What? Embezzling money? Are you serious? How?"

"The board claims I opened some offshore account and diverted funds to it. The documents have my signature on them. I don't know how they did it, but this is complete nonsense."

"That just makes no sense. I'll get in touch with the corporate attorneys right now. I'll call you back as soon as I know something. Are you okay?"

"No, I'm not okay. I want to kill those two."

"Try and calm down, we'll get to the bottom of it."

"Oh, we will, you can count on it."

With that, they hang up. Maggie is beyond angry as she speeds along the highway, headed home.

Dante and another demon suddenly appear, hovering above Maggie's car. "Nothing like some lust, deceit and deception to stoke the flames of anger. Stay on top of them and keep pushing their buttons." With that, Dante and the demon fly away and vanish in to the California sky.

CHAPTER 3

<hr />

Impulse Reaction

ater that same evening, Maggie is sitting in the living room of her penthouse apartment, feet up and sipping on a glass of red wine. The living room is adorned in expensive white Italian leather furniture, with accents of red, giving it a feeling of elegance and class. The apartment is spacious, with an open-concept kitchen and high-end stainless-steel appliances. In the oversized dining room sits a glass table that seats ten. On top of the table is a pricey silver-and-red vase, something Maggie acquired on a trip to France. The views are striking with its floor-to-high-ceiling windows, and like most places on the Malibu coast, the apartment overlooks the Pacific Ocean. As Maggie sips her wine, still feeling rather agitated from the day, her cell phone rings.

"Hello, Bill," she sighs deeply.

"Hey, Maggie."

"Well, what did you find out?" Maggie queries.

"I talked with the corporate attorneys. Maggie, whoever did this to you set you up pretty well. They have your actual signature on a fund transfer approval to an account offshore."

Maggie walks over to the window with the glass of red wine in her hand and looks out.

"Tell me something I don't know," she replies as she guzzles down what's left inside her glass.

"Your name is the only name on the account."

Maggie walks over to the kitchen, grabbing the half-empty bottle of wine and pouring what's left into her glass.

"That's impossible. I did not set up that account," she states adamantly. "It's a setup by Kara, I know it. She did this to me."

Bill, sounding less than promising, says, "Maggie, unless you can prove she did this, they're moving to have you terminated and stripped of your shareholder equity. They are going to take legal action and have you arrested for embezzlement. They will be filing charges. We may go before the judge in the next week. I'm so sorry."

"I can't believe this is happening," she responds.

Bill remains silent for a moment.

"I don't know what our options are at this point. I'll find something. I just need some time," Maggie responds, gulping down the rest of the wine. She then goes over to her bar and pours something a little stronger into her glass—Irish whiskey.

"I hate to say it, Maggie, but we're running out of just that—time. But we'll keep digging on our end. You may need to hire a private investigator."

Maggie walks out to her terrace, looking down at the beach below.

"We'll speak soon." Bill hangs up.

Maggie quickly gulps down mouthfuls of whiskey. She's an emotional wreck. She pours more whiskey into her glass, guzzling it down, one, then two, and then three, until the bottle is empty. She then takes the empty bottle and throws it over the terrace to the beach below in a fit of rage. She sobs loudly, dropping down onto the flat surface of the terrace.

THE NEXT MORNING, MAGGIE AWAKES TO THE WIND BLOWING through the open terrace door of her apartment. She's on the couch, pretty much still intoxicated from the night before. She can barely open her eyes, swollen from her emotional outbursts. She sits up slowly and carefully. Her head is pounding. She's somewhat disoriented as she stumbles over to the terrace door to close it. It's obvious that the wine and whiskey from the night before didn't necessarily mix well as she gets up enough energy and tries not to vomit along the way to the bathroom. Maggie steps out of the bathroom, her energy depleted from all the booze. She slumps down onto the couch, reaching for the remote control. She channel surfs for a few moments and then lands on the tabloid news of the day from TMZ. Something immediately catches her attention.

She sits up from her slumped position and tipsy state. It's breaking news concerning the unsanctioned release of information about the embezzlement scandal of the senior partner and Founder of Text Styles Inc., Maggie Hargrove. Maggie perks up, listening to the report on the news, and doesn't even hear her cell phone ringing in the background. Instead she listens as the reporter says they have a comment from someone at the company, Brad Collins. Maggie is now enraged.

"That SOB, how could he?" Maggie shouts, infuriated. "He did this deliberately. I bet he and Kara leaked this information. He's trying to destroy me and everything I built!"

She starts roaring at the television.

"So, you want to play dirty, huh? Okay, okay!" she screams at the top of her voice. "You pathetic excuse for a man!"

Maggie drunkenly gets up from the couch and tosses the remote at the television, cracking the screen. She grabs her keys from the glass table by the door and storms out of her apartment, still wearing the same clothes from the night before and clearly not in the right state of mind to drive.

Maggie staggers to her car, parked across the street from her apartment building. She gets in and manages to start it up and pull out of the space, lightly scraping the front of her bumper on the car parked in front of her. She speeds down the highway toward the office, weaving and swerving in and out of traffic.

At Text Styles Inc. headquarters, she haphazardly parks across two spots and stumbles into the entrance of the building. Her actions are disoriented as she stumbles toward the elevator near the lobby. The smell of alcohol on her breath is overwhelming. She repetitively pushes the elevator button. Luckily, no one is on the elevator. As the elevator arrives on the company's executive floor, she steps off, drunk, infuriated and aggressive.

As she storms through the hallway toward her office, she mutters and slurs to herself, "They think they're going to get away with this. She started this and I'm going to finish it."

Maggie charges towards Kara's office. Kara's executive secretary, Stephanie, sees Maggie heading her way and immediately calls security.

"Please get up here now, Maggie's in the building," she yells nervously into the phone.

Stephanie steps in front of Kara's door to block Maggie from entering.

"Maggie, you're not supposed to be here."

Stephanie is clearly no match for Maggie's frenzy and frustration. She shoves Stephanie violently to the floor and bursts through Kara's door.

Kara is on the phone and caught off guard as Maggie slams the door closed behind her and lunges toward Kara. She grabs Kara by the throat, tackling her on top of the desk.

Maggie screams, "I'll kill you before you take my company, you lying bitch. I'll kill you!"

Kara struggles to breathe as she tries to release Maggie's grip from around her neck. It is apparent that even in Maggie's drunken state, her rage has given her an increased amount of strength as her grip gets tighter and her resolve to cause bodily damage is intensified. Just as Maggie gets on top of Kara, choking her unmercifully, two bulky security guards burst through the doors of Kara's office. One grabs Maggie as she struggles to hold on to Kara's neck, screaming, "I'll kill you, you hear me, bitch?"

The security guard yanks Maggie off Kara as she screams and struggles to grab Kara again. Kara stumbles onto the floor, and another security guard helps her up onto her feet. "Are you okay, Ms. Kline?"

Kara, stroking her neck, responds, "Hell no. No, I'm not okay. She's crazy, call the police!"

Maggie's still screaming at the top of her voice as she fights and struggles with security as they carry her out.

"We've called the police, Ms. Kline, they're on their way."

Maggie can be heard through the door. "You won't get away with it, you bitch. You hear me!"

Kara tries to regain some composure. She's nervous and upset.

"Get her out of here now!"

Security drags Maggie out toward the elevator as Stephanie steps into the office. She helps Kara get herself together.

"I'm so sorry, Kara, I tried to stop her but—"

"It's okay," Kara reassures her. "She needs help. She's mentally unstable. It's obvious she's not well."

Kara gets up from the chair and fixes her clothes and her hair as Stephanie picks up the papers that were thrown to the floor from the desk. Once the office is pretty much back to its original state, Kara leads Stephanie out of the office, reassuring her again, and closes the door behind her. She sits down and dials Brad.

"Hello?" Brad seems surprised that Kara is calling his private line.

Kara blurts out, "That crazy bitch just tried to kill me." The line is silent. "Hello, did you hear me?"

Kara, upset, repeats herself. Brad is about to get into his car. He looks a bit tousled as he waves and blows a kiss of sincerity to a woman across the street from an apartment building.

"Yes, I heard you. Tell me what happened."

"She showed up here, drunk and belligerent, and she starts screaming and choking me, yelling 'I'm going to kill you.'"

"Are you serious? I didn't think she had it in her. I guess she lost it."

"Lost it?" she questioned. "I knew she'd be pissed off, but I didn't expect her to burst into my office and try to choke the life out of me."

"Well, I did leak the story to TMZ. I made sure they ran it repeatedly. I guess she saw it or heard about it."

Kara walks around her office, unnerved, looking out the window below. She sees the police car pull up.

Brad continues, "Well, she wasn't going to let us destroy her and not do anything. She's impulsive, but I never thought she'd get violent. I knew she would eventually do something rash, but this little stunt will finish her for sure. She'll be out of our way sooner than we anticipated. Now you can threaten to press charges if she doesn't relinquish her share of the company. She may have done us a favor."

Kara takes a seat behind her desk and leans back in her chair.

"Little stunt? She almost killed me. I've never seen her that angry. She snapped. Yeah, you better believe it, now I'm going to make her pay." Kara is rubbing her neck, still in pain. "She may have dug her own grave, but she almost dug mine as well."

Kara leans back and looks out the window again as the police enter the building. "I want her gone and now. The sooner the better. I'm going to bury her reputation. After this, she'll never get another customer in this industry. Listen, I must go talk to the police. I'll call you later."

Brad puts Kara on speakerphone in the car and fixes his tie and belt around his pants. "Stay calm. Compose yourself and act scared for your life when you talk to the police."

Kara leans up against her desk and lets out a gasp of air. "I don't have to act, Brad. If security hadn't come in, she would have killed me. I've gotta go and get myself together."

Kara hangs up and heads into the bathroom in her office as Brad starts his car and drives off.

Unbeknownst to Kara, lurking outside the window of her office is Dante; his expression is one of pure delight.

"Two souls for the price of one," he utters to one of his demons. "Kara will be easy, and the other one…I knew she had it in her. We've got her just about completely over the edge now," he hisses.

As Kara looks at herself in the mirror, tossing her hair a bit, Dante shoots a flame-like invisible vapor through the window at her throat. It causes her immediate pain and frightens her. She grabs her neck quickly as the pain lasts for a few seconds. She clears her throat until the pain subsides. Dante laughs out loud, watching Kara in pain.

He turns to one of his demons. "We better leave her be. She needs to focus on burying the brunette to the police."

Kara applies a smidgen of lipstick and inspects her teeth and then her neck again, which is slightly bruised. She tucks in the collar of her white blouse for the bruise to be more visible to the police. She fixes her eyebrows and hears a tap at her office door. She then dabs a little water around her eyes, as if she's been crying, shuts the lights off and opens the door to her office.

There are two police officers standing on the other side of Kara's door. A young female officer and, to Kara's surprise a rather attractive older male officer. "Ms. Kline, may we step inside?"

Kara invites them in, opening the door wider and peeks out to tell Stephanie to hold her calls. Both officers step inside and Kara offers them a seat on the brown leather couch adjacent to the door of her office.

"Would either of you like a bottle of water?"

They both respond no. Kara then takes a seat in the chair behind her desk.

The male officer begins to question her as his female counterpart takes notes. "First of all, are you okay?"

"Considering she almost choked me to death, I'm a bit shaken up, Officer."

"I'm sorry you had to endure this. Can you tell us what occurred?"

As Kara is explaining the details of that morning, Dante continues to observe her from outside the window. His pure evil intent is written all over his face. He grumbles, "Atta girl, pour it on thick. Play the poor innocent victim."

Dante turns to one of his demons, laughing. "Stay here and observe this. Report back to me later with the details."

Kara gives the police a complete description of the attack and how she feared for her life. Dante turns and flies off into the sky in a burst of black dust.

THE AFTERNOON HAS BECOME CLOUDY. NOT A GLIMMER OF sunshine can be found. The police station is in Calabasas, not far away from Malibu and its beautiful beaches and oceanfront properties. It sits alone on a long stretch of road. The red brick building in the middle of nothing demands respect and is notably a place of authority. Inside, police officers are situated at desks, processing incoming offenders. Maggie sits on a cot in a jail cell, alone for the moment. It's nothing compared to her penthouse apartment. It's clean enough for a lady of the night, but not Maggie, the founder and partner of one of the largest and most notable firms in Malibu.

It's apparent she's not happy with her surroundings. Bill, her lawyer, is on the other side of the bars. A police officer taps on the bar to get Maggie's attention and allows Bill inside.

"You have a few minutes," the officer states.

Bill steps inside and looks around, shocked that Maggie has stooped this low. He stands there silent for a moment. He then sits beside her.

"Maggie, what did you do?"

He puts his hand on her shoulder. She doesn't move.

"This is a real mess. You're in deep trouble."

Maggie remains silent, looking down at the gray floor and up at the cracks in the concrete walls. She lifts her head and looks at Bill with a look of desperation and despair.

Maggie wipes a tear from her eye. "I don't know, Bill, I was drunk. Honestly, I don't know what came over me. The scary part is, in the heat of the moment, I think I really wanted to kill her."

"Listen, you were drunk and upset. The combination made you act crazy. You know that's not who you are."

"Maybe it is me. Maybe I'm capable of that behavior. How could I snap like that?"

"Nonsense. Once we get you sobered up and out of here, you'll clear your mind and start to think rationally. I've posted your bail, but let's not kid ourselves, this is serious. You've been arrested for assault."

She looks at him with disbelief. He continues, "If they press charges, you could be looking at attempted murder."

Maggie looks at him in disbelief. She is shocked. "I just snapped, Bill. I was drunk." She jumps up from the cot. "I don't know what came over me."

He walks over to her to comfort her. "Look, don't say any more. Let's get you out of here and we'll talk outside."

Bill is allowed out of the cell and goes up front and gets the paperwork for Maggie; he signs the documents and then waits outside the building. Around thirty minutes later, Maggie appears. They walk a few feet away from the entrance of the jail.

"I've spoken to Kara's attorney. She might be willing to drop the charges, but there's a catch."

Bill lights a cigarette for himself, offering one to Maggie. She takes it and he lights it for her. She takes a drag from the cigarette. "What do you mean, a 'catch,' Bill?"

Bill takes in a long drag of his cigarette. "Kara will drop the charges for the attack and say she provoked you…if you sign over the company to her."

Maggie's mouth drops. "What? That devious bitch! This can't be happening. The fact that I attacked her had nothing to do with her stealing my company out from under me."

Bill takes in another long drag. "Otherwise it's jail, Maggie."

He looks at her pensively. "Look, she's willing to give you a severance deal, but you have to sign a noncompete. If she drops the criminal charges, you're off the hook for any jail time."

Maggie begins to pace back and forth. "Yeah, no jail. No criminal record and no career. Boy, did I really screw myself over. But what about the embezzlement charges?"

"They won't pursue those charges. The company doesn't want the negative publicity in the press. You go away quietly; they'll just say there was a mutual agreement for you to leave."

Bill continues, "There's more. She also wants you to attend anger management therapy. Basically, this stunt is costing you your company and your reputation."

Maggie is struggling with the idea of losing her company, but she's also struggling with the notion of losing her freedom while staring out into the road.

"You screwed up big-time with this drunken stunt."

Maggie looks back at Bill.

"Damn it, Maggie, what were you thinking? You assaulted not one but two people in front of witnesses."

Maggie throws her hands up. "I barely touched that girl."

"Maybe that's what you think, but you did, and you tried to choke Kara to death. You tossed your whole case out the window. Unless you want to go to jail, you have no option."

She walks back over to Bill and stands in front of him, fighting for her right to keep her company, but she knows there's no other way out.

"Do you how hard I worked to build this company? The sacrifices I made. I built it. Not her, me!"

Bill rubs his chin. "If you don't take the deal, they'll press charges. Sure, we can fight it, claim temporary insanity, the booze, the anger from her sleeping with Brad, but it won't be easy. They probably can push for first-degree attempted murder charges, which is a life sentence."

Maggie throws her hands in the air. Bill continues.

"But a lesser charge in California is five to ten years in state prison," he informs her.

Maggie is stunned, and it shows all over her face. She knows she's not built for a jail sentence, let alone five to ten years, but she also knows what she and her family sacrificed to get what she accomplished thus far and she's not sure if it's worth it.

"Maggie, fighting assault and attempted murder charges would be an uphill battle at best, and you have to seriously consider whether you're willing to take that chance."

Bill takes in another long drag of his cigarette and then drops it to the ground and stamps it out.

"Look, take the deal and get the criminal assault charges dropped. Once that's out of the way, we can see if we can prove how they framed you. If you go to jail for assault, trying to get the company back won't matter. At least this leaves a slight opening to find evidence they set you up. Why don't I take you home and you think about it?"

Maggie agrees as they head to Bill's car in the parking lot area of the police station. She buries her face in the palms of her hands, wondering how she'll get herself out of the mess she's in, and then looks out the window as they drive away.

IT'S MIDNIGHT. MAGGIE'S PENTHOUSE APARTMENT IS QUIET AND dark except for the moon shining through the open glass doors of the terrace. You can barely hear the ocean splashing against the rocks. The stars are in rare form in the sky, shining ever so brightly. Maggie is sitting outside on her terrace. She's coddling a bottle of whiskey that's almost empty. She's in deep thought and getting drunk again. It's been nearly two days since her release from jail and the debacle she caused for herself. She's gone over the scenario in her head a thousand times, thinking about what the best would be concerning her life and the company she built. But nothing seems to make sense to her. She knows deep down inside what her only outcome should be, but she's afraid of what would come next. She's emotionally drained and distraught.

She reaches for her cell phone on the railing and dials a number. "Bill, it's me." She pauses for a moment. "I'll sign the papers." She sighs heavily.

He responds softly on the other end, "I am so sorry, Maggie. It's the only solution."

Maggie gets up and goes inside. "Thank you... really, for every-thing. I'm sorry I let you down. Can you bring the papers over in the morning?"

Bill responds somberly, "Of course. Take some time and let the dust settle and then we can look into investigating them."

Maggie sips on the whiskey inside her glass. "I really need to get out of here. I plan on leaving for New York tomorrow evening. I'll be gone for a while; it's just been way too much for me to handle… and now this…I've got to go."

"I understand. A change of scenery may do you some good. I'll make sure everything gets executed properly. I can get any of the business papers you need to see sent to you in New York."

"I'm sorry, Bill. Thanks for not giving up on me."

"Hey, you know I'll always be on your side, Maggie. I'll talk to you soon."

Maggie hangs up and looks around her penthouse apartment, knowing her life is about to go through some huge changes.

She yells out to God to help her. "Please, if you're out there, help me. I don't deserve this."

Stepping back out onto the terrace, she looks out at the beach and silently sobs.

EARLY EVENING THE NEXT DAY, MAGGIE GATHERS HER SUITCASE by the door and heads for the elevator.

There's a heaviness in the air as she walks out to meet the waiting Uber car that's taking her to the airport. The driver takes her suitcase and places it in the trunk. Maggie takes one last look at her high-rise apartment building as memories flood her mind of the first day she moved in. How excited she was when the moving truck pulled up and how she immediately started decorating her new place. She was elated to FaceTime Kate, displaying the view of the beach from her terrace. It all seems so long ago. Her thoughts are quickly interrupted as the Uber driver slams the trunk closed.

The drive seems long and she's somewhat impatient. "Could you hurry, please? I don't want to miss my flight," she voices to the driver.

"You won't miss it. According to my GPS navigations, it clears up after this bit of traffic."

Soon enough, the traffic does start to diminish.

Maggie arrives at the airport with lots of time to spare. She sits at the gate, waiting to board her flight. In her hand is a copy of *Fashion Weekly* magazine from a few months ago. Her picture is on the cover, with Kara beside her. She sneers a little and then her face takes on a serious expression. The flight attendant announces they're ready to board. Maggie stands up, gathering her things, looks down at the magazine in her hand once again, rolls it up tightly and then tosses it in the trash as she walks down the jetway out of sight.

CHAPTER 4

Escape

It's an early morning in New York City. Haze from air pollution hangs over the skyline. Way back when, you could almost touch the air in New York, looking out into a yellowish horizon, a far cry from now. You can hear the echoes of fire trucks, an ambulance and police cars and the mumbles of busy pedestrians. On the Upper East Side there's a small brown brick building that contains multiple studio apartments and a bodega below it. A garbled but steady flow of voices can be heard going in and out of the bodega.

The second-floor walkup staircase leads to two studio apartments. To the back of the hallway is Apartment 2B. It's small and basic, rather drab and in disarray. The floors are a dark scruffy wood and newspapers are scattered about. The bare walls are a muted gray. There's a small black couch adjacent to a window with views of another brick building with a fire escape and a glaring red flashing neon sign that can be seen through the window late at night. A full-size bed sits a few feet away from the couch with a small television on a stand nearby, in addition to a small kitchen containing a four-foot refrigerator and old stove. There's a bathroom to the left of the entrance into the apartment where clothes hang along the shower bar. On the floor leaning against the wall is a framed award covered in light dust that never got hung up: "Fashion Designer Guild, Designer of the Year 2012: Maggie Hargrove." This is a far cry from the penthouse apartment in Malibu. Maggie's psychological state is so weakened, she just doesn't care about her surroundings. This apartment is simply a place to crash. It's emptiness, in stark contrast to her place in LA, reflects the current state of her mind. Nothing seems to matter to Maggie anymore, as she is a depressed and lost soul. When you lose the will to fight, life becomes irrelevant and meaningless.

The television is on in the background, reporting the news of the day and the impending heat wave. Maggie is pouring a cup of coffee in her to-go cup. She looks fatigued, as if time has not been kind to her. Maggie takes a sip of coffee and then looks at the time on her wristwatch and quickly turns off the television, cuts the lights out and heads out the door. On the way down the stairs, she pulls out her last cigarette from the pack of Newport Lights. She lights it and pulls in a long drag.

She heads out the side entrance of the building where a few sketchy characters congregate, but they don't seem to frighten Maggie. It's obvious she's gotten used to it. It seems to be a daily and nightly occurrence. She tosses the empty pack of cigarettes in the large dumpster located under her window. Her cell phone goes off as she stops inside the bodega for a new pack. She doesn't answer it when she realizes it's her sister. However, Kate is persistent and calls again.

Maggie answers, annoyed. "Yes, Kate, what is it?"

"Sorry—geez, hopefully I'm not interrupting anything important," Kate responds.

"Nope, just on my way to work," Maggie reacts nonchalantly while blending in with the crowd along the busy streets of New York.

Kate, Maggie's younger sister, lives in Upper Westchester with her fiancé in a quiet and upscale part of Scarsdale. There was always a bit of sisterly competition between the two, Maggie in fashion and Kate an abstract artist. Kate was always a little envious of her big sister Maggie getting a full ride to FIT while she worked at nonprofits, barely scraping by. Nevertheless, that's where Kate gained her interest in and passion for art. She'd become a quick study and later had been offered a full scholarship to art school. They were both ambitious and had huge aspirations of making their own way in business, willing to sacrifice whatever it took to obtain it. Like Maggie, her artistic talent was her ticket out of blue-collar Elgin.

Kate always felt as if she had to prove herself to Maggie, being that Maggie's career skyrocketed way before hers. Yet Kate was also climbing the ladder of fame and had received a great amount of recognition and accolades for her art, as well as owning a small art boutique in Westchester.

"Oh, that's right, the former world renown fashion executive is on her way to her new career serving breakfast specials to the hungry masses."

"Ef you, Kate. What do you want?"

"I'm sorry, that was unfair." Kate quickly changes the subject back to the reason why she called. "Listen, mom says you haven't called her. She's worried about you, Maggie."

"I'm fine; she needs to lighten up on me. I'm not a child."

"She's well aware of that, Maggie."

Maggie wedges her cellphone between her ear and shoulder while continuing the conversation. She opens up the new pack of cigarettes, takes one out, lights it and takes a drag. "Did she forget I went to college in New York and I lived in California? She thinks the only safe place in the world is Elgin."

Maggie stops; she takes a few more puffs before putting out the cigarette and crossing the street.

"Give Mom a break, Mag. Just call her, okay? You and I really need to sit down and discuss things. I'm worried about you."

"Look, I don't have time for this right now."

"Fine, but promise me you'll call mom and we'll get together soon."

"Whatever. I gotta hang up."

"Love you."

Maggie hangs up and crosses the street. She knows she needs to call her mother and at least reassure her with the illusion that she's okay.

Maggie's mother, Jane, has always been proud of her accomplishments, but she never liked her LA lifestyle and especially didn't like her ex-husband, Brad. Jane was and always will be a small-town girl, so the trappings of the big cities like Los Angeles and New York always made her worry about her daughters. With Maggie's current situation and hasty departure to New York, Jane was now worried more than ever. She has no idea Maggie lives in a cheap apartment and works as a waitress.

A few blocks away from Maggie's apartment and around the corner is the Empire Diner, a classic stand-alone old-school diner frequented by busy New Yorkers. It's described as a classic for its lunch counter comfort and convenience as well as its reminiscence of the fifties, with its soda fountain and famous milkshakes; old-school for its vintage metal-finish tables and retro leather booths. The diner is owned by Erastos Vassos, a stocky middle-aged man of Greek descent whom everyone calls Earl. Earl is tall, with striking features, with a full head of black hair with touches of gray. His family has been in the restaurant business for generations, but Earl wanted to carve his own path in life. After graduating from NYU's business school, he became a stockbroker at a top firm on Wall Street. After years of making lots of money, Earl suddenly shifted gears, left Wall Street behind and opened the Empire Diner with his uncle Stavros.

Maggie quickly walks inside, greets a few patrons, and heads toward the back of the diner and through a door that reads Employees Only, where she puts her purse in a locker and puts on an apron. Earl is in the kitchen area. He sees Maggie.

"Good morning, Maggie," says Earl.

"Good morning to you, boss."

"Late night?" Earl asks, referring to Maggie's rather disheveled look, which really isn't out of the ordinary. Since Empire isn't a business suit attire establishment, she isn't concerned about her baggy jeans, T-shirt and drab no-makeup appearance. Yet there's still a smidgen of light in her eyes.

Maggie smirks at his comment and heads to the counter to wait on customers. Unfortunately, her claim to fame in serving the fashion industry has now been altered to serving breakfast, grilled cheese sandwiches, French fries and coffee.

Two New York City cops walk in. Officer Kevin O'Connell is a fit, clean-cut, redheaded Irish bloke in his early forties. His partner is Officer Tony Benuti, a rather handsome, soft-spoken dark-haired Italian. They're regulars at the diner and have a friendly rapport with Maggie, often engaging in playful banter.

Maggie wipes down the counter and pours a cup of coffee for one of her patrons. She looks up and sees the two cops enter.

"Well, if it isn't my two favorite cops."

She glances out the window at their police car parked across the street, right next to a fire hydrant. "I see some rules don't apply to New York's finest."

Both sit down at the counter.

"We were in such a hurry to see your pretty face we didn't have time to find a real spot." Officer O'Connell smiles.

Maggie smiles back and leans in, placing her elbow on the counter. "Who are you kidding, O'Connell? You'd park on the damn sidewalk if you could."

They both laugh and he retorts quickly, "I'd park in here just to be closer to you. So…when am I taking you out for drinks?" he asks.

Maggie grabs her pad from her apron pocket. She looks up at Officer O'Connell, tilts her head to the side.

"Wait, let's see." She looks down and then up at him. "Nope, hell hasn't frozen over yet," she laughs, prompting Officer Benuti to gesture with a fake handgun.

"Bang! Shot down again! Stick to those bar tramps, Kevin, who find your line of BS so irresistible."

Maggie pours them both a cup of coffee. Officer O'Connell gives Maggie a look. He lifts his chin and smiles seductively. "Yeah, but I'd rather just sit in the squad car and dream of you in nothing but my police shirt, playing with my nightstick."

Maggie's not the least bit impressed or offended as she's always prepared for Officer O'Connell's sexual undertones. After all, Officer O'Connell's phony charm is nothing compared to her ex, Brad. She's well versed in BS.

"*Dream* is the operative word, Officer O'Connell. Try the hookers on Tenth Avenue. Even your *nightstick* will look good to them for twenty bucks."

Officer Benuti, impressed with Maggie's quick comebacks, says, "Ouch!"

Maggie lets out a big sigh. "Too bad you're married, Tony. I have to get hit on every day by *luck of the ol' Irish* over here." Benuti blushes.

Officer O'Connell looks over at Benuti and then at Maggie. "Wow, Tony, I guess she prefers Italian sausage to Irish corned beef."

Benuti shoves O'Connell with his shoulder. "Knock it off, jackass." He looks over at Maggie. "Sorry, Maggie. It's time for us to get back to work, lover boy. Have a good day, Maggie. See you tomorrow."

Earl sees the two cops bantering with Maggie and jokes, "You guys hang around here much longer, I've got some dirty dishes in the back that need washing."

O'Connell looks over at Earl. "No, thanks—it'll ruin my manicure."

"A cop with a manicure. Did you paint your toes too?"

They all break out in laughter. Officer O'Connell winks at Maggie as he gets up. Maggie shakes her head at him as they walk toward the door.

"Always a pleasure, boys. Be safe, Tony. You too, Rico Suave." They both laugh on the way out.

"Who's Rico Suave?" O'Connell asks Benuti as they walk to the car.

"Man, you're lame."

Benuti waves to Maggie from the window; she gives him a wave back. O'Connell blows a kiss. Maggie responds with a simple sarcastic smirk, then goes back to attending to other customers.

CHAPTER 5

The Element and Cost of Corruption

On the other side of town, near the train tracks, in a not-so-nice neighborhood, sits a dingy dark gray building covered in graffiti that serves as a clubhouse. The area is not frequented by many people due to the fact it attracts a criminal element. Even the once-green grass that surrounded the building has been reduced to a brown and brittle appearance and is covered in weeds. Strewn about are beer bottles, cans and cigarette butts. In the back of the building are old rusted car parts and tires.

The clubhouse building belongs to an outlaw motorcycle club known as the Rojos gang. The Rojos have vehemently established themselves as a feared organization, commanding recognition and respect. They're notorious for illicit activity, from extortion to assaults, gun possession to drug activity and even murder.

The Rojos make money illegally in many ways, one of which is transporting drugs for the cartel to New England and as far away as Ohio and south to Virginia. They are a clever bunch of rebels that sometimes "clean up" and dress like day-trip bikers, riding on unassuming motorcycles or in ordinary SUVs. They often split up so as not to attract attention. They are a shifty group and have often eluded police and the FBI due to their affiliation with a few corrupt cops.

The head of the Rojos gang is Victor Valles, a stocky six-foot-tall tattoo-covered Mexican. Victor is considered a no-nonsense leader and has little tolerance when it comes to rules. You either follow club rules or you don't. If you don't, you answer to Victor. There's no middle ground.

Upon walking into the clubhouse, you can feel the eeriness of aggression. The inside of the building feels damp and cold, with barely any natural light. Its walls are dark blue and red. The carpet is a dirty dark green color and a pool table sits in the middle. There's a wood bar with an abundance of liquor behind it. Two low black couches, old and torn up, are in the middle of the room, facing an old floor model television, which sits up against the wall. Above the TV is a large painted version of the Rojos Motorcycle Club logo.

Victor is slouched down on one of the couches, drunk. He takes a swig of Jack Daniels whiskey. He's watching the news about an incident fourteen months ago, involving two officers, John Moran and Kevin O'Connell. He is the same Officer O'Connell and counterfeit Casanova from the diner. Officer John Moran was O'Connell's original partner, before he shot and killed twenty-year-old Manny Medina, who was reported to have affiliations with the Rojos gang. In reality, Medina had nothing to do with the Rojos gang. He'd had his issues with childhood pranks in the past, one of which had led him to be placed in juvenile detention for a few weeks. But after that ordeal, he'd cleaned up his act and started working with other youths in his neighborhood and building up his community in the hopes of turning around a few others, like his childhood friend and Rojos member Ruben Castilla.

Victor leans in and listens to the television commentator. "Today the grand jury will present its verdict. According to Officer Moran, Manny Medina was shot in a struggle while resisting arrest following a traffic stop. Moran told the grand jury that Medina had a knife and lunged at him, and he shot him in self-defense. But there was a witness who told a different story. Ruben Castilla, also twenty years old, was with Medina the night of the incident and describes in his version of the story as being set up by police."

As Victor awaits the verdict on TV in the case, he recalls what Ruben told him actually transpired that night. Victor knows they were set up by O'Connell.

The following are the details and backstory of what actually happened to Manny and Ruben that night.

The story and events surrounding the killing of Manny Medina go back to when Ruben became a Rojos member at a young age. Ruben had been initiated into the Rojos MC when he was only fifteen. He'd pursued a family connection to the club as a young boy, not having a father in the household. He'd desired respect from his peers and his community, and the only way he could obtain it was by joining the Rojos. Although Ruben and Manny shared a fatherless bond, their mindsets were quite different when it came to belonging to any type of group or gang. Manny had pursued his love of baseball, while Ruben pursued gang life.

Prior to Manny's death that evening, Ruben and Manny were at Father Murphy's church, St. John's. Father Murphy had been assigned to St. John's parish for years. He made a strong effort to reach out to the kids in the neighborhood, using sports as a vehicle to help them stay away from trouble, something that had assisted him early in his own life. He has been referred to as the "savior of baby angels," a nickname given to him at his previous parish, after steering a lot of the young boys and girls in a positive direction. Many spoke highly of Father Murphy for his work and his caring and kind demeanor. He was beloved by many of the parents of his parish, as well as nonmembers who recognized his impact on the community. For a quiet, soft-spoken priest, Father Murphy seemed to be a beacon of hope for many in the neighborhood.

Early that evening on that fatal day, Manny had pressed Ruben into taking a ride with him to St. John's to help out at a basketball clinic, something Father Murphy organized every Friday night for the youth. They had just finished helping Father Murphy with a basketball game and were headed out to their car. Father Murphy was out front talking with some parents. As he saw Manny and

Ruben walking towards him, he turned to greet them with a warm smile on his face.

Father Murphy extended his hand in gratitude to both of them. "Thanks again for helping out. We had some good games going on tonight." Both Manny and Ruben shook his hand.

"You're welcome, Father. Yeah, it was all right," Manny conveyed, smiling.

"You know we couldn't keep it going without your help, Manny." Father Murphy looked over at Ruben. "Glad you came tonight, Ruben."

Ruben looked over at Manny. "Yeah, I was sort of told to come."

Manny shook his head and coyly rolled his eyes.

"Ruben, maybe you'd be interested in helping out at our youth soccer program on Saturdays?"

He handed them both a flyer about the soccer program.

"Please tell the neighborhood kids about it. It's free and we'll have lunch afterwards."

Manny and Ruben both looked at the flyer. Manny folded it and put it in the breast pocket of his leather jacket. Father Murphy looked down for a moment, paused, and then looked up at Ruben.

"Ruben, I see your mother a lot here on Sundays. She always talks about you, and if I'm not mistaken, I remember her telling me you were once quite the soccer player."

Ruben smiled. "I guess. That was a long time ago, though, Padre."

Father Murphy smiled. "Not too long ago. Matter of fact, I used to play too, you know."

"Is that so?"

"Yeah, back in the day. I wasn't that bad either. We could really use your help if you could spare the time. Any chance you can assist us on Saturdays?" he inquired.

Manny interjected, "Yeah, Ruben, I remember those games. Your team was pretty good. I'm sure Father Murphy could use your help teaching the kids the game. Maybe once the baseball program starts up, we can come together and both coach. What do you think?"

"I don't know. We'll see, Padre."

"Okay, I'll just pray on it, then."

Father Murphy shook both their hands again and started walking back to the church. Manny and Ruben headed across the street, got in Manny's car and drove away.

As they drove, Manny kept looking over at Ruben. "How did you feel about tonight? You know, helping out the kids with Father Murphy?"

"Like I said, it was okay."

Manny looked at him seriously. "You have no intention of going on Saturday, do you?"

Ruben, who had been a Rojos for well over five years, understood his commitment to the gang and to Victor. He knew if he were to tell Victor about wanting to help out with the soccer program, Victor would not agree. The Rojos always came first and as Victor was fond of saying, "*You either follow the club rules or you answer to me.*" Ruben was still pretty much in the early stages of the gang and still needed to prove himself and working with Father Murphy would not be part of demonstrating his commitment to gang life.

Manny felt differently about Ruben and what he was capable of if he was no longer a Rojos. He knew his friend was smart and had potential and could achieve a lot of good things if Victor and Rojos weren't running his life. Manny had confidence in Ruben and always felt if he just applied himself in the right way, he could make a difference, not just for himself, but for the kids in the neighborhood as well.

"All you're doing is helping kids play soccer. I don't get you sometimes," Manny exclaimed. Ruben started getting a little agitated, but he knew Manny's heart was in the right place.

"I love you, Manny, but I'm a Rojos. That's my choice. Helping kids is great and all, and I get why *you* want to do it, but I took an oath to my brothers and that's the way it is. Now drop it."

"Your brothers?" Manny responded sharply. "We are like real brothers, Ruben, do you realize that? Do you remember all the shit we went through growing up? Have you forgotten about that? I'm the closest thing to a real brother you've ever had, not those bikers. They don't really care about you or give two shits about anyone else."

Ruben remained silent, looking out the window. He knew Manny cared about him, and maybe to some extent, the words he spoke were true, but the hand he had been dealt in life and the situations he encountered had ultimately led him to become a Rojos. They were now his family.

"Just drop it." Ruben turned his head and continued to stare out the window.

Manny shrugged him off for now, in hopes of changing Ruben's mind in the future. Manny made a right turn onto the avenue. As he drove about a block or two, police car lights suddenly flashed behind him, followed by their siren. Their loudspeaker came on and one of the officers said, "pull over." Manny looked back in his rearview mirror and quickly pulled over to the side of the road.

"What the—? What's this about?"

Officers O'Connell and Moran stepped out of the police car and approach Manny's car. Apparently, there had been a robbery at a convenience store earlier that evening. The report had stated that the perpetrators were two young Latino men in a dark colored, two door Chevy. Officer Moran came up to the driver's side window and asked Manny to see his license and registration. Manny, agitated, took out his license and handed it to Moran. Officer O'Connell shined his flashlight into the backseat of the passenger side of the vehicle. Ruben sat quietly in the front seat. He saw Ruben's Rojos vest on the back seat and motioned to Moran to look in through the window. He also saw it.

"Step out of the car and put your hands on the hood," Officer O'Connell instructed Ruben. Moran told Manny to do the same.

"For what?" Ruben retorted.

Officer O'Connell proceeded to tell them that the car fit the description of one used in a convenience store robbery earlier. Yet now, knowing one of them was a Rojos member, O'Connell wanted to see if this might turn into something more.

"That's bullshit. We just came from a basketball game at the church," Manny responded aggressively.

"Yeah, right," Officer O'Connell retorted sarcastically. "And I bet you said a few rosaries too. Now calmly and quietly step out of the car."

Manny became more and more agitated as he and Ruben got out of the car.

"This is bullshit. We did nothing. Stupid-ass cops. We were coaching basketball, like I said. Call Father Murphy at the church."

"We will, but for now just shut up and get against the car!" Officer Moran exclaimed, grabbing Manny's arm.

Manny, agitated, pulled away and shoved Moran. He began reaching into his breast pocket to pull out the soccer program flyer to show the cops. But Moran thought Manny was going for a weapon. He instinctively pulled out his gun from his holster and shot. The force of the bullet made Manny fall back against the car. As he fell backwards, the soccer flyer in his hand dropped to the ground. Manny's body slid down against the side of the car and collapsed on the ground near the flyer. Manny was bleeding profusely. Moran quickly realized he just shot an unarmed man.

Ruben had seen his fair share of violence with the Rojos, yet for the first time in his life, he had seen someone shot in front of him. Not just anyone, but his best friend. Ruben became hysterical.

"You shot him!" he yelled. "You shot him. Manny! Manny!"

O'Connell looks over at Moran. Grasping what had just happened, he sucker punched Ruben, knocking him unconscious. The next thing Ruben remembered when he came to was lying on the ground, with his head swollen and bleeding from hitting the curb.

What happens next, unbeknownst to Ruben or anyone else, is what actually happened.

Moran was in shock, looking down at Manny, who wasn't moving. Officer O'Connell bent down, checked Manny's pulse. He looked up at Moran with a concerned look on his face. Manny is still alive, but in bad shape. O'Connell quickly grabbed a pair of rubber gloves from his back pocket and started searching Manny's car while Moran stood there, stunned and motionless. O'Connell found a knife in the glove box. It was a simple pocketknife. Not exactly a weapon, but it would suffice.

He mumbled excitedly, "Bingo!"

Unbeknownst to O'Connell, the clouds in the sky above became dark and a shadowy figure appeared. It was Dante. He looked on at the two cops, Manny and Ruben. Looking at O'Connell, he grumbled, "A man after my own black heart." Dante smiled a sinister smile as he looked on.

O'Connell grabbed the knife and placed it in Manny's hand.

"Kevin, what are you doing? Shit, I shot this kid. I thought he was going for a gun. Is he dead? Oh my God, he's dead, isn't he? I killed him, didn't I?" Now panicked, Moran is trembling as he begins to pace back and forth.

O'Connell grabbed him by the shoulders, shook him hard and stared directly in Moran's eyes. "Get yourself together and follow my lead, unless you want to spend the rest of your life on Rikers Island." Moran, in shock, just stood there as O'Connell went to work.

Officer O'Connell picked up the flyer from the ground and placed it in his own back pocket. He opened the back door of the car and checked Ruben's Rojos vest. He found a small amount of marijuana and some Vicodin in the pocket.

"I knew these dirtbags would have drugs on them. Now we got them on attempted assault on a police officer with a deadly weapon and drug possession." He smiled. "Stick to the story, John, and we'll be okay."

Moran wiped the sweat from his brow while panting heavily.

O'Connell radioed in. "Ten-thirteen, ten-thirteen, officers need assistance."

Ruben, who'd been knocked out for over fifteen minutes, started to regain consciousness. The street was now flooded with police. He saw Manny's lifeless body lying in a pool of blood in the street and noticed the knife in Manny's hand. Ruben was handcuffed on the ground. Other officers now at the scene got him to his feet and put him in the back of a police car. Ruben started yelling through the window.

"Yo, they planted that knife! He had no knife, this is bullshit! This is a setup! He didn't do anything."

Officer O'Connell and Officer Moran stood to the side, speaking with their sergeant, as the police car Ruben was in pulled away. Later that evening, Manny died from the gunshot wound.

During the investigation, Ruben was grilled repeatedly about that night and yet always told the same story, steadfast to what happened. Now it's up to the grand jury.

Back in the present moment, Victor sits anxiously replaying what happened over and over in his mind. A million thoughts are running through his head. He stares at the TV screen, still sitting in the same position, downing the bottle of Jack Daniels, anxiously awaiting the verdict. By rehashing the details, he knows these cops are guilty. The door to the clubhouse opens wide and the warm sun shines in, prompting Victor to look away from the television at Ramon, another Rojos member. Ramon grabs a cold Corona from the fridge behind the bar and quickly downs it. Soon after, Jose, new to the gang, steps into the clubhouse.

"*Qué onda, Jose?*"

"Speak English, Ramon. Remember, I was born here," he jokes.

Victor drunkenly looks over at the both of them. "Shut up, the both of you. I'm trying to hear this."

Ramon grabs another Corona and takes a seat next to Victor.

"You know, one of my informants tells me that cop O'Connell goes to the Empire Diner in the morning for coffee. They say he's a cocky ass, always flirting with the waitresses."

"Good to know," says Jose. "We just might have to pay him a visit one day."

"All I know is, this pig better go down," Victor slurs.

Ramon retorts, "Yo, Victor—this Manny dude, he's not a Rojos. I know he's Ruben's friend and all, but we don't owe him no revenge."

Victor shoots Ramon a piercing look. "How about the fact this pig cold-cocked Ruben, knocked him out and planted a knife to save his buddy's ass? How about they arrested Ruben on some bogus drug charge? Don't you get it? That asshole will railroad every one of us if he gets the chance."

For Victor, it isn't about Manny not being a Rojos. It's more about cops like O'Connell setting people up by planting evidence to save their own asses. Victor knows dirty cops are working with the cartel. It's one of the reasons the club isn't harassed too often by the police. Victor doesn't like it, though, as he doesn't trust cops. He suspects O'Connell is working a side deal with the cartel and may have had more to do with Manny's death than anyone is saying. He trusts what Ruben told him and that's good enough for him. As far as he's concerned, O'Connell will pay the price for knocking out Ruben.

Victor, although drunk, listens even more intently to the news. On the screen, he watches the reporter, who is standing outside the courtroom, waiting to hear the official verdict. The reporter is silent for the moment as the camera pans in on a crowd of protestors. The reporter suddenly cups his hand over his ear piece to listen more intently to the breaking news he is receiving. He turns and stares into the camera and begins to speak.

"This just in. The grand jury has returned a verdict of not guilty against Officer John Moran in the shooting death of Manuel Medina. I repeat, the jury has returned a verdict of not guilty. The jury has found that the officers acted in self-defense." Suddenly, the doors to the courtroom open abruptly. Officer Moran walks out with his lawyer beside him. He is surrounded by police officers who escort him outside as reporters swarm them. He refuses to make any kind of statement as they rush him into an awaiting unmarked police SUV. Outside the courtroom, representatives and protestors from the Latino community loudly voice their displeasure.

Victor snaps. He stands up and growls like a grizzly bear and throws the bottle of Jack Daniels against the wall in a fit of rage, just missing Jose's head.

A menacing obscure figure emerges from the shadows of the corner of the room. Dante, with his demons in tow, look to seize on Victor's rage. He laughs vociferously, seeing Victor's eyes turn fiery and filled with hate. Dante's whisper vibrates in Victor's ears.

"It's your time, Victor. I've been waiting for this moment. Seek your revenge. Don't let these pigs get away with murder. You know what you have to do."

Victor screams loudly and stomps around, not knowing how to control himself. He storms toward the door. His fists are clenched. Ramon tries to stop him but knows it's pointless. Just as Dante saw that fire burning in Victor's eyes, so did Ramon. Ramon is taken aback by the shear rage possessing Victor. Victor brutally shoves Ramon out of the way as he heads for the door. Ramon falls back and hits the floor. He has never seen rage like this before. Victor pushes the door to the clubhouse open and steps outside. He goes straight to his motorcycle, kick starts his bike and screeches off.

Jose looks over at Ramon and reaches out his hand to help pull him up. "I got a bad feeling about this one right here. I've never seen him this pissed off. We better follow him."

"Leave him be, bro. Let him blow off some steam. He'll calm down once he rides a bit."

"I don't know, bro. Did you see the look in his eyes? He's out for blood."

Victor, consumed by anger, speeds down the road, darting in and out of traffic. Dante and his demons fly in sync with Victor's motorcycle, just above his head. Dante's face turns from humanlike into a skull, with flames trailing his body. Victor continues to cruise the streets of New York. He remembered Jose say O'Connell often goes to the Empire Diner. Victor takes the chance and rides by the diner and sees two cops sitting in their car. By coincidence, one is O'Connell. Victor, realizing he just stumbled upon O'Connell, quickly drives around the block. He finds a place to park his bike two blocks away and out of sight. He takes off his Rojos vest and packs it on the back of his bike. Underneath, he's wearing a plain black T-shirt, jeans and boots. He puts on a Mets cap and dark shades and tucks two semiautomatic pistols under his shirt. Victor walks the two blocks to the diner where he observed the police car. Dante follows him closely.

With a fiery rage in his belly, Victor crosses the street and steps up to the car. He looks straight through the windshield at O'Connell and quickly pulls a semiautomatic from under his shirt. O'Connell catches him out of the corner of his eye. He tries to open his door and go for his gun, but it's too late. Rapid gunfire disengages from Victor's gun. The bullets pierce the windshield. O'Connell takes multiple shots to the chest and falls out onto the street. Officer Benuti is able to get out of the passenger side of the car. He attempts to draw his gun. Victor is upon him and shoots him twice before Benuti is able to get off a shot. Victor then turns, firing bullets into the Empire Diner window to create a distraction. The diner window shatters into a million pieces, the crowd inside scrambling to the floor in sheer terror. Earl grabs Maggie and pulls her down behind the counter in an act of bravery. Shards of glass cut his forearm and hands as he ducks down and hits the floor.

Benuti and O'Connell are both on the ground, clinging to life. O'Connell is conscious, Benuti isn't. Victor hauls ass, running down the block. A bystander calls 911.

Outside of a bodega, Franklin Watson, a seventy-five-year-old man who's well known in the community, sits on a milk crate. Watson is a sweet old guy, kind of the neighborhood watchdog. He keeps an eye on the streets. Watson is reading a newspaper when he looks up from his seated position and sees a familiar face crossing the street, Cookie, a transgender sex worker. She saunters across the street and greets Franklin before heading into the store for a pack of condoms. Watson has known Cookie since she was a kid. He always looked out for her as she had it rough growing up. He did that with all the kids, but especially with Cookie.

Cookie, aka Dwayne Jones, grew up in Harlem as an only child. She was somewhat of a loner. She knew she was different from a young age and so did everyone else. She was constantly beaten up and bullied. Nothing was ever easy for her. Her relationship with her father, a long-distance truck driver, was severely strained. He frequently told her he was ashamed of who she was and what she represented, and eventually the embarrassment he harbored caused him to throw her out of the house to fend for herself when she was just fifteen.

Cookie's mother, however, loved her unconditionally and wanted only the best for her. If it wasn't for her mother, Lila, Cookie would have nowhere to go. When Cookie's father was on an overnight truck delivery, Lila would often let Cookie stay at the house, but eventually her father found out and gave Cookie a fierce beating that landed her in the hospital. The incident ultimately ended her parents' marriage. Despite everything, Lila accepted Cookie. Her unconditional love as a mother ran deep. She knew Cookie was different and did her best to raise her the best she could.

After she died, Cookie lost her greatest ally, her mother that she loved deeply. Her life spiraled out of control for a few years. She was so depressed, she once attempted suicide, overdosing on pills in an alley near the bodega. It was none other than Franklin Watson who found Cookie and called 911. If not for Franklin coming to her aid, the suicide effort would've succeeded. Her life is still a struggle to survive. All she wants is to be accepted for who she is.

Before going inside the bodega, Cookie lights a cigarette.

"Hey, let me get one of those, Cookie," says Franklin.

"Mr. W., now you know you shouldn't be smokin'. These things will be the death of you," Cookie responds.

"I can think of a few things that can be the death of you too, Cookie."

They both exchange a friendly laugh.

"I got you, Mr. W. Besides, if I count all the cigarettes you've given me, I'd owe you a whole truckload by now. I'll be right back, Mr. W. I've got to get my stuff for my dates tonight. A girl has to be safe, you know, because these streets ain't loyal to no one."

Cookie steps inside the bodega. She walks around the small store. Everyone pays her no mind as she's a regular from the neighborhood. The occasional customer who doesn't know her will give her an uncomfortable stare. A man near the beer cooler does just that and stares at her awkwardly.

Cookie says coyly, "I hope you're just admiring my dress."

The man puts his head down, grabs a cold six-pack of Modelo and heads for the register.

"Have a nice day, sugar," says Cookie, chuckling.

Watson is preoccupied, sweeping trash and humming a tune with his back to the door by the garbage. He lives a simple life, tending to little things at the bodega. He keeps the front of the store neat and tidy. It's like his personal front yard. As Cookie steps out, Victor is running up the block with his gun in hand and slams into her, both falling to the ground. He gets up and points his gun at her.

"Stupid freak," he yells.

Cookie looks at Victor in stunned fear. Watson turns around and sees Victor pointing the gun at Cookie. In the heat of the moment, he reacts. He hits Victor across the back with his broom, and with all his strength, he hits him again. Cookie quickly crawls into the street in an attempt to get away. Victor is dazed by the sudden blows and drops to one knee. Victor shakes his head, regains his balance and looks up at Watson in anger. He slowly lifts his gun and, with no qualms about shooting a man he doesn't even know, fires multiple rounds into Watson's chest.

"Stupid old fool," says Victor, who turns and runs.

Watson falls back onto the ground, gripping his chest.

Cookie is horrified. She jumps to her feet and runs to Mr. Watson's aid. "Somebody, help. Please!" she yells, helplessly cradling Watson's head in her lap.

"Hang on, Mr. W. Hang on! Somebody get an ambulance… please!" screams Cookie. Cookie, in shock, doesn't know what to do. As she begins to sob, she holds his hand and strokes Mr. Watson's forehead, hoping help will arrive.

In the distance, sirens are blaring as the cop cars are getting closer and closer. Victor knows they're closing in on him. He runs down the block and into an alleyway with no exit. He's trapped.

Cookie continues to comfort Watson as he lies on the ground, bleeding. He looks at Cookie briefly and says in a low, struggling tone, "You okay, Cookie?"

"I'm all right, Mr. W. You hang on. Help is coming."

Franklin slips into unconsciousness. People surround him and Cookie, continually dialing 911.

The police respond to the 911 call that a gunman is on foot near the bodega. They pull up and spot Victor in the alley.

Victor has no way out. The cops jump out of their police cars with their guns drawn, coercing Victor to give up.

"Put down the gun!" they yell. Victor knows he's trapped. There's no way out, and he refuses to let them take him alive. Victor points his guns and yells, "Come get me, pigs."

Bullets fly from his gun. Multiple police officers, taking cover behind their cars, return fire. One of Victor's bullets hits a cop. He grabs his bleeding shoulder and continues to return fire. Multiple bullets hit Victor in the chest, the force knocking him backward. His body jerks violently as each bullet pierces his chest. He falls to the ground.

The shooting suddenly stops. In the chaos, there is an eerie moment of silence. The police cautiously approach Victor's lifeless body and surround him, guns pulled.

One cop bends down to check his pulse. "Low life loser. He's dead."

Suddenly, a bright light appears in the darkness of the alleyway. It's Victor's guardian angel, sobbing nearby. The angel is unable to approach, unable to claim his soul. The bright light softly fades away and a fiery red flame approaches Victor's corpse.

Dante swoops in through the cloud of flame. He looks at Victor. "Well done, Mr. Valles, well done."

Dante then points at Victor's dead body and pulls a ball of murky smoke from Victor's chest and immediately casts it down through the ground towards hell. Dante looks up and sees Matthias not far away. He laughs with great pleasure and vanishes. Matthias looks down in sadness and flies away into the shadows of the alley.

Back at the diner, Earl and Maggie are lying on the floor behind the counter, covered in glass from the window and various debris from the counter. Broken bottles of ketchup, coffee cups and sugar bowls litter the floor. The shooting has stopped for a while now. Earl cautiously gets up and looks around. He then helps Maggie up.

"Maggie, are you okay?"

"Yeah, I'm fine. But your forearm is bleeding."

"I'm okay. It's just a cut."

Earl gets up and looks around the diner. He starts helping other customers who are slowly getting up from the floor. Luckily, no one is seriously injured. Maggie wipes off her apron and shakes some sugar out of her hair. Her forearm is bruised, and she has some minor cuts on her arms and her knees. Maggie looks out the window and sees the cops that were shot lying on the street. In horror, Maggie instinctively runs out of the diner, stepping over more broken glass on the sidewalk. She sees Officer O'Connell lying on the ground. She runs to his side and collapses to her knees next to him as the others rush to assist Officer Benuti. O'Connell, who's covered in blood, is struggling to breathe. Maggie gently cradles O'Connell's head in her lap. O'Connell knows he's been shot. He glances up and sees Maggie. Despite his condition, he mumbles, "So, you do want me after all?"

O'Connell is trying to ease the tension in a horrific moment by being playful. He doesn't realize how seriously he's hurt.

"I dropped my damn coffee. Can I get one on the house?"

"Sure thing Kevin. Just be quiet and lay still. Help is on the way."

Turning serious, O'Connell says, "Where's my partner? Where's Tony? Is he okay?"

"We're helping him. Help is on the way. Just lie still."

"That effin' bastard shot us. I know who it was. I saw him. I'm gonna kill that bastard."

She focuses on comforting him until help arrives. O'Connell is coughing up blood. As Maggie tries to hush him, he is losing consciousness. She removes her apron and applies pressure to the gunshot wound near his neck. O'Connell loses consciousness. Maggie can hear the ambulance sirens getting closer.

"Oh God, come on. Stay with me! Breathe. Come on, Kevin, breathe. God, please!"

Maggie is panicked. She doesn't know what to do. She glances down and sees that her hands and lap are covered in O'Connell's blood.

One of Dante's demons is standing over Maggie, staring at O'Connell—a menacing creature with a gargoyle-type face. There is a sinister look to him. He glances up to see an angel nearby, just a short distance away. The angel is big and strong, an imposing figure. It has a human soldier-like quality, there to protect and defend the good from evil. The demon sneers at the angel and vanishes. As wailing sirens from a nearing ambulance approach, the angel turns and vanishes too.

Police officers and EMS personnel finally arrive and frantically rush to assist Officers O'Connell and Benuti. As they approach Maggie, an officer says, "We'll take it from here." Maggie moves aside, then drops back on her ankles and continues to sob uncontrollably. An EMS worker helps her to her feet and walks her away from the site. Still in shock, she glances back at O'Connell and collapses briefly in the arms of the EMS worker.

After attending to his customers to make sure everyone is all right, Earl runs outside and sees the cops have been shot. He sees Maggie with the EMS worker and runs to help her. What was a perfectly calm and ordinary day in the city has turned into complete and utter chaos. Evil has a way of disturbing the peace.

CHAPTER 6

Victor's Reality

Victor Valles is a badass biker through and through. He grew up in the roughest part of town with a poor representation of an alcoholic father and a mother whose vice was hard drugs. His father was in and out of prison most of his life and barely home when he wasn't incarcerated. The times he was around usually wound up ending in the verbal and physical abuse of Victor and his mother. As Victor got older, he became stronger and fought back, beating his father after watching him smack his mother around. Growing up in that environment hardened him immensely. He never knew what it was like to be normal. It wasn't living, it was simply surviving. All Victor ever knew was pain, violence and hardship. From a young age, his anger and resentment at the world led him to a life of crime. He got involved with the Rojos club at fourteen and quickly wound up in all kinds of trouble. The Rojos were his true family. Unlike his parents, his biker brothers always had his back. The brotherhood of the club was a bond of friendship. He finally had a sense of security he never knew growing up in his dysfunctional home life. The club brought purpose and meaning to his life. He finally had people who actually cared for him and respected him. It's the one thing that's ever made him feel in control of his dark world. Yet, as club president, he wields his power with no regard for anyone. He will fight and protect his brothers till death, but he expects them to toe the line at all times. There is no room in his eyes for weakness. To him, letting your guard down makes you vulnerable to your enemies. As he rose to the head of the Rojos MC, he demanded respect and loyalty and ensured that all its members were individually tough, yet inseparably bound together by the blood oath in their allegiance to the club.

Victor Valles eyes open suddenly. He looks around at his surroundings. He's sitting on the floor of a prison cell. It's cold, dark, damp and dirty. There's a stench that fills the room, like a rotting dead animal. The walls are solid concrete cinder block, drab and covered in dark soot. There is a steel door, but no window. A single small, dim bulb swings from a wire on the ceiling, barely lighting the room. Victor stands up and walks around the tiny, drab room. There is no air in the room, making it feel like being locked in a cargo container. The steel door is so tight that no natural light is visible whatsoever through the seams where the door meets the frame. Victor has been in some bad prisons before, but nothing like this place. It was very different.

"Is this some kind of joke?" Victor voices out loud in an annoyed tone. "What type of bullshit is this? What shithole prison did they put me in?"

Victor starts banging on the steel door.

"Hey, I got rights. I want a lawyer."

There is no response. Victor goes back to the far wall and sits on the floor, directly across from the door.

"These bastards can't leave me in here forever," he says to himself.

After about a half hour, the steel door creaks and slowly opens. It's still hard to see, but in walks a tall, burly man with dark, bushy unkempt hair and a dark beard. His eyes are hollow and black as coal. He's a commanding figure at about six feet seven inches tall. He's wearing a long dark coat with a pair of calf-high spiked black leather boots. He carries a whiskey bottle in his left hand. As he walks in, he looks down and sets the whiskey bottle on the floor to his left, about five feet away from Victor. He looks down at Victor and says slowly in a gravelly voice, "Victor Valles…"

Victor looks up at this imposing figure. "Who are you? Where's my lawyer?"

The man stares at him. "Victor Valles, the badass Rojos biker," he says after a pause.

"You know me?" asks Victor. "You from some other motorcycle club?"

The man paces slowly back and forth, not making eye contact with Victor. "Oh, I know all about you. Let's skip all the BS about your shitty life. You've killed more men than you care to remember. The number is eighteen. That doesn't include the other twenty-six you shot, stabbed and beat within an inch of their lives."

Victor retorts, "I don't know who the hell you are, but I ain't saying shit to you. I want my lawyer."

The man looks at him and replies in a controlling tone, "Lawyer? You want an effin' lawyer, Mr. Badass Biker? Since when does a tough-ass guy like you want to lawyer up? Well, unfortunately, it's too late for that…Victor. Lawyer? No, you're right where you belong and you ain't going anywhere."

At that moment, the room gets intensely hot; sweat begins to form across his forehead. Victor feels like his skin is about to melt off his face. He is having trouble breathing as the intensely hot air fills his lungs. Fear suddenly grips him; he has never experienced anything like this.

"What's happening to me?" he screams. "Who are you, man? What are you doing to me? What the hell is happening?"

The burly man looks at him. "You got that right," he says eerily. "Hell is happening…to you." The intense heat suddenly stops, giving Victor momentary relief.

Victor looks into his hollow eyes. "Hell? Who are you? Wait, are you saying I'm dead?"

The burly figure leans up against the cinder block wall. "Well, what did you think happened in that alley? Let's see, you had two semiautomatic Glock pistols with about twenty rounds of ammunition left. There were about ten cops shooting at you at the time. You do the math."

Victor looks around, looking down at the palms of his hands, touching his chest, his legs, his arms in disbelief.

70

"Well, if I'm really dead, I don't deserve to be in hell. This is bull crap."

The dark figure's laughter echoes loudly. "Were you expecting a cute puppy dog to come and lick your face on some sun-drenched mountain, surrounded by beautiful flowers? Hey, come on now, you're Victor Valles, the badass biker. Don't go soft on me now. Besides, you're gonna need every ounce of fight you have left in you down here. It gets a little rough."

Victor, getting scared, starts pleading his case, "A little rough? Hey, look, I'm no choirboy. I'm a survivor. I grew up in the hood, man. I dole out my own justice."

"Yeah, with your justice, people keep winding up dead," the imposing figure says.

"All those bastards deserved to die. Eye for an eye, tooth for a tooth. Ain't that what it says in the Bible? Like my drunken old man. He beat my mother every time he came home with a load on and she'd shoot up to heal her wounds. He deserved what he got from me. I saved her life from that prick, but the drugs took hers. Anyway, he deserved it. He made her who she became."

The man continues in a sarcastic, judgmental tone, "Victor Valles…the badass Rojos biker. This is not a trial where you get to state your case. I frankly don't give a shit what you think or say. But I'll indulge you for a few minutes. Everyone deserved what they got, you say? Like the man who cut you off on the freeway three years ago? Yeah, you got away with that one. No one could ID you. You followed him home and beat him within inches of his life—in front of his young daughter, no less. You left him there to die."

"He died from that beating?"

The burly man's voice echoes in the cell. "You know damn well how he died. You saw it on the evening news. You were playing pool at your clubhouse, acting like you knew nothing about it to your brothers. That guy you killed was named Charles Rivera. He had beaten cancer a year before. He was just a simple family man. A Latino like you. By the way, the bulb in his car blinker had burned out. He never cut you off deliberately. His signal didn't work. But, no, Mr. Badass Biker thought he deliberately cut off a Rojos. How dare he! No one cuts off an MC member while riding their sled, especially on the highway, right, Victor? When you got to his house, he barely stepped out of his car and you beat him with a lead pipe. His daughter witnessed it. Poor kid, she's scarred for life. Now she must go through life without a father. All because you thought he disrespected you. You want me to keep going? I'll just cut to earlier today and save myself the boredom of rehashing what a complete piece of shit you are. You shoot two cops out of revenge and then you shoot that old man. That old man just wanted to protect his friend from you. You were gonna shoot his friend for what? For accidentally running into you? The nerve of him. He deserved it, though, right?"

The man continues, "No, Mr. Badass Rojos Biker, you deserve to be here."

Victor stares at him with a stone-cold look on his face. The intense heat starts again as fear grips him.

"Screw you."

As the heat gets more intense, Victor screams, "Okay, okay. Make it stop. I was wrong. I screwed up, all right. Is that what you want to hear? Cut me a break. I'll change."

Victor now makes a weak attempt at showing he's not all that bad.

"Hey, I've done some good shit in my life. I tried to help kids when I could—with the club."

The man sarcastically replies, "Oh…the Christmas toy drive when you and your MC buddies dropped off toys to the hospital? Yeah, that was nice. You did steal some of the stuff to give to the kids, though. Kind of like Robin Hood, eh? How sweet. You guys even chipped in some cash. How thoughtful. Yours came from the heroin you sold to those dealers. Nice little business venture. Beats working in the factory, right? Do you want me to go over how many kids overdosed from the smack you sold? Nah, I ain't got time for that crap."

The man walks towards the door, then turns back. He shoots a deadpan look at Victor and in a frightening, deep tone says, "It's too late for you. Goodbye, Victor." He walks out the door and slams it shut, echoing into the air.

"Wait. Come on, man! Cut me a break. I've done some good shit. I don't belong here."

No one answers.

The intense heat briefly stops, and the room cools down, giving Victor momentary relief. It's eerily calm. Victor is shaking. He doesn't know what to expect next. He's starting to feel trapped, like a caged animal. Is this really hell? He looks around the room. He sees the bottle of whiskey, about a quarter full. Victor crawls across the floor and grabs the bottle. There's a rolled-up note stuffed in the opening where the cap would normally be. Victor is so parched from the heat, he pulls out the note and drinks the whiskey. He can't quench his thirst as the whiskey is warm, but at least it's wet.

When he's done, he glances down and picks up the note. He unfurls the paper, which reads, "You reap what you sow."

Victor mumbles, "What is this garbage?"

He crumples the paper and tosses it across the room. He takes another swig of whiskey. Victor's mood swings back and forth between fear and anger. The room is eerily quiet since the burly guy left.

Victor takes the last gulp of whiskey and wipes his mouth with his sleeve. From a dark corner of the room, a rat comes toward him. Victor reacts without hesitation and throws the bottle at it. The bottle smashes and shatters into pieces, killing the rat.

He screams out, "Hey, let me outta here! There's damn rat in here."

Then a second rat, a third rat, a fourth rat, and more and more rats come from the corner, charging towards him. He jumps up to avoid them. More rats keep coming. Victor starts freaking out. He runs over to the door, beating it with fear.

"Let me outta here, let me outta here," he screams over and over to no avail.

More rats come, crawling up his legs and over his body. Victor shrieks in fear as he pounds the door. Hundreds of rats bite him all over his body, ripping at his flesh in an insatiable, ravenous manner.

Victor is covered in rats as they begin to consume him. His screams are so piercing, they sound inhuman.

"Help. Help. Help," he cries repeatedly.

Victor falls to the floor. There are so many rats you can no longer see his body. Suddenly, the room is black. There is no sound.

Victor's eyes open. He is sitting on the floor as he was earlier, but the rats are gone. There are no bite marks on his body. It's as if it never happened. The fear is real, though. Victor is shaking and can't calm himself from the terror. Was it a nightmare? He glances across the room and sees another bottle of whiskey, same as before, with a note stuffed in the neck. There is no broken glass from the bottle he threw. Maybe it was just a nightmare.

He grabs the bottle of whiskey and takes a sip. This time it's more bitter and warmer. He opens the note, again. It says the same thing: "You reap what you sow." The room gets burning hot and from the corner, the rats come again, crawling all over him, biting at his flesh. Victor throws the bottle at some of them, but there are just too many rats this time. Victor is tormented and screaming. Suddenly, after what seemed like an eternity of being attacked by the rats, it stops again.

Victor's eyes open again. Now he is gripped with more terror. Once again, the room is empty. The bottle of whiskey is standing there again with the note inside, like before. The scenario starts all over again. Each time it starts over again, Victor becomes more terrified. He will spend his damnation in this recurring torture. There is no escape. This is his personal hell.

"All souls are immortal, even those of the wicked. Yet, it would be better for them if they were not deathless. For they are punished with the endless vengeance of quenchless fire. Since they do not die, it is impossible for them to have an end put to their misery."

—St. Clement of Alexandria

74

"The road to hell is open for the wicked. Once they enter it, they will never come up again. They will be without glory or bliss and will be filled with misery and everlasting reproach."
—Christ to St. Bridget of Sweden, The Revelations

CHAPTER 7

Critical Situations

It's a typical morning at Lenox Hill Hospital on the Upper East Side of Manhattan, but that's about to change soon. Ambulances are en route with the shooting victims. Throughout the hospital, the staff attends to their normal duties. Claire Monroe is a head nurse at Lenox Hill Hospital. She's in her late fifties, kind of a plain Jane, with graying brown hair. There's nothing that really stands out about her.

She has been a nurse for over thirty years. She grew up in a strict religious home in Youngstown, Ohio. Her parents moved out east when the factory her father worked in closed and he needed work. Her parents both served in the military and raised their daughter in that vein. They always had a regimented schedule for her. Her early life was by the book: up early, chores, school, more chores, homework and early to bed. There wasn't much time for socializing, and whenever there was, it was limited. Her parents always told her she needed to make something of her life, so she studied to be a nurse. She joined the military after nursing school and served as an Army nurse. After many years of service, she retired and came to work at the hospital.

From her upbringing and military background, Claire is a stern, old-fashioned type of woman—no nonsense, everything according to standards and procedures, just like she was raised. That's how she manages her nursing staff. She's fair, but at times, inflexible. She's empathetic, but her empathy doesn't necessarily adhere to those same standards and procedures.

Claire makes the rounds on the second floor, checking up on her nurses. She goes into 227A, the room of an elderly female patient, Mrs. Abigail Reinhardt. Abigail is asleep. Claire walks over to Abigail and stands by her bedside, checking the vital signs on her monitors. Abigail is in her late eighties, suffering from dementia. She recently broke her hip in a fall. She is not doing well at all and has been going steadily downhill. The pain meds have her pretty much asleep most of the time.

Claire is dressed in white uniform scrubs. She has a needle in her hand while holding the patient's IV bag. She's about to insert the needle in the portal of the IV line when another nurse runs in, prompting Claire to step away from Abigail, quickly hiding the needle behind her back.

"Claire, we need you in the ER, stat! We've got gunshot victims coming in. Someone said police officers were shot," says the other nurse, who quickly turns to rush back out the door.

"I'll be right there," Claire replies.

The nurse leaves Claire alone again with Abigail. Claire puts the cap back on the needle and places it in her front pocket. She bends down.

"Don't worry, dear. I'll help end your misery soon," Claire says in a haunting whisper, although Abigail is fast asleep.

Claire hurries out of the room and heads to the ER, which is in complete bedlam as the two police officers are rushed in. The room is filled with many cops as the shooting victims are Officers O'Connell and Benuti. EMS personnel frantically wheel them in as doctors rush to their sides. Both officers are unconscious and bleeding profusely. More police officers follow them in with deep concern for their fallen brothers. The atmosphere is tense and frantic.

Rita Damaso, an attractive Latino woman in her early fifties, is a seasoned triage nurse. She also happens to be the mother of Rojos MC member Ruben Castilla. Rita was born and raised in the Bronx. She grew up in a large family, with two sisters and three brothers. She was the oldest. Living in a cramped apartment, they

77

always had to make do, and sharing became necessary for survival. Rita did her best to avoid trouble. She stayed in school and got her nursing degree from City College. Her boyfriend, Ernesto, got her pregnant with Ruben just after she graduated. He skipped out on his responsibilities as a father and left her to raise Ruben alone. She persevered, and with the help of family, she raised Ruben while starting her career as a nurse.

She is an excellent nurse, as her strong street sense makes her a perfect fit for the fast-paced environment of the ER, where acting quickly is critical. Her biggest disappointment has been not spending enough motherly time with Ruben as he grew up. Her work schedule and the need for money left her less time for parenting. She loves Ruben deeply, but over time, he fell in with the wrong crowd and became a Rojos. She hasn't given up hope of getting him out of it.

As the EMTs wheel in Officers Benuti and O'Connell, Rita looks intently at O'Connell. Suddenly, she realizes he's the same cop who punched Ruben in the face and knocked him out when Manny Medina was killed. She stops and stares at him. A feeling of rage comes over her, but she keeps a calm, outward demeanor so as not to let on she knows who O'Connell is. Struck by the coincidence, she stares at him in amazement, almost as if to positively identify him.

Claire rushes in through another set of ER doors.

"What are we dealing with, Rita?" says Claire in an authoritative tone.

"These two officers were shot. I don't know any more details," Rita says hurriedly.

A concerned police officer overhears them. "Officers Benuti and O'Connell were ambushed by a Rojos biker."

The officer seems agitated. He turns and points to another gurney, on which is the dead body of Victor Valles, who died from gunshot wounds sustained during his brazen gunfight with multiple police officers.

"Over there. That scumbag shot them in their patrol car."

Rita's face turns white as she wonders if it's her son, Ruben. Could she be staring in the face of her worst nightmare?

"Hey, Rita, are you okay?" Claire asks.

Rita disregards Claire's question; her only concern is who might be under the sheet on the gurney. She walks slowly toward the dead body with Claire close behind her.

"Please, God. Don't let it be my son," Rita whispers softly to herself.

Rita reaches over and, with some anxious reservation, slowly pulls back the sheet. It's Victor Valles, not Ruben. Rita feels a tremendous sense of relief, almost bringing her to tears. She quickly pulls the sheet back over Victor's face.

Claire looks at Rita and inquisitively asks, "Do you know him?"

"No," Rita replies quickly, walking away from Victor's body.

Claire looks at her, a bit puzzled by why Rita looked at the dead body in the first place. Rita starts heading for the ER door to go outside.

"I'll be back in a few minutes. I need to make a phone call."

"No problem, but don't be too long."

Rita must have known him, Claire thinks, but she lets it go and walks back into the main area of the ER.

Rita heads outside, about a hundred yards from the entrance. She frantically dials Ruben, but his phone goes straight to voicemail. On the third attempt, she leaves a message.

"Ruben, where the hell are you? Victor is dead. He shot two cops. They brought them here to the hospital. What the hell happened? Are you okay? Where are you? Call me or text me and tell me you're okay. Please... love you."

Rita slips her phone in her pocket and turns to hurry back inside. Standing outside by the door is Cookie, looking scared and disheveled.

"Nurse, excuse me. My friend Mr. Watson, he was shot. Is he okay? Is he alive?"

"Are you family?" asks Rita.

"No, but yes, kind of.." Cookie stutters. "I mean, no, I'm not. I was there when it happened. He's my friend…he…saved my life."

Cookie starts crying. Rita puts her arm around her shoulder.

"He's in pretty bad shape, but he's fighting. We're doing the best we can. Stay strong, okay?"

"I'm trying, miss."

Rita takes out a pad and pen and scratches her cell phone number down and hands it to Cookie.

"You call me later and I'll see if I can give you an update."

"Thank you. God bless you. Thank you."

Rita gives Cookie a hug. It's just her motherly instinct.

She heads back to the ER. The automatic doors open and quickly close behind her as she heads back into the chaos. A little while later, the ER doors open and in walk Reverend Ezekiel Pitts and Grace Williams, both from the local East Side Evangelical Church. Reverend Pitts is a tall, slender man in his late sixties. He was born and raised in Brooklyn. The son of a Baptist preacher, he followed in his father's footsteps and was ordained thirty-five years ago. His church is a small but tight-knit congregation. He is known for his steady hand, inspiring sermons and kind heart. Grace, a full-figured woman in her late forties, is a pastoral assistant to Reverend Pitts. The congregants refer to her as the angel on Reverend Pitts' shoulder, helping him run the day-to-day outreach programs in the community. Grace was raised in a strong Christian home. She is deeply spiritual. She also sings in the choir. She inherited her singing gift from her Auntie J, a well-known gospel singer in the New York church circles back in the early 1960s.

Pitts looks around as if he doesn't know where to go. He spots a group of police officers standing by a wall.

"Excuse me, Officers. I was told one of my parishioners was here. A Mr. Franklin Watson? We heard he was shot today."

One of the officers, not really knowing, points to the doctor coming out of the emergency surgery area.

"I'm not sure. Multiple people were shot. Ask him," says the cop.

Pitts and Grace rush over to the doctor. The doctor is Stephen Kirkland, a well-known trauma surgeon at Lenox Hill.

"Doctor, my name is Reverend Ezekiel Pitts. I received a call and was told to come down here regarding Franklin Watson?"

"Yes, Reverend Pitts," replies Kirkland. "I had the staff call you. Mr. Watson was shot today during a police chase. He had your information in his wallet. He had no other family contact information, so I figured you would be the best person to contact."

In a deeply concerned voice, Grace asks, "Oh, dear Lord. Is he okay?"

Kirkland looks at them both. "His wounds from the gunshot are pretty bad. We just operated on him. We've made him as comfortable as possible, but he's in critical condition. If you're his pastor, now would be a good time to pray for him."

Reverend Pitts is anxious to know more details of the shooting. "How did this happen?" he inquires.

"I'm not really sure of the specifics, Reverend. You'll have to talk with the police, but I do know two police officers were also shot."

"Oh my Lord, this is terrible," says Grace. "Can we see Franklin, Doctor?"

"Yes, but he is heavily sedated. Please keep it brief," says Kirkland. "Follow me."

Kirkland leads them down the hall and into the trauma surgery postop area. Grace has tears in her eyes. Pitts places a reassuring hand on her shoulder.

Across the crowded, chaotic ER, Maggie is sitting on a hospital bed in an area for ER patients, the partially drawn curtain separating her from the next cubicle. Her shirt is covered in blood. She's not hurt, but she was brought in by the EMS team after she collapsed while assisting O'Connell. She has been treated for minor cuts and abrasions.

She has a blank stare on her face. She's in shock. Everything happened so quickly. The sight of O'Connell bleeding on her lap has now overwhelmed her. Nurse Claire pulls back the curtain to check on Maggie. She wraps the blood pressure cuff around Maggie's arm as Maggie continues to sit there with a blank stare on her face. When Maggie picks her head up and notices Dr. Kirkland from across the way, tending to another patient in the ER, her face turns pale, as if she's seen a ghost. Dr. Kirkland looks back at her and offers a friendly gesture in a smile. Claire closes the curtain for privacy.

"I heard you saw everything," Claire says. "The officers said you ran out to help Officer O'Connell. They said you kept the pressure on his wound till EMS got there."

Maggie remains silent as if in deep thought. Claire finishes checking Maggie's blood pressure and gets sanitized hand wipes and begins cleaning Maggie's bloody hands as well as the splattered blood from her face.

"Physically, you're okay and free to go. Is there anyone here for you, someone that can take you home, or maybe someone I can call?" probes Claire.

Maggie stays silent.

"How 'bout I get you a clean shirt and a ride home, okay?" says Claire. "Here, take these." She hands Maggie two mild sedatives. "They'll help you sleep tonight. They'll just take the edge off a bit."

Closing the curtain behind her, Claire leaves Maggie and heads down the hallway to get Maggie a clean scrub shirt from the nurse's supply room.

Detective Sal Petrizzo, a short Italian man in his late forties with a bristling black mustache, is walking down the hallway. He sees nurse Claire and walks towards her. He is a twenty-five-year veteran of the NYPD and the head detective for the Upper East Side Homicide Unit.

"Excuse me, Nurse, I'm Detective Petrizzo of the NYPD. I'm looking for the woman from the diner. The waitress. Do you know where I can find her?"

"Oh, sure—yeah, she's just down the hall," says Claire. "Follow me. I was just grabbing a clean shirt for her to change into. She was covered in blood. Her name is Margaret Hargrove."

"That would be great, thanks," says Petrizzo.

As Claire is leading the detective back to Maggie, she says, "It's really a shame what happened. These gangs are out of control, shooting cops in cold blood. That one biker they brought in is dead. I hope those two cops pull through. Such a tragedy." She pauses. "Do they know why it happened?" she asks, hoping to hear some details.

Petrizzo, in a disinterested tone, replies, "We don't know. We're still investigating." Quickly changing the topic, he asks, "Where did you say she was?"

"She's right over here."

Claire walks over and pulls back the curtain. Maggie is gone.

"She was just here. I told her I was getting her a clean shirt to go home in."

Petrizzo looks at Claire, frustrated. Claire turns to another nurse.

"Carol, did you see Miss Hargrove? She was here a few minutes ago in cube 12C."

"I saw her before when you were talking to her. I didn't notice her leave."

Petrizzo says to Claire, "Walk with me around this area and see if you can spot her."

Claire and Petrizzo walk around for a good five minutes. Claire even checks the restroom.

"She must have left," she states.

"If you see her, call me," says Petrizzo, handing Claire his card. He walks away, a bit disgusted.

"Where the hell did she go?" Claire mumbles to herself. She leaves the clean shirt on the edge of the bed in cube 12C and walks away, still looking for Maggie.

Maggie walks out the back of the Lenox Hill Hospital ER doors and into the clear evening skies. The hospital is on Seventy-Seventh Street. She wanders east on Seventy-Seventh Street towards Lexington Avenue, her shirt still covered in blood from Officer O'Connell's wounds. She is still in an almost zombie-like trance, now walking south down Lexington Avenue. A few passersby notice her blood-stained shirt, but in typical New York fashion, no one says anything to her, they just stare. She continues to walk south on the avenue for a while, dazed and clearly in a state of shock. Her mind is fixated on the incident. She can't get the image of O'Connell bleeding in her lap out of her head. She is lost in emotional pain. Maggie quietly wonders how much more she can endure. First the business scandal and now the shooting. Why are these things happening? Why is she engulfed in a mess she didn't create?

As Maggie reaches the corner of Sixty-Sixth and Lexington, she comes upon St. Vincent Ferrer Catholic Church. The striking fourteenth-century French Gothic Revival church was built in 1918 by the Dominican order. It's one of New York's architectural marvels. Maggie looks up at the awesome structure and ascends the concrete steps that lead to the church doors.

The interior of the church is a beautiful and stunning sight. The walls are made of limestone, with large stained-glass windows throughout. Maggie's attention is immediately drawn to the high altar in the front of the church. At the center of the altar is the tabernacle, covered in gold and precious metals. The tabernacle is backed by an enormous carved stone reredos, which is like a massive screen altarpiece. Above it is a huge blue stained-glass window.

Maggie grew up attending Saint Mary's church and school in Elgin. Saint Mary's was an old, pretty church, but it pales in comparison to what she is looking at now.

The church is empty except for one older woman, who sits in a rear pew, silently praying. Her name is Yolanda. She is small, in her late seventies with grayish-white hair, wearing dark clothing. Maggie does not notice her as she walks up the center aisle towards the altar. The large empty church has a cold feel to it as the lights are dimmed. Only the area around the altar is illuminated. Maggie takes a seat in a carved wooden pew near the front.

Recalling the day's events, she begins to sob with her head in her hands. After a few minutes, she looks up and stares at the cross above the altar.

"Help me, God," she says in a low, tear-filled whisper. "Please help me."

Maggie continues to sob with her eyes fixated on the crucifix on the altar. Time seems to stand still as the waves of emotions fill Maggie's thoughts. She feels lost and alone. She continues to pray, hopeful God will give her answers to all these things that are happening to her. She prays He speaks to her in some way. Yet the church is so quiet, she feels alone. Lost in her thoughts and pain, she continues her silent prayers. After fifteen minutes of sitting in silent tears, Maggie gets up from the pew to leave. As she walks out, wiping the tears from her eyes, Yolanda approaches her and hands her a tissue. Maggie looks at Yolanda with a blank stare, wondering where she came from.

Yolanda has this loving, maternal quality. She's a calming presence. "Looks like something is deeply troubling you. I've been to hell and back many times myself. Many times. Whatever it is, it will get better, if you look in the right places. You walked in here for a reason. God led you here. I hope you realize that. What's your name, dear?"

Maggie clears her throat and responds, "I'm Maggie."

"I'm Yolanda. I'll pray for you, Maggie. It's what I do best. He listens to me… sometimes," she says jokingly.

"Thank you. I've always had faith, but my life lately has become filled with darkness. I just don't understand. Things have happened to me that I didn't cause, yet they're ruining my life. Why does God allow these things to happen? It makes me wonder if God really exists, or if He even hears me after what I've been through."

With a gentle look of reassurance, Yolanda grabs Maggie's hand. "Life can be hard. It's not about what happens to us but more about how we react to it. We can let the events of life destroy us, or we can use them to make us stronger. With the power of God, nothing can defeat you, if you only believe. Just remember, faith is about seeing light with your heart when all your eyes see is darkness. The light that comes from the heart is the brightest light that shines. Don't lose faith, dear, God hears you. He's listening."

"That seems to be difficult for me to believe right now."

"I understand. Don't worry. Through our darkest moments, it's human nature to have doubts. Yet God transcends all things, and nothing is beyond His omnipotence. God hears you. I know He does."

"I hope so. I don't know how much more I can handle."

"You're stronger than you know. You'll see. What you probably need is a good night's sleep. Get home safe, my dear."

"Thank you," Maggie replies. She looks at Yolanda with an appreciative gaze, then walks to the back of the church.

Yolanda's simple and kind words were comforting. For a moment, Maggie feels a sense of calm, something she hasn't felt since the shooting turned her life upside down. She turns around to see Yolanda, but Yolanda is gone. Maggie is bewildered. How could the older woman be out of sight so quickly? Instinctively, she looks up at the cross on the altar again. What just happened?

Maggie pauses and walks down the wide aisle, heading for the doors at the rear of the church. Matthias, with some of his angels, walks out of the sanctuary near the front of the altar. They watch as Maggie pushes open the door. Some of the angels follow her out.

Maggie walks out of the church and is back on Lexington Avenue, heading home. She walks up the street, takes a deep breath and wipes the tears from her eyes. She needed that time inside in the peace and serenity of the quiet church to calm her. She needed Yolanda's kindness and her prayer.

Across the street, Dante watches her. He says to one of his demons, "I hate that wretched place. Every time we have one of His worthless humans at the point of despair, He leads them into one of His buildings. If it wasn't so well protected by His soldiers, we could go in and burn the damn place to the ground. Stay on her. Follow her wherever she goes. We're not done with her by any means. We pushed her to the breaking point before. We can do it again."

They fly off and vanish into the sky.

Back at Lenox Hill Hospital, through the ER glass, we see Reverend Pitts with a Bible in his hand. Next to him is Grace Williams. They're praying at the bedside of Franklin Watson. Franklin opens his eyes and sees them. He motions with his finger to the pastor to come closer. Reverend Pitts leans in as Franklin, in a low, almost inaudible tone, says, "Pastor, I'm in bad shape. Pray for me." His speech is labored as just those simple words were a struggle for him.

Pitts grabs Watson's hand and bows his head in silent prayer. After a few moments, he stands upright.

"May our Lord Jesus Christ absolve you; and by His authority I absolve you and give you pardon and peace, as far as my power allows and your needs require." Reverend Pitts makes the sign of the cross. "Therefore, I absolve you from your sins in the name of the Father, and of the Son, and of the Holy Ghost. Amen."

Watson manages to crack a smile and whispers, "Thank you, pastor. God bless you."

Watson's eyes close. Pitts and Grace know he is close to death. They join hands and softly pray for their brother. After a few minutes, Franklin Watson slips into unconsciousness. His head falls to his side. He takes his last breath. The heart monitor flatlines as the alarms go off. Nurses and Dr. Kirkland rush in.

"Pastor, please step outside," implores Dr. Kirkland.

Reverend Pitts and Grace leave the room. Grace has tears in her eyes and begins to cry. After a few minutes, Dr. Kirkland comes out to them and solemnly says, "I'm sorry. He's gone. We did all we could. He fought hard, but his injuries were just too severe."

"Thank you, Doctor. We know you did your best," responds Reverend Pitts.

The pastor and Grace slowly walk away. The room clears of hospital personnel as a nurse covers Franklin's face with a sheet before they remove him from the room. Grace pauses to look back at Watson. Reverend Pitts gives her a moment and continues down the hospital corridor.

Grace is saying in a low whisper, "Almighty God, take care of my friend Franklin's blessed soul. I know how much he loved You."

As Grace wipes a tear from her eye, the room suddenly fills with an illuminating light and a multitude of angels surround Franklin's body. Are her eyes deceiving her? A tremendous sense of calm and peace comes over Grace. The angels lift Franklin's soul towards heaven. In an instant, they're gone. The light vanishes and the room goes back to normal, with Franklin's body lying there covered by the sheet. Grace looks on in astonishment. Did she just witness a divine event? She knows the feeling of joy she just experienced is indescribably beautiful.

She looks up towards the sky. "Praise the Lord!"

In another area of the ER, Rita Damaso decides to finally take a break from the chaos in the ER and go outside for a cigarette break. She pulls a pack of Newport cigarettes from her pocket, removes one cigarette and lights it. She takes her first drag while she paces back and forth. Ruben has not answered any of her numerous phone calls. She mumbles quietly, "Where the hell is he?" Suddenly, Ruben approaches, wearing a dark hoodie and a baseball cap. She runs towards him, grabs his arm, turns him around and starts to walk him away from the hospital and towards the parking lot.

"What are you doing here, mijo? The hospital is crawling with police officers. The cop who punched you when Manny was killed, he's one of the two cops Victor shot. O'Connell's his name."

"Screw that bastard. I hope he dies. His partner killed Manny and he covered it up. I owe him a punch in the face for knocking me out. I can't believe Victor's dead. He was my brother. I know he was getting revenge for Manny's death and for what they did to me. Those cops set us up to save their own asses."

Rita angrily shoots him a piercing look and gives him a scathing slap across his face, showing her disappointment. "He's not your brother! How many times do I have to tell you that? He's not your real blood! If you don't change your life, you'll wind up just like him. I begged you to get out of that gang. Victor's put a target on all your backs."

Ruben looks down in embarrassment. "I'm sorry," he whispers.

Rita grabs Ruben's face and stares into his eyes. "You need to get out of here. Go somewhere and hide, okay? I'll call you later."

Ruben, realizing the severity of the situation with cops all around the hospital, responds, "Okay. I'm outta here."

He kisses his mother on the cheek and hastily walks off into the darkness. Rita waits until he is completely out of sight, then glances around to make sure no one saw him. She drops the cigarette butt, steps on it and heads back into the ER.

As Ruben leaves, an ambulance pulls up. The EMS workers jump out, open the rear doors and remove a stretcher with a man on it. They begin to wheel him inside. The man on the stretcher is dirty and disheveled. His clothes are old and worn. He is deceased.

Rita, who is heading back inside, says to the driver, "Get him straight into Unit B. I'll alert the doctors."

The driver says, "Too late on this one. He's dead."

"Where are you coming from?"

"We got a call from a liquor store owner who said he was passed out on the sidewalk. He was unresponsive to treatment in the ambulance. He passed away. Store owner said he was a homeless drunk. A bit of a whacko, not all there mentally."

"Sad. Truly sad. Another wasted life." She pauses momentarily. "Okay, you guys know the drill. Check in with the head nurse. She'll have the ER doctor pronounce him dead and they'll send up someone from the morgue to get the body."

Rita makes the sign of the cross as they wheel him through the ER doors.

CHAPTER 8

....

Casualties of War and Life

ather Murphy stands in the front of the altar at Saint John's church. There is a closed casket covered in an American flag. It's the funeral mass for John Michael Nevins, the homeless man who Rita saw being brought into the ER a few nights earlier. Next to the casket is a photo of John in his Army dress uniform from 1971, when he served in the Vietnam War.

John Nevins was an Irish kid who grew up in a predominantly Irish neighborhood in Queens. He was one of three kids, with a younger sister, Mary, and an older brother, Kevin. Their dad, Liam, was a strapping Irishman who moved from Donegal, Ireland, to Queens as a young boy with his family. He was a hardworking man and a proud member of the Longshoreman's Union. John was never the best student, so he saw himself following in his dad's footsteps. It was hard work, but a solid job with steady pay and benefits.

As a young teen, John's focus was stickball, hanging with friends and sneaking beers under the stands at the high school football games. He was carefree, just waiting for the day he was old enough to join the union. Then it happened. Vietnam brought about the draft lottery and John's birthday was selected early in the process. April 11—the fourteenth number called. John's older brother Kevin was June 20, number 360. He wasn't called. Liam was proud to live in the US and, although apprehensive, he told John to serve his country with honor. John, though, was scared as hell. Like so many other boys across the country, his simple, carefree life just ended, and he was headed to war. John entered the Army, went to boot camp, and in short order was on a military transport plane to Vietnam.

John, like many other young boys, was right in the middle of the fighting. A young boy of eighteen, barely mature, was fighting to survive in the jungles of Southeast Asia. He watched in horror as platoon mates were killed, some in the most horrific ways. No one should ever experience the horrors of war, yet it was front and center for him every day. This would be too much for anyone to take, but to late teen boys, the harsh reality of war forced them to grow up fast, and in a way no one would ever choose.

Death was all around. There was no escaping it. One day you're with your platoon mates, trying to keep each other sane, and then suddenly, you watch them killed in front of you. The images of death would scar these boys for life. How John longed for his carefree days of playing ball and hanging with his friends back in Queens. He'd shut his eyes and try to escape by dreaming of being home. Then he'd open them, and reality would smack him in the face. He was still in the steamy jungles of Vietnam. It was a constant battle of the mind between fear and survival. Sanity was beginning to escape him as the fight for survival and the thought of dying so far away from home erupted constantly in his mind.

John did survive his tour of duty and was sent home after a few years of service. He returned to Queens, but he would never be whole again. What happened to him there changed his life forever. The scars of what he saw would never go away. The death and destruction all around were just too much for him. He suffered from post-traumatic stress disorder, to the point he couldn't function. Back in the early '70s, PTSD was not really diagnosed, so John kind of fell through the cracks. He was in and out of mental hospitals. Most doctors said it was depression. He began drinking heavily and abusing drugs. His father and family tried to help him. His dad got him that union job, hoping it would help him, but John's mental state was too far gone and the constant revolving doors of the psych wards were no help either.

As the years went by, one by one, John's family passed away. With no safety net or family support, he wound up on the streets, homeless. He found some comfort with fellow brothers at the local VFW. He tried to be active. At least they knew what war was like. Yet the scars on his mind were just too much for him to bear. His life had no meaning or purpose. Drugs and booze just numbed the pain.

The church is empty the day of his funeral service, except for a few Vietnam vets. John was once an active legion member, before his condition worsened. Some of the men from his legion post are at the funeral. They arranged it with Father Murphy, as all of John's immediate family predeceased him.

Father Murphy is finishing a brief eulogy to the few mourners present.

"John would be viewed by many as a lost soul, as he had no family, was destitute and suffered from various afflictions. The effects of the Vietnam War robbed him of his innocence. He went there a carefree Irish lad from Queens but returned an empty shell of himself. The damage was irreparable. But in the eyes of God, he is not lost. Just like you and me, regardless of his circumstances, John was made in the image and likeness of God. As you and I have the hope and trust in God's love and mercy, even though at times we don't feel we deserve it, it's there for us and it's there for John. Only God can give John the peace that has eluded him his whole life.

"Although it would seem to many that John had nothing, from the testimony of his fellow vets, he still had faith in God. Even though at times he questioned why God would allow such horrors, he knew in his heart that God could one day answer it for him. That's why it's called faith. Trusting when there seems to be no reason to trust. Having faith when there seems to be no answer or reason. We can, therefore, take comfort in the mercy of God, a God who understands all our pain and suffering. We may not fully understand the depths of John's pain and the emptiness of his mortal life, but we have the hope that God understood John and was with him through it all. At the moment of his suffering and death on the cross, Jesus commended himself to the Father. Jesus, in His deepest moment of despair, knew He was never alone. We can take hope in the promise that God was at John's side."

Father Murphy finishes his eulogy and continues with the final blessing. As the service ends, two gentlemen from the local funeral home remove the casket and place it in the hearse. There is no funeral procession to the cemetery, as there are only a handful of mourners. There will be a private burial at a military cemetery later that day. The few vets who are there thank Father Murphy with a handshake.

On the day of his death, just a few days prior to his funeral, John awoke after taking his last breath in the ambulance on the way to the hospital. He was no longer drunk and dying on a New York street. He was at a national park in the mountains of Oregon, near a campsite. It was an amazing place, with evergreen trees and a mountain range serving as the backdrop for a beautiful shimmering lake. Further down the banks of the lake were a few fishermen, casting their lines into the water, creating a momentary ripple as their lures hit the surface. The sun was shining brightly in a clear blue sky.

There were three men about twenty yards away. They were sitting in chairs with a cooler of beer, simply relaxing and enjoying the peaceful tranquility of the lake.

"Hey, John, are you going to stand there and stare at the lake all day? You city guys need to get out in the wilderness more often."

John turned around and saw Curt Reynolds, Devin Boyd and Charles Whitaker. These were his Army buddies, members of his infantry division in Vietnam. He had watched all three of them get killed. Curt was a redheaded kid they called 'Carrot head', born and raised nearby in Oregon. He was killed at the age of eighteen. Devin Boyd was from South Carolina—a strong, athletic African American youth, a high school football star. He was the son of a Baptist preacher. He was nineteen when he died. Charles Whitaker was a blond-haired, blue-eyed kid from Topeka, Kansas. He worked in his father's hardware store right up until the day he was drafted. He was killed at the age of twenty-one.

John looked at his friends in both disbelief and joy.

"Curt, Devi, Chuck...I can't believe it's you! Where are we? How'd I get here?"

Curt replied, "This is my little piece of heaven. We all decided this would be the best place to welcome you."

"This is amazing. Where are we? Is this really heaven?"

"I just told you, Johnny Appleseed," he said, using their nickname for the kid from the Big Apple, "this is a piece of my heaven. You'll see the rest of it and your own piece of it a little later. Come sit over here and grab a beer."

John walked over and sat next to his buddies. They handed him a can of beer, but he couldn't stop looking at the natural beauty all around him.

"I always wondered about you three. After that horrible day in Khe Sanh in 1968, my life was never the same. One nightmare after the next. That day played repeatedly in my mind. I should have been killed with you guys."

Devin patted John on the shoulder. "Hey, man, it just wasn't your time. All that doesn't become clear till you get here."

Chuck added, "We were all terrified that day. The death we saw all around us was horrifying. Yet, at the moment we died, it was over. It was calm. We were here."

Curt said, "John, for all you endured—all the pain and misery—you had no peace. The booze, the drugs and painkillers—none of that erased the memory of the war. Yet, despite you questioning whether there was a God, you never stopped believing in Him."

"Watching you three die destroyed me. Oh, you're right, Curt. I spent my whole life questioning if there was a God. Why did He leave me behind to suffer that pain?"

Devin spoke up. "It doesn't make any sense on the other side, but soon enough it will. It will all be revealed to you. Every life is different. Some are easier and some are hard, but it's God's plan, not ours. Through it all you never lost faith. Oh, you fell hard and suffered, you did things to escape the pain, but deep down you begged God for an answer."

Chuck continued, "War, death and destruction are the actions of men. We were sent to Vietnam to fight a war we wanted no part of. We were drafted. We were just kids. They gave us a uniform and a gun, dropped us in a foreign land and told us to kill the enemy. It wasn't God's original plan for it to be that way. He gave man free will to choose to share in His infinite happiness, but man chose otherwise and brought sin into the world. With it came evil, hatred and the lust for power. Christ changed all of that on the cross. Although sin and death remained part of our human existence, if we believed, we were saved from it."

Curt interjected, "We were all scared. All we had was our faith and each other. Think about it—amid all that chaos, God gave us each other. We all came from different places, yet we laughed, cried, lived and even died together. Yet at the moment of my death, in the blink of an eye, I was here in paradise. The evil was gone."

John looked at them. "I don't know why I was left behind. From that day forward, I wished I had died that day with you guys. My life was pure torment. I could never understand why I lived that day. I was left with a life of loneliness and despair. The images are burned into my memory. I could never escape them."

Devin said, "I can't answer that for you, John. I don't know why you suffered, but your life will all be revealed to you shortly. What I can tell you is this. Despite all you suffered, you still tried. You stayed connected to other veterans. You made a difference to some of your fellow veterans in that American Legion post you belonged to. You helped each other as survivors of the war. Like us, you were a band of brothers who stuck together through the worst nightmares imaginable. You honored each other as someone passed, making sure no one was ever forgotten, just as those fine men did who eventually arranged your funeral. You see, through it all, whether we realize it or not, God's love for us is always at work in our lives.

But, at least now you know. There is a heaven. We are here and you're with us. You ain't seen nothin' yet! Welcome, my brother."

John had tears in his eyes. "I love you guys. You've always been my brothers and in my heart. Not a day went by when I didn't think about you."

Curt replied, "Hey, Johnny Appleseed, in all the excitement, did you realize yet that you're eighteen again and not that old man who died on the sidewalk?"

John looked down at himself and realized he was a healthy eighteen-year-old once again. "How about that? This will work... and there's beer in heaven! What more could an Irish kid ask for?"

They all burst out laughing. For the first time in a very long time, John felt like the carefree kid he had been before the war.

Curt said, "Yeah, and your old man, Liam...he's a cool dude. He's just like you used to describe to us back in Nam. I had a hard time understanding that Irish brogue at first, but he's all right."

"My dad? You spoke to my dad?"

"Sure thing. Your mom, your brother and your sister too. They're waiting for you."

John's eyes teared up. Curt put his arm on his shoulder.

"It's all good now, bro. No, it's not good. It's all perfect now. You'll see. Now drink that beer before it gets warm."

With that, they clinked their beer cans together and smiled. For John, every bit of pain, sorrow and despair was now gone. He finally felt the great sense of peace and joy he had always hoped would be there one day.

CHAPTER 9

The Power of a Mother's Love

The East Side Evangelical Church, run by Reverend Pitts, is located on Sixty-Ninth Street, between Lexington and Third Avenue, not too far from the hospital. It's a small building that has been the home to various church denominations over the years. It's relatively small but has a vibrant congregation. Today, sadly, is the funeral of Franklin Watson.

Reverend Pitts stands over the casket of Mr. Watson, carefully fixing Mr. Watson's tie, making sure it's perfect. Grace walks over to the casket and starts to tear up as she tenderly looks at his body lying there so peacefully.

A flood of childhood memories of Franklin come back to Grace. "I can't believe he's gone. I've known him since I was a kid."

"Yes, it's so sad. He was a fixture in the neighborhood. He kept an eye on things, kept a lot of kids out of trouble. They looked up to him."

Grace looks up at the altar. "We always felt safe around him. I remember he used to plant quarters in our braids so when Mr. Softee would come around, we'd have enough money to buy ice cream. That was just his nature, kind and giving."

Reverend Pitts turns and looks out over the church's pews. "Sister Grace, I expect a full house today. Mr. Watson knew a lot of people and touched a lot of people's hearts. He was a simple but good and godly man."

"The choir will be in full voice today, Reverend." She looks up at the ceiling with a slight smile and then back at Mr. Watson lying in the casket.

"We'll be singing 'Hosanna Blessed Be the Rock.' I know it was one of his favorites."

"That will be wonderful."

The door to the church opens slowly as Pitts and Grace are conversing. A person walks in and takes a seat toward the back of the church, not wanting to intrude as the service hasn't yet started. It's Cookie. Reverend Pitts glances out to see the person and waves her over. Cookie walks to the front, nervous and out of place. She walks up to the casket and stands near Grace and Reverend Pitts, looking down at Watson.

"He was a good man. A friend of yours?" Reverend Pitts asks.

"Yes, he was. He basically saved my life," Cookie responds.

Reverend Pitts puts his hand on Cookie's shoulder. "So, you're Cookie?"

"Yes, I'm Cookie. I don't mean to intrude. I just wanted to pay my respects to Mr. Watson. I hope that's okay?"

"Of course, but the service is later this morning, at ten."

"Yes, I know. I figured I could maybe come by now and just pay my respects quietly, Reverend. I don't want to cause a distraction or anything at the service."

"And why would that be?" Reverend Pitts replies.

"I'm sure you've noticed, Reverend, I'm not like everyone else around here. A lot of people look down on me and don't want me around, so I try not to—"

Grace interjects, "Nonsense, child. You are always welcome in this house of God, especially to pay respects to this fine man."

"Yes, you're always welcome here. God loves you just as much as He loves anyone else," Reverend Pitts replies, furthering Grace's sentiment.

Cookie seems touched by their words but still uneasy. "I appreciate that coming from you both, but if it's all the same, I prefer just to pay my respects and be on my way."

"Certainly, we understand. Take as long as you need." Reverend Pitts reaches out and gently touches her shoulder briefly in a consoling fashion. He hands her a small packet of tissues from his coat pocket.

Reverend Pitts and Grace retreat to the back of the church, allowing Cookie to have her time with Mr. Watson in peace. Reverend Pitts gathers some of the Bibles from the pews and places them in the slots on the back of each pew. Grace looks at Cookie with empathy.

Cookie approaches the casket, looking down at Watson with deep sorrow. Tears form in her eyes. She touches Watson's hand, gently embracing it. She smiles at him and then from her bag she pulls out an unlit cigarette and touches it to his hand.

Softly, she says, "I never got to give you this. I'll have it for you. I guess I still owe you one." She smiles. "You were the only one who cared about me. You never judged me or said anything that was unkind. You always made me feel important."

As her emotions grow, tears fall from Cookie's eyes. "You take care now, Mr. W."

As Grace looks on, tears fall from her eyes as well. She wipes them away quickly as Cookie starts walking to the back of the church, where she's standing. She looks over at them both.

"Thank you kindly."

"If there's ever anything we can do for you, come see us," Reverend Pitts utters.

Cookie simply smiles. Grace grabs her hand.

"We mean that—we're always here for you, no matter what." Grace looks over at Mr. Watson's casket. "Just like Mr. Watson. Okay?"

Cookie looks Grace right in her eyes. "Thank you—thank you both. I best be going."

Cookie quietly walks towards the door. At that moment, Grace senses an angelic presence. She yells, "Wait, don't leave yet."

Cookie turns around and looks at Grace.

"I've got a message for you. But wait, they're still talking to me..."

Cookie looks confused. Grace is looking to the sky as if seeing something. After a moment, she looks at Cookie. "Lila. Your mom, Lila. She saw you here and wants to tell you she loves you."

Cookie, astonished, says, "My mama? How do you know my mama?"

"I told you, she saw you here and wanted me to tell you how much she loves you."

Reverend Pitts is dumbfounded. Cookie begins to tear up.

"It's all right, child," Grace reassures her. "The good Lord gave me this gift, and sometimes He permits those that have passed to speak to me."

"Where is she?"

"Oh, she's in heaven, darling. She's fine. She told me to tell you how much she loves you and misses you. She also said to tell you to fix the things in your life that need fixin'. I don't know what she means, but I'm sure you do. You know your mama better than anyone."

Cookie, still in shock, feels a brief sense of joy.

"I miss my mama so much. She loved me, no matter what."

"Child, that's what we're supposed to do. Love each other. No conditions. You come back here and chat with me in a few days when you clear your head, okay? God loves you."

"I think I'll do that. Thank you so much."

For the first time in a very long time, Cookie feels a sense of joy and relief as she steps outside the church doors.

Grace sighs heavily as the door shuts behind Cookie. "That child has seen more trouble in a day than most people have in a lifetime. Watson always looked out for Cookie, especially when she was little and bullied by so many kids."

"It would be good if you could try reaching out to her. Offer our assistance," Reverend Pitts utters.

Grace looks over at the reverend. "I certainly will, Reverend."

"I remember her mother now," says Pitts. "Lila. Lila Jones. She started coming here in the later years of her life, before she passed.

That woman had a good soul. I remember her mentioning she had a child going through some difficult times. I'm so happy that you remembered her as well as a member of our congregation to say those kind words to Cookie."

"Oh no, Pastor, Lila was talking to me, just like I'm speaking to you now."

"Her mother spoke to you just now?"

"Oh yes. Clear as a bell."

He pauses. "Sister Grace, sometimes you simply amaze me. The words you told that child were comforting."

"Amen to that, pastor!" Pitts starts to walk away, but Grace grabs his hand. "Reverend Pitts, these messages from God are happening more frequently."

Reverend Pitts turns to face her. "Sister Grace, really. You are dead serious?"

She looks away for a moment and pauses, as she isn't sure how Reverend Pitts will respond. She leans up against one of the pews, clasping her hands together, and swallows deeply.

"What happened just now, it's been happening to me a lot. I feel the good Lord is not just sending me messages. When we were at the hospital, when Mr. Watson passed, I glanced back at him and… and I saw…I saw…"

She pauses for a few more moments.

"It's okay, Sister Grace. What did you see?"

"I saw angels, Reverend. Beautiful, peaceful angels all around Franklin."

He raises his eyebrows. "Angels? Well, like I said, Mr. Watson was a God-fearing man. I'm sure the good Lord sent angels to escort him. There's nothing wrong with believing in that, Grace."

She exhales intensely as Reverend Pitts resumes walking to the front of the church.

"No, Reverend, you don't understand. *I saw actual angels*. I can describe them as if they were standing right here in front of me and you at this very moment!"

Reverend Pitts turns and faces her. He then puts his head down to gather his thoughts.

"Sister Grace, sometimes in moments of extraordinary circumstances, we bring our faith to the forefront and we believe we see what we earnestly feel. I'm sure that's what happened with you."

"Reverend, I've known you since I was a little girl, and I'm pretty sure I know what I saw."

He nods. "I see. Sister Grace, I'll take it on faith you saw what you saw, and that Lila Jones spoke to you. Far be it from me to question the power of Almighty God."

She smiles. "Thank you, Reverend Pitts. I know it's real."

He raises his hands to the heavens above. "Praise the Lord. Now, I need to go finish preparing my sermon for this morning. I'll see you in a bit, okay?"

He embraces Grace and leaves her standing at the front of the church while he vanishes into his office. Grace stands and watches over Watson. She hears a slight whisper in the air, and as she turns, she sees angels flying out of the church. She looks down at Mr. Watson's body and mutters, "They may have taken your body, but the angels have your soul. Rest well in heaven, Franklin."

Franklin Charles Watson was born in South Carolina. He came from a poor family who worked as laborers. In search of a better life, as soon as he was old enough, Franklin joined the Army. He was always good at fixing things, so they trained him to be an auto mechanic. Franklin was well known in the motor pool as the guy who could fix almost any engine. He just had a knack for it. After the war, Franklin moved to New York. One of his GI buddies' dad had a gas station and auto repair shop in Brooklyn. It was the perfect place for him, working as a mechanic for someone he trusted. Back then, he was still a simple southern country boy, not quite ready for the big city. He was a good-natured soul but sometimes a bit naïve to city life.

Over time, he learned his way around and started to feel more comfortable. Franklin met some fellows who realized he had excellent mechanic skills. They befriended him and conspired to use his talents to their advantage. They offered him some side work that wouldn't interfere with his job. Franklin saw it as a way to make some extra cash. What Franklin didn't realize was they were stealing cars and wanted him to remove the parts. They lied, telling Franklin they'd bought the cars cheap from people who needed the money and that the parts were more valuable than the whole car. Franklin naively went along. The extra money was good.

Franklin started hanging around with them more often. They were nice enough, and always good to him, but they partied and drank a little more than he was used to. They started taking Franklin to the racetrack. They also taught him how to play poker and shoot dice. Franklin just thought this was the way of life in the big city. Their car parts business seemed to be steady. Franklin never questioned how they got such good deals all the time—until the truth came out, in a harsh way.

One day, while Franklin was removing some engine parts from an old Buick LeSabre, the police raided their backyard garage and busted them for grand theft auto. Poor Franklin had no idea what was happening and was shaken by the allegations. As the police handcuffed him, he looked in disbelief at his so-called friends, who wouldn't look him in the eye. At that moment, he knew he was being used. He was arrested along with five others. Turned out they had stolen about twenty-five cars over a year, and all the while, police detectives were watching them. They all went away for grand theft on twenty-five counts, including Franklin.

Prison in New York was tough on the simple southern kid. It truly hardened Franklin. He endured many fights in jail, fights that added to his jail time. When he eventually got out, he bounced around from job to job, as it was hard for an ex-con in those days to find work. Even his friend's dad who'd originally hired him wouldn't take him back. He finally found work as a mechanic in a small mom-and-pop shop. He didn't make much money, but at least they gave him a chance. As the years went by, his hands were just too arthritic to hold the tools to continue doing it as a steady job. He wound up on welfare and spent most of his time watching ball games. When he took the part-time job at the bodega, he became known as the guy who could fix things. He became a fixture in the neighborhood. People would bring their cars to the bodega just to ask him what was wrong. His advice saved people lots of money. His friend owned a repair shop a few blocks away. If Franklin sent anyone there for service, they would give him a few extra bucks for the referral. All legit. Everyone knew Mr. W.

At the moment Franklin passed away in the hospital, he suddenly awakened in a field full of daffodils. The dancing bright yellow-and-white flowers stretched endlessly as far as the human eye could see and with each step he took, they turned from bright yellow to an array of beautiful colors. There was a sweet fragrance in the air, one that couldn't be described nor mimicked. For Franklin, it was one of a kind. There was an almost ethereal sensation as he walked further into the field and looked up into the sky at what seemed to be the sun, but its light was greater, and a mixture of rainbows surrounded it. The clouds were soft and billowy, smooth to the touch, and they hovered just above him. The cool air was consumed by a sweet humming voice as if calling out to him.

He gazed upon a lightly shaded blue house with a huge wrap-around porch, and like the field, it was surrounded by vibrant and colorful flowers, blossoming one by one while the aroma of freshly cut green grass could easily be detected. The vision of it brought about calmness, tranquility and a certain familiarity. And that sweet scent of honeydew and marmalade was more robust, consuming the air. He looked back at the field and the ever-changing flowers now turned a hue of orange, and beautiful trees appeared. The sweet sounds of birds chirping high in the sky could be heard at the very top of the trees, and a natural stream of water emerged, flowing steadily from a path nearby.

On the porch of the house was a round white wrought-iron table with two chairs. Perched on top was a glass pitcher, filled with lemonade and fresh-cut lemons. Two glasses filled with ice sat beside the pitcher. The door to the house was wide open and it looked warmly inviting. A woman, short in stature, somewhere in her early forties, stepped out onto the porch. Her hair was woven into two long plaits, resting on her shoulders. She was dressed in a knee-length bright pink-and-white dress, which was complemented by a bright yellow apron hanging loosely around her waist. She was beautiful and aware of Franklin as she saw him coming towards her. She excitedly waved to him.

"Franklin, come on now. Dinner's 'bout ready, son."

Franklin was confused, but he felt a powerful sense of peace as he moved closer.

"Mama? Mama, is that you?"

She smiled. "Of course, son. Come and have a sit-down with me while we wait. I made all your favorites when I heard you were coming."

He took in a deep breath. "Is that your famous apple spice pie I smell, Mama? I've been dreaming about it every day since you passed."

"It sure is, son, and my homemade biscuits and gravy too. Nothing but the best to welcome my boy."

Franklin stepped onto the porch. He realized that it was the home he had grown up in. His mother greeted him with a heartfelt and tender hug, one that he'd been missing for years. Tears cascaded down his cheeks and dissolved into the air. His mother softly grasped his hand and led him over to the table, where they sat.

She reached across the table and grabbed both his hands, caressing them. "It's been a long time, Franklin. I've missed you so much, son."

"Mama, I don't understand. You look exactly the same as you looked before the cancer took you."

She smiled with an endearing expression and took a sip of lemonade.

"Yes, baby, I know, and I'm sorry I had to leave you so early, but it was my time and I knew the good Lord would watch over you. The angel told me so."

"The angel, Mama?"

"Yes, Franklin, your guardian angel. He's always been with you."

Franklin looked down as if ashamed. "Mama, I ain't always been a God-fearing man. I had a lot of struggles in my life. I've been in prison. I've done a lot of bad things that I wasn't proud of. I decided to change those wrongs, but I still didn't think I was worthy enough. I didn't think God would want me, Mama."

"My boy, God is a forgiving God. There is no sin too big or too small that God won't forgive. You had to repent, Franklin. When the good Reverend Pitts gave you absolution, son, you were asking for God's forgiveness. You were confessing your sins. See, God will forgive all unrighteousness, including anything you've done, if you are willing to bring it before Him. So, son, you are worthy."

Franklin wiped the tears from his eyes.

"It's okay, Franklin, you can cry. Those are cleansing tears; they're good for the soul. You're a godly man, Franklin. Always were, deep down in your heart. You struggled; all of us do. But you trusted the Lord. Just before you came here, you saved Cookie from being shot by that man who killed you. Cookie had a troubled life, yet you always looked out for her. Son, that's the love of God in you. He resides in your heart, always has."

Franklin took in the view and the beauty of where they were. "This place here, Mama, it's beautiful. The house looks exactly the same from when I was a child."

She let out a slight giggle. "Yes, son, it is, but there is so much more. I want you to come with me and let me show you." She stood up and looked at him. "Come on now, baby. You have lots to see. God's beauty is ever-changing and His love is overwhelmingly vibrant, just like them there flowers that sprout from the ground, the trees that rise up into the sky, the air that flows around you with the sweetest taste of beautiful emotion you ever felt and the water that not only quenches your thirst"—she laughed— "but feels like silk. It's all around us, Franklin."

She grabbed his hand, and they walked down off the porch and towards the ever-changing field.

"Mama, this really is heaven, isn't it?"

"Boy, you ain't seen nothing yet. We're just at the start. Come now, we've got lots to do."

They walked off, arm in arm, still conversing and admiring the beauty surrounding them, fading into the field of daffodils.

"Love is what we bring with us at the end of life. We will be judged by our love..."

—St. John of the Cross

CHAPTER 10

The Angels are Watching

Back at Lenox Hill Hospital, Abigail remains asleep from all the pain medication. Claire returns to her room to finish what she started before she was called away to the ER.

Claire pulls the syringe from her pocket. It contains her own concoction of meds, which will cause Abigail to lapse into unconsciousness and never recover, killing her.

The IV connected to Abigail's arm still hangs alongside her bed. All Claire now needs to do is inject the needle into the IV tube leading to the port and the drugs will slowly enter Abigail's bloodstream. Abigail's breathing is labored and somewhat wheezy. Given her weakened condition, the drugs will work rather quickly. Claire stands silently alongside Abigail, looking down at her. It's time to release Abigail from her painful existence. Claire thinks she's being merciful and is just doing what society won't allow a seasoned nurse to do for a patient in distress. She truly believes she is putting the woman out of her misery, ending a life that has seen better days. After all, Claire thought, who would want to go on this way?

Claire bends down and once again whispers in Abigail's ear, knowing full well she can't hear her.

"It's time. I know you're tired; you have no more use here. You've had a good life. You got to see your children grow up and you had the joy of spending time with your grandchildren. Not many people get to experience that."

Claire takes the cap off the needle and gets ready to inject the drugs into the IV tube. She whispers, "I'm going to give you the greatest gift of all—the peace of death. I remember the first time I gave that gift. It was to my father, a sickly seventy-four-year-old man. He had suffered so much in the latter part of his life. I gave him peace, that kind of peace I'm sure he wanted. He wouldn't have lasted much longer anyway. Unlike you, he was awake, barely able to breathe. He was extremely afraid as I took that needle and injected it into his IV. He struggled for air, which made me feel terrible. Luckily it didn't last long, and he died shortly thereafter. But no worries, over the years I've gotten much better at it. I know exactly what dosage to use. You'll just drift off to sleep. No pain, no worries, just a deep, deep sleep."

Dante is watching Claire through the window with a sinister grin on his face. As she is about to administer the deadly dose, the chair in the corner suddenly slams into the wall. Bang! The window flies open, and a brisk wind blows into the room, knocking over the flowers on the table. Dante sees his adversary, Matthias, standing in the corner of the room. Suddenly, the blood pressure sensor starts beeping loudly. The once-quiet room is now full of noise. Claire, bewildered, swings around and quickly goes over to the window and closes it. She picks up the flowers, arranging them back in the vase. When she turns back around, Abigail is sitting upright in bed. Startled by the noises, she is now awake, but still groggy.

"What happened?" Abigail says out loud.

Claire is shocked and silent. Dante is annoyed. He flies away in utter disgust, cursing Matthias. Claire notices that during the commotion, she dropped the needle on the floor and stepped on it. The drug leaked out and is now useless. Annoyed, Claire bends down and picks up the broken needle with some tissue, hiding it in her pocket and wiping up whatever spilled on the floor. She then resets the steadily beeping BP monitor, which immediately goes silent.

Claire turns to Abigail. "No worries. That gust of wind knocked over the vase and the flowers fell. It's all taken care of. Go back to sleep, Mrs. Reinhold."

Abigail, still startled, replies, "Oh, Okay. Thank you, Nurse."

Claire puts on her caring demeanor and politely says, "You get your rest. Go back to sleep. I'll be back later to check on you."

Abigail slowly closes her eyes and drifts back to sleep. Claire, obviously annoyed, hastily leaves the room. Matthias watches Abigail fall back to sleep. Another angel appears to stay and watch over her. Matthias walks across the room, changes into his spiritual form and flies out the window.

Dante is outside with one of his demons. He is angry.

"We've got this nurse about to take another life and these cursed creatures keep stepping in. Keep the pressure on her. She'll be back to finish the job. If not, she'll just meet her own demise a little sooner."

With that, Dante flies away.

A FEW DAYS LATER, MAGGIE DECIDES TO RETURN TO WORK AT the diner. Earl gave her a few extra days off to gather herself. She really needed it. She is apprehensive about returning to work. She can still sense the horror and fear of what happened that day. In the time she was off, Maggie met with Detective Petrizzo of the NYPD. She detailed what she could for him about the shooting, although, because it all happened so quickly, she never saw the gunman, explaining to Detective Petrizzo that she was on the floor behind the counter after the window shattered. Petrizzo thanked her for assisting his brother officer and told her if she ever needed anything just to let him know.

The traumatic events of the shooting weigh heavily on Maggie's mind, but she knows she needs to confront them and therefore has to go back to the scene. She debated quitting and finding a job elsewhere. Perhaps, but for now, she needs to return to the diner. Maggie showers, gets dressed and heads out for work. Today is a calm day, but so was the day of the shooting. At least it started out that way, before all hell broke loose.

Maggie arrives at the diner to see a large piece of plywood covering the frame where the glass window used to be. Taped to it is a handwritten sign, simply stating, "We're open."

Maggie walks into the diner. Earl comes right over, gives her a reassuring hug and says with a smile, "Welcome back, Maggie. How do you like our new wooden window?"

"It's different."

"Yeah, one thing is for sure—it stops all the creeps from staring in. The new glass one will be in tomorrow. Since the insurance is covering it, I'm going to have a professional sign guy make a new logo. I know you used to be a designer, but would you mind looking at it?"

Maggie, still in her coat, pauses. She's gone from being one of the top textile designers in the country to helping Earl design his window logo for the diner, she thinks, but she can sense Earl is excited about it.

"Sure thing, Earl. I got you."

Earl runs over and pulls out a rough sketch and shows it to Maggie. She studies it.

"I like the font. I'd add a New York skyline. After all, it's the Empire Diner."

"I love that idea! I'm going to go call him right now and give him the edits. Thanks, Maggie."

"My pleasure, Earl."

Maggie finally goes into the employee room, hangs up her coat, puts on her apron and goes behind the counter, just like she would any other day. She heads to a booth in the corner of the diner to serve a couple who has just been seated.

The diner isn't as busy as it usually is, but considering the shooting that took place only a few days earlier, there are a few regular patrons showing their support. After all, the diner has been a fixture in the neighborhood for years.

A young, pretty blond college student, named Jennifer Peterson, walks into the diner. She sits at the counter, staring at her iPhone. Maggie goes behind the counter and stands in front of Jennifer.

"What can I get you, dear?"

Jennifer looks up at Maggie, then looks back down at her phone and starts texting.

Maggie rolls her eyes a bit, which Jennifer doesn't see as her eyes are still glued to her phone.

"Would you like something?" Maggie says again.

Jennifer finishes her text and finally looks up at Maggie.

"Can I get a venti macchiato latte?"

Maggie, now a little annoyed, replies, "That's Starbucks, sweetie—across the street."

Jennifer is still looking at her phone. She glances up briefly. "You can't make it?"

Maggie replies, "Just regular coffee—hot or iced coffee. Regular or decaf. Macchiato? No can do."

"Whatever," Jennifer says sarcastically. She gets up, still texting, and heads for the door.

Grace Williams walks into the diner and passes Jennifer, who bumps into her. Jennifer doesn't pick her head up. Grace pauses and takes a long look at her. Jennifer says nothing and keeps on going out the door. Grace just shakes her head and takes a seat in a booth across from the counter. Maggie comes over and hands her a menu.

Grace smiles. "Kids these days with those darn phones. Hope she doesn't walk out into oncoming traffic with her head buried in that thing."

Maggie smiles back. "Yep, it's a new world of high-tech rudeness. She came in with her eyes glued to that thing, then asked for a macchiato latte."

Grace chuckles. "A macchiato latte? In the diner? She needs to go to Starbucks."

Maggie laughs. "That's what I told her, if she even heard me. What can I get you, dear?"

"I'll take the turkey club and the French fries—well done, I like them crispy. And a glass of water."

Maggie jots the order on her pad. "You got it. Can I get you anything else?"

Grace pauses, debating about a cup of coffee, but doesn't order it. "No, that's it, thank you. Oh, wait—I'll take one of those double mocha espresso chia cappuccinos, with whipped cream," she jokes.

Maggie laughs. "Sure. You can pick it up across the street at Starbucks—right after you walk over there and order it."

They both start laughing. Grace looks around and continues to make small talk. "It's pretty quiet in here today. I thought it would be busier, considering its lunchtime."

Maggie, placing silverware and a glass of water in front of Grace, says, "It usually is, but since the incident, people might be a little leery."

Grace suddenly realizes where she is. "Oh, you mean the shooting. That was horrible. Those two police officers are still in critical condition. Were you here?"

Maggie, still uneasy when talking about it, says, "Yeah, I was here. They're replacing the window tomorrow."

Maggie points to the large plywood now occupying the place where the window shattered from the gunshot.

"You okay, dear? That must have been a horrible experience. That crazy biker shot and killed one of our church members, Franklin Watson. He was a sweet old man. I've known him since I was a little girl." Grace has a tear in her eye as she remembers Franklin.

A rush of memories from that day suddenly fills Maggie's mind. She pauses and then says calmly, "I'm okay. I'm so sorry about your friend. I heard about him when I was at the hospital that day."

Grace touches Maggie's hand in a reassuring way and glances to Maggie's right. Just outside one of the windows that wasn't shattered during the shooting, she sees a dark, disturbing figure. It's Dante. Grace gets a chill down her spine. It's the opposite of what she felt when she saw the angels around Franklin. She has a sixth sense when it comes to the spiritual world. Dante is looking right at Maggie, and then he turns his head and shoots an evil look directly at Grace. Grace can't help but notice how his black eyes pierce right through her like a laser beam. She sees the demonic look on his face as he turns back and stares at Maggie.

Grace turns to Maggie and asks, "What's your name, dear?"

"Maggie."

Grace looks back out the window. Dante is gone. She can sense Maggie is being watched and decides to inquire a little deeper. "That shooting must have been horrible. What did you see?"

Maggie doesn't really want to discuss it. She replies quietly, "More than I needed to. More than anyone needs to."

She turns away to avoid continuing the conversation. In her mind, she can clearly see the image of O'Connell in her arms, bleeding profusely. Maybe she did come back to work too soon. Maybe she needs to get out of this place. Her eyes well up with tears. Grace sees this and quickly offers some further reassurance. "Whatever you were involved in, it's now in the past. You must put it behind you. Thank the good Lord you're okay. If you ever need someone to talk to, come by the Evangelical Church and ask for me. I'm Grace."

Maggie, somewhat disinterested but appreciative of the offer, says, "Thank you. That's sweet. You're very kind."

Grace smiles. "I'll be praying for you. It's what I do best."

Maggie recalls that this was the exact same thing the older woman, Yolanda, said to her in the church.

Maggie responds, "Can't hurt. I'll take all I can get. Let me go check on your food."

Grace can sense that Maggie is deeply troubled. Maggie brings out Grace's food and places it on the table. Grace enjoys her lunch. When she finishes, she gets up from the table and leaves cash to pay for the bill, with an extra big tip—she figures Maggie can use a little extra kindness. Along with the money and tip, she leaves her church card, which has her phone number. On the back of her card is printed a quote from the Bible: "For I am the LORD, your

God, who takes hold of your right hand and says to you, Do not fear; I will help you. Isaiah 41:13."

Grace gets up to leave. She looks at the man in the booth across from her, who smiles at her. It's Matthias, who is dressed like a construction worker. She smiles back at him.

Matthias stands up and says to Grace, "You have a nice day, ma'am."

Grace smiles again and replies, "You too, sir." She pauses. "Do I know you?"

"Maybe you've seen me here before. I stop in for lunch whenever I'm working in the area."

Grace can't place him, but there is something familiar about him. She replies, "Well, it's nice to make your acquaintance."

"I apologize, but I couldn't help but hear your encouraging words to the waitress. That was very kind of you. You know, kindness has a way of helping troubled souls to heal. Those who spread kindness regularly are truly blessed."

Grace smiles. "Well, thank you. How nice of you to say that. I agree with you completely. We need to be doing the Lord's work by helping each other in any way we can."

"I couldn't agree more."

"Are you a godly man, sir?"

"I would say that's a pretty accurate statement."

"Well, praise be."

She hands him her card. Matthias reads the biblical quote on the back. "Isaiah 41:13. One of my favorites. I always tell him that when I see him." Matthias puts the card in his pocket.

He gets up to leave, and she realizes he just said that he tells Isaiah he likes the quote when he sees him. An odd response, she thinks, and then realizes that there is something special about this man. "Stop by the church sometime," she says.

Matthias smiles. "I already have."

He winks, tips his cap and walks out. Grace is a bit surprised and confused, but she has an overwhelming feeling of joy. With a puzzled but happy look on her face, she replies, "Bye now."

As she heads for the door, Grace walks over to Maggie and says kindly, "You take care of yourself, Maggie. Please come see me. The macchiato latte is on me."

Maggie laughs and gives Grace a brief hug. Grace heads out as Maggie returns to Grace's booth to clean away the dishes. She notices the big tip. She picks up Grace's card, reads it and smiles. She puts it in her pocket and heads for the kitchen.

Maggie's shift ends later that day. She hangs up her apron in her locker, grabs her jacket and heads outdoors. Her first day back at the diner was a bit emotional. She's not sure how much longer she can go on being a waitress. The whole point of taking on basic employment was to escape the reality of her executive life in LA for a while. The shooting changed that. What she thought was a way to blend into the crowd actually threw her into more chaos, made her more visible. She realizes there is no escaping the world. It just keeps going on around us, regardless if we try to hide from it. She thinks maybe it's time to start dealing with it, to fight back and move forward. She just needs to muster up the strength and courage. She had it once. She needs to get it back.

Maggie heads out to meet her sister for drinks. She is sure she'll get an earful about not fighting to prove that she got screwed over by Brad and Kara. Maggie, realizes, though, that instead of fighting, she chose to escape to New York.

Maggie walks out and hails a cab. One pulls over right away. She jumps in the back and the cab heads downtown. The cabbie is a small fellow from India. He seems to be in a good mood, but a little too talkative for Maggie's taste.

"Good evening, ma'am. Where are you headed on this fine evening?"

"Finnegan's Wake. It's on First Avenue and Seventy-Third Street."

"Oh, I'm so sorry. How did he die?"

"How did he…what? It's a bar. Oh… very funny, very funny."

The cabbie starts laughing and smiles. This stupid, corny joke makes Maggie laugh.

"I bet you were just dying to use that line."

"I've got a million of them. If you're hungry, I know a great Chinese place—Wok This Way. Steven Tyler of Aerosmith recommends it."

"Oh, God. Okay. You got me. That's enough."

The cabbie speeds along. Maggie looks at her phone to pass the time. The ride doesn't take too long. The cab pulls up in front of Finnegan's Wake Irish Bar. Maggie slides a twenty for an eight-dollar fare into the payment slot. As he goes to grab the bill, she says with a deadpan look through the glass separating her from the driver, "Harry...keep the change," referring to the Harry Chapin song "Taxi."

"Not bad. Not bad at all. Very funny!" says the cabbie. "Give Finnegan my condolences," he chuckles.

Maggie rolls her eyes, laughs, and gets out of the cab. She walks into the bar. Kate is seated in the back of the bar at a small round table with two chairs.

"Maggie, over here!" Kate calls out, jumping up and giving Maggie a big hug.

"Hey, big sis, what's up?"

Maggie looks around. It's a traditional Irish pub with brick-and-mahogany walls and a long mahogany bar with brass accents.

"Nice place. Is it Guinness Night in here?"

"Well, I did say drinks. Were you expecting to sip champagne at the Waldorf Astoria?"

"No, I'm kidding. This is fine. Where's Finnegan's body laid out? I want to pay my respects."

"Ha, good to see you haven't lost your sense of humor, Mag. Other than that, you look like shit. When's the last time you put on some lipstick?"

"Well, thank you. I do work in a diner. My current career choice doesn't require makeup like yours. So, is that a token insult for the night, or are you just getting warmed up?"

"You're right. I'm sorry. I'm so glad to see you. How are you? You know, after the shooting. I still can't believe you were there."

The barmaid comes over and places a freshly poured Guinness stout on the table.

"What can I get you?"

"I'll have a Guinness too."

"Another Guinness coming up."

Kate takes a sip of her beer. "Well?"

"Well what?"

"How are you getting along after everything that happened?"

Maggie says sarcastically, "Life's just one big party for me."

"Damn, Maggie, what's up with you? I know you just went through hell, but you need to snap out of it. You look like shit and you act like you're in another world."

Maggie looks at Kate, annoyed. "Wow, same old Kate. You're still the same straight shooter you've always been, aren't you? What is it that you want to hear, Kate? I'm depressed? I can't cope? My job sucks? Well, yeah, all of the above. I'm miserable. Shit, I almost lost my life in an execution hit on two cops, both customers of mine at the diner. What else is it you want me to say or do that will make you feel better?"

"Look, I apologize. Maybe I did come on a little too strong."

The barmaid comes back over and places Maggie's beer on the table.

"A little too strong? Yeah, you can put the sledgehammer back in your purse. You think I want to be in this position, Kate? You think I don't look at myself and wonder what happened to my life?"

Grabbing Maggie's hands, Kate softens to a concerned tone. "I'm sorry, I didn't mean it that way, Mag. It's just you're so withdrawn from everyone. I feel like I can't reach you anymore. You're not the Maggie I used to know. What happened to the confident fashion guru? The woman who knew exactly what she wanted and wasn't afraid to go after it? I'm really, really worried about you."

"I'm just having a really hard time with all of this," says Maggie.

"Maggie, let's face it—you got screwed in LA, point-blank, period. You didn't deserve it. But you've got to snap out of it. You need to take your life back. I feel like you just gave up and accepted what happened to you. You deserve better, and that jackass of an ex-husband of yours deserves to be in jail, or better yet, under it."

Maggie takes another sip of her beer and looks squarely at Kate. "You're right, Kate, it's true. Maybe I did give up, but I tried to kill Kara. Remember? I threw away everything I worked for due to my own drunken stupidity. Do you have any idea what it's been like for me? I married that self-centered jackass Brad. He never gave a crap about our marriage. He married my career, not me. I was good for his ego and his business. I was ashamed at what happened. How could I have been so blind to everything? It was all right there in front of me, right there in black and white, and I just chose not to pay attention to the signs. I needed to get as far away from that life as possible. Coming to New York let me escape the guilt and the embarrassment."

"I get that, Maggie. We all make mistakes and bad decisions. Things happen. It's how we respond that makes the difference. I know you feel like there's no way out. But you have to fight. You just can't give up and accept the way things are. You know they set you up. You didn't steal anything. Don't let them beat you."

"I know, I know. I didn't have it in me to fight. Hey, I don't plan on spending the rest of my life pouring coffee. I just needed some mindless simplicity for a while to sort things out. After what happened in LA, I needed that, but the shooting shook me to my core. I really need to decide how to go forward with my life. Just give me some time, okay? I'm getting there. I promise. I'll get it together."

"Why don't you get a private investigator?" says Kate. "Somebody has to be able to find the truth."

Maggie takes a sip of Guinness. "I've thought about it. I just haven't had the strength or courage to try. I'll think about it. I promise."

"Fine, but you need to find the courage soon. Otherwise, you'll keep beating yourself up and you'll get nowhere. I'm not going to let you give up. I'm going to stay on you. That's what kid sisters are for."

"Is that what they're for?" Maggie says inquisitively.

"You're an ass, but I do love you."

"Yeah, I know. Now finish that damn beer so we can order another, and a few shots!"

The tension of the straightforward discussion has ended, and the two sisters switch focus to just having fun drinking and being sisters again. Maggie needed this. A little dose of straight talk from Kate always makes her feel better. For the first time in a long time, Kate helped her feel like herself again.

CHAPTER 11

————————

In the Blink of an Eye

It's early in the evening and the Empire Diner is quiet. Earl's uncle Stavros is getting ready to close up. Earl will stay a little longer and close at around 10 p.m. Stavros walks through and inspects the kitchen one last time. He hangs up some frying pans and puts away a few newly washed utensils, glasses and plates. Stavros likes a neat kitchen. That's how he was taught by his father and his grandfather. There was always a lot of pride in how they ran their restaurants. Not only was good-tasting food important, but how the place was kept and cleaned were just as important. He believed the only way to run a great restaurant was to ensure everything was done properly.

He puts on his coat and stops by the counter to speak with Earl. "We've bought too much beef. I'm going to make a beef stew in the morning as a lunch special tomorrow. The beef stew is always popular."

"That's a good idea. I was thinking the same thing. Your beef stew is the best in the city."

"You're right. Who am I to argue?"

They both laugh as Earl pats his uncle on the back.

"By the way, the produce delivery was missing some vegetables. He's supposed to come back in the morning with the rest of the stuff. You'll be here before me, so I'm just letting you know."

"What did he forget?"

"Some carrots and red onions. He brought some, but not the full order."

"No problem, nephew. I gotta go pick up your aunt Lexi. She's making me go shopping for a new tie for your cousin's daughter's birthday party."

"But doesn't she pick out all your ties?"

"Apparently, they're all ugly now. I know better than to argue with your aunt Alexis."

They both laugh.

"See you tomorrow, Uncle Staav."

Stavros heads out the door. He drives home and picks up his wife, who is waiting for him in front of the driveway.

"You're late."

"Lexi, my dear, I can't control the traffic."

"Well, let's get moving. I want to get to the store before it closes."

"Do I really need a new tie?"

"If you don't keep quiet and drive, you'll be trying on suits too."

They drive to the local mall to a Macy's and head to the men's department. After looking at just about every tie in the store, Lexi finally picks one she likes. Stavros says, "Don't I have one just like this?"

"No, the pattern is different, and the shade is darker."

"If you say so, my love. Do you want to stop and eat on the way home? I could go for a nice bowl of pasta at Mario's."

"No. I cooked this afternoon. I made moussaka."

"Well, nothing tops your moussaka. Home it is."

They drive home to their house in Forest Hills, where they have lived for thirty-five years. Stavros pulls up and opens the electronic garage door. Lexi gets out and heads for the staircase. Stavros pulls the car into the garage. He gets out and hits the remote to close the door. As he rounds the corner, Lexi is lying across the threshold of the door. Stavros lets out repeated screams.

"Lexi! Lexi! Oh my God, Lexi!"

A neighbor is walking his dog nearby and hears Stavros's screams. He quickly dials 911 and runs to help Stavros. Lexi is not responding. She is unconscious. In the blink of an eye, she suffered a massive heart attack. She's dead.

Stavros lifts her head and gently places it on his lap and cries uncontrollably.

"Somebody help us, please. My beautiful wife, Lexi. Oh no. God, no!"

The ambulance arrives at the scene, along with the police. Stavros asked the neighbor to call his nephew Earl and his brother Spiro, Earl's father. Both men are in shock and head straight to the house to comfort Stavros. The EMTs at the scene examine Lexi and pronounce her dead. Now they must wait for the coroner to arrive to remove the body. Earl and Spiro arrive. Stavros is sitting on the stairs outside his home with the EMTs attending to him. As soon as he sees Earl and Spiro, he breaks down again, sobbing uncontrollably.

"Spiro…she's gone…my Lexi is dead. Oh God, no!"

Spiro and Earl are both crying as well. They are speechless but doing their best to comfort Stavros. The coroner arrives and places Lexi's body in their transport vehicle. Earl and Spiro are trying to get Stavros to stand up to bring him inside the house. He is devastated as he turns and sees them place Lexi's body in the vehicle. At the sight of them closing the door behind Lexi's body, he collapses. The EMTs run over to assist Earl and Spiro. The four of them help get Stavros up and bring him inside the house. The coroner drives away. All that's left is the pain and the heartbreak.

A few days later, there is a packed house at Christos Funeral Home in Astoria, New York, for Lexi's wake. The funeral home is well established in this strong Greek community. Lexi's body lies in a half-open casket, revealing her body from the waist up. Her hair and makeup have been meticulously done. The only jewelry she is wearing is her wedding ring. She is dressed in a beautiful light blue dress, reminiscent of the beautiful blue waters of her native Greece. Sitting atop the unopened portion of the casket is a cross.

Mourners are lined up from the casket through the memorial chapel room, out into the hallway and almost out the door. The Vassos family is a large Greek family and they have hundreds of friends and workers from all their restaurants. One of the mourners in the line is Maggie. She waits a long time to pay her respects. As she reaches the family, Earl runs over to greet her.

"Maggie. Thank you so much for coming. You didn't need to come, especially after all you've been through, but I'm so glad to see you here."

"I'm so sorry, Earl. Your aunt was a wonderful lady. She always made me laugh. May God give you strength to bear the loss of your beautiful aunt."

"Thank you. My aunt was a special lady."

"Yes, she was. She always took time to chat with me when she visited the diner."

"Not only that, she was a big fan of yours, Maggie. When I told her about your past, she spent time researching your work. She absolutely loved it."

"Really?"

"She would tell me and my uncle to fire you so you'd go back to being a designer!"

"Thank you for sharing that, but please don't fire me yet…"

Maggie's comment allows her and Earl to have a light moment. Maggie realizes how crowded it is. She hugs Earl and starts to move towards Stavros. Earl stops her briefly.

"The diner will be closed a few more days. My cousin Pete will be filling in for Stavros until he's ready to come back to work."

"Sounds good."

Maggie goes over to Stavros. He stands up and hugs her. Tears come to Maggie's eyes.

"I'm so deeply sorry, Stavros. May Lexi's memory be eternal."

"Thank you for coming, Maggie. You know she loved seeing you at the diner. When she found out who you were, she looked up all your designs. She loved them. Did Earl tell you she jokingly told us to fire you so you would go back to being a designer?"

"Yes, he told me."

"You know, Maggie, you obviously have a gift. We love you, but you don't belong working as a waitress. Lexi's passing is a reminder we're not promised tomorrow. Go be what you were meant to be, an amazing designer."

Maggie starts to cry and hugs Stavros.

"Let me get to the rest of these people in line. I'll see you in a few days, back at the diner."

Maggie gives him another hug and kisses him on the cheek. She walks away and starts to head to the exit, wiping tears from her eyes with her hand. She can't believe how Stavros, a man who just lost his beloved wife, took time to give her encouragement. It was one of the most touching moments she ever felt in her life. As she walks towards the back, a tall, handsome man with black hair and striking features, dressed in an impeccably tailored suit, hands her a handkerchief.

"Here, looks like you could use this."

"Thank you. I get a little emotional at these things."

"I'm Matthias. I'm a friend of the family. I guess we all get a little emotional when someone passes. It's sad to see these things happen. Yet this family is a family of tremendous faith, especially Lexi."

The man is actually Matthias, the angel. He looks completely different from the other times he has presented himself to Maggie.

Maggie says, "I work with Stavros and Earl at the diner. I've met Lexi on many occasions. They are truly wonderful people."

"I couldn't agree more. In difficult times like these, the family can use all the love and support they can get. Glad you could come to pay your respects."

"So am I. Funny, though, in the midst of his grief, Stavros took time to encourage me on some difficult things going on in my life."

"I'm not surprised. That's the sign of a truly blessed man. We are all here to help each other, comfort each other and get each other through difficult times. Kindness and compassion have a way of uplifting our souls."

"Yes, they do, don't they?"

"For sure. Well, the line is moving. It was nice to make your acquaintance. Have a nice evening."

"Wait, here's your handkerchief."

Matthias pulls out another from his pocket and shows it to Maggie.

"Keep it. I always carry an extra at wakes and funerals for someone in need."

Maggie smiles. She impulsively reaches forward and hugs Matthias.

"Thank you for your kindness."

"Get home safe now." Matthias winks at Maggie as she turns away and heads towards the door. Maggie smiles as she realizes she left the funeral home with more than she came with.

Alexis Vassos was born Alexis Skordalos in the coastal town of Chora, Greece. She grew up in a large, traditional Greek family with seven siblings. As a teenager, she came to America with her family to start a restaurant business. They moved to Astoria, Queens. While at a church function at St. Demetrios Greek Orthodox Cathedral, she met Stavros. The two instantly fell in love and were married, and their wedded bliss lasted for over thirty-five years. They eventually moved out of Astoria to a bigger home in Forest Hills so they could raise their family, but they always stayed connected to the Astoria community. Stavros helped run the family restaurants, until he helped Earl open the Empire Diner.

Lexi awakens to the sight of a beautiful seaside town, much like Santorini in Greece, where she honeymooned with Stavros. She is in awe of its sapphire waters and clear blue sky. She is in a state of inexplicable joy. She has never seen or experienced such beauty. She feels a complete sense of peace. She cannot recall ever feeling this way. As she looks down toward the ocean, she sees a woman waving to her from a beach below. Who could this be? She walks from the top of the cliff, overlooking the ocean, and over to a path that leads to the water.

As she makes her way down the path, the sunset is simply breathtaking. The sea air has a sweet crispness to it. Its salty feel is intoxicating to the senses. The woman on the beach continues to wave. Lexi continues down the path, feeling light on her feet, almost as if her feet are not touching the ground. She is wearing a flowing white cotton summer dress that rustles with the ocean breeze.

Lexi gets closer and closer until she can finally see the face of the woman. She drops to her knees and with tears of indescribable joy she yells out, "Yia-Yia!"

It's her grandmother, Nefeli. Lexi gets up and runs to her grandmother, who opens her arms and embraces her in a hug that Lexi can feel to her very soul. Her grandmother raised her after her mother tragically passed away in a car accident when Lexi was a young girl. When Yia-Yia passed, Lexi had an emptiness in her heart that remained her entire life—until this moment. The emptiness is now gone and replaced with a sense of fullness and love.

Her grandmother lovingly lifts Lexi's head in the palm of her hand and looks her in the eye and simply says, "I love you. Come, child. Walk with me, my sweet Lexi. Your mama is waiting for you."

Lexi's eyes swell with more tears of joy. She embraces her grandmother so tightly as if the two had become one. With that, Lexi strolls off peacefully with her grandmother's arm wrapped around her waist and her head softly resting on her grandmother's shoulder. They walk into the setting sun.

"God sends us friends to be our firm support in the whirlpool of struggle. In the company of friends, we will find strength to attain our sublime ideal."

—St. Maximilian Kolbe

CHAPTER 12

Distractions and New Beginnings

ennifer Peterson has just finished her classes for the day. She's the same girl who was at the diner earlier, trying to order a gourmet coffee from Maggie while texting. Jennifer heads to the student parking lot and gets into her blue 2017 Toyota RAV4 hybrid and drives out of the parking lot of Iona College in New Rochelle, New York. Her iPhone is on the seat next to her. Jennifer is in her sophomore year, studying psychology. She's not the most ambitious student. She's a former high school cheerleader who's into the party scene. She'd really like to be a party planner, but her parents were insistent she give this major a try.

As she leaves the campus and drives away, her phone dings, indicating a new text from John, a guy from the rugby team that she's dating.

"Party 2nite. Frat house," texts John.

Jennifer picks up the phone. "Yuk. That place smells," she texts back while driving.

Jennifer is on the way to her off-campus apartment on Union Avenue, just over a mile from the school and just past Montefiore Hospital.

Dr. Kirkland, the ER doctor from Lenox Hill, has just finished spending a day at a medical conference at Montefiore. He sat through a long day of lectures and was now looking forward to heading home. He gets into his late-model Mercedes-Benz sedan and leaves the parking lot.

Jennifer is driving but continues texting John. Preoccupied with her phone, she's now exceeding the speed limit. Not paying attention, she suddenly runs a red light, at the precise moment that Dr. Kirkland's Mercedes is passing directly in front of Jennifer's Toyota. Suddenly, there's a sound of screeching brakes and tires skidding, with a loud violent smash as two cars violently collide. Jennifer's car slams into Dr. Kirkland's driver-side door. Her airbag deploys, but the strong impact causes her car to fold instantly like an accordion. She wasn't wearing her seat belt. Her head hits the steering wheel with tremendous force, so strong that she goes through what used to be the windshield. She dies instantly.

Dr. Kirkland's car is also so badly mangled upon impact that his door is pushed into his body, pinning him up against the passenger door. It is a horrific, grisly scene. Kirkland's airbag also deployed, but the blunt force of the high-speed impact caused massive internal bleeding.

A passerby runs over to both vehicles as they frantically phone for help. It's too late as, after a few minutes, Dr. Kirkland is dead as well. The street instantly fills with flashing red lights in every direction and the distant sounds of sirens.

***

BACK IN THE CITY, MAGGIE IS HANGING AROUND HER APART-ment, just watching television, constantly changing channels. Her cell phone rings. She doesn't recognize the number and doesn't answer it. The caller doesn't leave a message. The phone rings again. Maggie hesitates and then decides to answer it.

"Hello?"

"Hey, Maggie, it's Don Phillips!"

"Don Phillips? How are you? God, it's been a while. How did you find me?"

"I tracked down your sister and she gave me your number."

Maggie replies with mild sarcasm, "Good ol' Kate. I can always count on her. So, what's new?"

"Don't know if you heard, but I'm back in New York, working for Regency Designs. As you know, it's a small new design firm, but I think it's going places. After you left Text Styles, I didn't want to stay. You were the main reason I worked there."

"Wow. I didn't know you left. Regency does nice work. They're lucky to have you. Congrats."

"Thanks, Maggie. Hey, I won't keep you long, but I have something you might be interested in."

"Really, what would that be?"

"FIT is looking for an adjunct professor a few nights a week to teach a textile design class. It's just part-time, but I thought, who better than the queen of textiles?"

"The queen? More like the court jester," Maggie says in self-deprecating humor.

"Nonsense. This is Don you're talking to. You're the best in the business. Remember, I worked for you."

"I once was. Teaching college kids? Sounds like a role for former 'royalty' like me. So, I guess my sister also filled you in on my current employment situation? I'm the queen of hot coffee and pancakes now. It beats staring at the walls of my apartment all day. It's good enough for me until I can get my act together."

"Hey, you're too talented to be slinging coffee and blue-plate lunch specials to a bunch of nameless faces. You truly have a talent that few possess. You used to tell me how your college days at FIT helped you to develop your style. Let's face it, what better way to get back in the game than to teach and enlighten young designers?"

"Yeah, I do love the designing part of the business. No BS, just creativity. I miss that."

"At the very least you can mentor and share your creativity with college kids. Give it some thought. It's yours if you want it. The dean is a friend of mine. When I mentioned your name, he begged me to call you."

Maggie replies jokingly, "The last time someone begged me was yesterday, when one of my customers wanted more decaf. Seriously, though, I'll think about it. You're sweet for thinking of me. How are you otherwise?"

"I'm great. You know me, always on the move. Look, I gotta run, but think about it and call me. If you don't, I'll just keep bugging you till I get an answer."

"Yes, you will, Don. That's for sure. It's no accident you're in sales. I promise you I'll seriously think about it."

"Great. Talk to you soon."

Maggie disconnects the call. She gets up and walks to the corner of her apartment. There are some stacked boxes of files from her old job. She opens one marked "Design Projects" and starts thumbing through some of the folders. She grabs a few to look through as she heads back to the couch. As she looks at designs she's created over the years, she smiles.

Matthias suddenly appears. He sees what she is doing, so he sweeps his hand to knock over the stack of boxes. As the files hit the floor, he pushes one file forward with his foot.

The file closest to her on the floor has its contents scattered. Maggie bends down and picks them up.

The folder is labeled "Trademark Infringement." She opens it. Paper-clipped to the first page is a business card: MARK HATCHER, Private Investigator. She pauses, staring at the card, then puts it on the coffee table. She sits down, lights a cigarette. She picks up the business card again and stares at it some more. She remembers her conversation with Kate about not even trying to investigate getting screwed over by Kara and Brad. She never embezzled that money. She never set up offshore accounts. Maybe it's time to have someone investigate it.

Matthias smiles and vanishes.

IT'S FIVE DAYS SINCE THE TRAGIC CAR CRASH THAT KILLED JENnifer and Dr. Kirkland. At a funeral home in the New Jersey town where Jennifer grew up, a closed casket sits in the front of the room.

The accident was so bad that Jennifer was disfigured and an open casket was out of the question. Next to the casket is a small table with framed pictures of Jennifer. There's also a collage of pictures of Jennifer on an easel, along with floral arrangements scattered about. The mood in the room is deeply sad. Jennifer's mother, sitting in the front, seems to go back and forth between deep shock and inconsolable sadness. Her anguish can be heard and viewed as each visitor pays their respects.

Jennifer grew up in the nicest area of Lawrenceville. Her father had an excellent job as a chemist for a major pharmaceutical company. Her family lived in a beautiful home, with another vacation home on the Jersey shore. Jennifer never wanted for much. She always had the latest clothes and cell phone, not to mention the new car her parents got her for her birthday after she passed her road test. Her sweet sixteen was the social event of the year, and her high school graduation party was held on the beach in Long Beach Island.

Yet suddenly, in the blink of an eye, she was gone.

John, Jennifer's boyfriend from college, is seated nearby, clearly shaken. He feels deeply guilty as it was his text that Jennifer was replying to. He has been speaking with counselors at the college, but he is really having a tough time with Jennifer's passing. Death is not easy on a teen, especially a sudden and tragic death.

Near the back of the room are two women who are acquaintances of the family. They seem to be preoccupied observing the mourners. A woman in her late sixties, a neighbor of the family, is speaking with another neighbor.

"What a tragedy. She had her whole life ahead of her. Such a pretty girl. Her parents will never be the same."

The second woman replies with questions. "I just don't understand. Why do these kids text and drive? Don't they know the dangers? When will these kids ever learn? And that poor doctor; Kirkland was his name. I heard he was the head of the ER unit at Lenox Hill in New York. Such a senseless tragedy."

"Terrible. I don't know how her parents are going to cope. She was the apple of her father's eye. Her mother was always bragging about her accomplishments. Losing a child is one of the most unnatural experiences. Believe me, I know."

"Sad. Truly sad. Ethel Turner from across the street said her younger brothers are in shock. They're really having a hard time."

"Those poor boys. God help them."

CHAPTER 13

Old Acquaintances and New Faces

Jennifer's eyes open and she's standing in the sunny hallway of her old high school. No one is there. She begins to walk around, looking for people. She sees a bulletin board with a flyer that says "Don't text and drive if you want to stay alive." Jennifer suddenly recalls her accident, but only to the exact moment of impact. She runs for the door, but it's locked. She runs to another door, passing the cafeteria. She sees a janitor mopping. A few feet behind him is a lone girl sitting at a table with a lunch tray. The janitor is Matthias. He walks past Jennifer while still mopping but doesn't speak. She walks into the cafeteria.

Jennifer calls out, "Hello?"

The lone girl sitting at the table keeps her head down and remains quiet. Jennifer walks further into the cafeteria. The janitor doesn't respond either.

"Hey. Hey, you. Do you hear me talking to you?"

She walks further and is now standing in front of the girl, whose head is still down low.

"Hello?"

The girl senses someone is there and finally looks up.

"Oh. I'm sorry, I didn't hear you."

"I was yelling from way back there. How could you not hear me?"

The girl removes the earbuds from her ears.

"Sorry, I was listening to my music."

Jennifer responds in an annoyed tone, "Where is everybody?

I've never seen the school this quiet. Is this some sort of day off?"

"No."

"Come to think of it, why am I back at high school? What are you doing here all alone?"

"I don't mind it. I'm used to being alone."

"Well, I'm not. Where is everyone? I was in an accident. I should be in a hospital. Why am I here?"

The girl disregards her comment but says, "I haven't been able to move on, but now that you're here, I can."

"What? Move on? What does that mean?"

"You don't remember me, do you? I'm Peggy Mulvey."

"Who?"

"You know, Peggy Mulvey, the girl you bullied and verbally abused all through high school?"

Jennifer suddenly has a flashback. It's clear as day in her mind as if it was happening at that very moment. Several girls are in the locker room. Peggy is sitting on the bench. Jennifer is taunting Peggy repeatedly.

"Where did you get those clothes from? The Salvation Army? Oh my God, those shoes. Don't you look at yourself in the mirror before you leave your house? Pathetic. What a loser."

Peggy tears up and begins to cry.

"You're gonna cry now? Oh, grow up. Do us a favor and keep your creepy, ugly ass away from us. We don't like you. No one does."

The flashback ends and Jennifer looks at Peggy and starts to act defensively.

"No, wait. I didn't mean all those things I said. We were just teasing you."

"You weren't teasing me. You tortured me every day. Why? I never did anything to you. Was it because I was poor? Was it because I wasn't as pretty as you? I just wanted to be your friend. Instead, you made me feel worthless. It got so bad I decided to kill myself. You convinced me I was a loser. People always looked at you as the popular girl. The cheerleader captain, the nice girl. But you were really a conceited bitch. You only cared about yourself."

Peggy looks over her left shoulder. As she turns her head, Jennifer sees there is an ugly rope mark around her neck, indicating her suicide was by hanging. Peggy was the girl who hung herself in the garage.

"What you didn't know was that my mother worked nearly twelve hours a day after my father died. She did her best for me and my brother. We couldn't afford nice clothes and other things. I would wait up for her every night when she got home late from work. She'd ask me about school, but I didn't want to upset her by telling her how you bullied me. She had so much on her plate trying to hold down two jobs. I didn't want to add to her stress."

Jennifer continues to be defensive. "I didn't mean all those things."

"You say that now, but you never showed me any kindness. Yet even though you were so mean to me, Jennifer, I forgave you as I put that rope around my neck. They gave me the chance to tell you this before it was time to go."

Peggy gets up as the janitor, Matthias, steps inside.

Jennifer is confused. "Go where? Who let you be here to tell me you hung yourself?"

Matthias walks over. He is not speaking to or even acknowledging Jennifer. It's as if she was not there.

"Time to go, Peggy."

Peggy gets up. She walks away with Matthias. Both head towards the door. Jennifer stands there in disbelief and shock. As they reach the door, Jennifer runs after them, but as she reaches the door, it turns into a solid brick wall. Jennifer turns around. Peggy is gone, but now she sees a different janitor mopping. This time it's Dante. He looks angry and unapproachable.

"Who are you? What happened to Peggy and the other guy? Where did you come from? Where did they go?"

Suddenly Dante drops the mop and addresses Jennifer. "She gets to leave with that despicable suck-up. He never could stand on his own, always taking orders from them," he says, looking up. "Yeah, too bad about her. With all that abuse you heaped on her, I thought she would turn to us for some revenge. She came close.

Almost followed you home once to kill you, but *they* stepped in. Curse their timing. I thought we had a real shot at her, but she kept praying to Him, asking for mercy. Oh please. She even forgave you. How nice, but that won't help you, *Jenny*. You're not going anywhere."

Jennifer quickly becomes frightened. "What do you mean you almost had her? How do you know my name? Why can't I leave? I want to leave!"

"Sorry, but you'll be staying with us. Everything she said was true. Oh, and there are other girls just like her that you bullied. They're pretty messed up too. We'll get a few of those souls thanks to your help. You helped to destroy their self-confidence. You were a self-centered little bitch. The phony, popular, pretty cheerleader. Do you want to discuss your abortion? Oh, yes, we know all your dirty little secrets, my dear. How about sleeping with that science teacher? Did you know you destroyed his marriage? Bet you didn't know that. Damn, you were a busy little bitch, weren't you?"

"There must be a mistake. I didn't hurt anybody on purpose."

"There's no mistake. You belong here, pretty Jenny. Or should I say 'ugly Jenny'?"

A small mirror suddenly appears in Dante's hand. He points it towards her. Jennifer sees her face is now disfigured, looking like she did after the car crash: deep gashes, swollen face and bloodstains.

Dante continues his condemning diatribe.

"Now your face matches your soul. You're uglier than anyone you ever bullied. Now we'll be bullying you, my dear."

Jennifer screams in horror, touching the mirror and her own face. Dante's face transforms into a flaming skull.

Jennifer screams the most horrendous scream of sheer terror. Demonic creatures suddenly come up through the floor and swiftly crawl towards her. Slowly, one by one, they grab at her legs and arms as the room gets dark. The darkness devours Jennifer entirely. She screams, but no one can hear her. Loud demonic groans fill the room. Jennifer is dragged to hell. Suddenly there is silence. Jennifer is gone.

CHAPTER 14

———

The Books Tell the Stories

The victim of the horrific car crash that also killed Jennifer Peterson, Dr. Stephen Kirkland, is being interred today. His family is holding a private service and burial for him, attended only by family and a few friends. His body was cremated, and his ashes are being buried at Ferncliff Cemetery in Hartsdale, New York, in the Rosewood Mausoleum. The Rosewood Mausoleum is constructed of the finest granites and marbles for their traditional beauty. His remains are placed in a stunning niche wall, near the indoor cremation garden. Each marble-front niche on the wall allows for the placement of cremains in an urn. Stephen J. Kirkland, MD, is etched into the marble facing.

After receiving his undergraduate degree in pre-med, Kirkland attended medical school at Columbia University. He graduated with honors and did his residency at Hackensack Hospital in New Jersey.

Kirkland left behind a wife and three children, aged sixteen, thirteen and ten. In addition to the family's private service, there was also a small memorial service held at Lenox Hill Hospital, put together by his colleagues to share remembrances of him. He was well liked by most of the staff, who knew him as an excellent doctor who always kept his cool under pressure.

Doctor Kirkland suddenly awakens as if from a deep sleep. He is dressed in plain white surgical scrubs, the exact kind he wears all the time at the hospital. He is barefoot. He finds himself seated at a large table in a library setting. The walls are covered with bookshelves from floor to ceiling. The shelves are filled with hundreds of volumes of leather-bound books. In fact, there are more books stacked high on the floor and more on the table where Kirkland is sitting. In walks Phillip, a tall, slender, unassuming man, dressed in plain blue hospital scrubs. He sits in the seat next to Dr. Kirkland.

"Dr. Kirkland, I'm Phillip. I've been assigned to you for your introductory stage."

"Where am I? An introductory stage? To what?"

"You died in that car accident. This is your transition place."

Kirkland suddenly recalls the accident and the events that led up to it. He recalls the impact of the collision, but that's the last thing he remembers before everything went blank.

"Yes, the car accident. A car must have run the light. My light had just turned green."

Philip just looks at him without speaking.

"You said this is my transition place? What does that mean? Where am I?"

"I really have no further information I can give you. I'm only here to brief you on your initial assignment and to briefly instruct you. Someone else will contact you after you have completed your task."

Kirkland is obviously puzzled and confused. He doesn't know what to think.

"Instruct me on what?"

"Mr. Kirkland, as I stated, I am only here to start you on the introductory phase. Please, let me begin. You are required to read all the books in this room. The first book, in front of you, is the book of your life. Once you read it, many things will become clear. You will see all your actions and decisions, both good and bad, and how they affected you and everyone you encountered throughout your life. This process allows you to see who you really were. It'll show you the way you lived your life and how you reacted and lived, day in and day out."

"Required by whom? So, what does all this mean? Am I in heaven? Hell? I saved a lot of lives in the ER. I've helped lots of people. Many people came into the ER and were close to death, and I saved them."

Phillip keeps his response instructional. "I'm sure everything about your life has been well documented. Again, I am only here to start your process. It is not my role to discuss anything with you. Many things will be revealed as you go along."

"If this first book is my life, what are these others?"

"I believe they are biographies."

"Of who?"

"Dr. Kirkland, I suggest you begin. You have a lot of reading to do."

Phillip gets up, heads for the door and leaves the room. Kirkland is still confused and unsure of what is happening. The only reality he knows is that he's dead. He doesn't feel any different. He sits for a few minutes, then looks down at the book in front of him. Engraved on the cover of the leather-bound book is his name. He pauses for a moment, staring at the cover, then slowly opens the book. He thumbs through it, glancing at chapters without really reading anything. In the first few chapters, he sees images of his early childhood, from his birth to his toddler days. He sees his birth certificate, baby photos, early school pictures, vacation photos with his family. Each chapter seems to be a detailed look at one year of his life. The chapters get longer as he gets older. After all, he starts to grow, experience life and make decisions. The book has piqued his curiosity.

As Dr. Kirkland flips through the chapters, he pauses on a page that says, "Lives Saved." He glances at it. It is a chronology of all the patients that came through the ER who he saved as a trauma surgeon. It includes victims of gunshot wounds, car wrecks, accidents, heart attacks and strokes. The list goes on and on. Dr. Kirkland remembers many of the cases, as the book gives detailed accounts and descriptions of each. One in particular was of a little girl he saved who was pulled from a frigid lake after falling through the ice one winter day. He remembered how her parents repeatedly thanked him and the rescue squad for saving their little girl. It made him feel good inside. It's one of the most rewarding accomplishments of being a doctor.

As he continues to flip through the chapters, he stumbles across chapter 27, entitled "Abortion Doctor Years." Suddenly, his face goes from happy to solemn. He hurriedly goes through the chapter. Each page lists hundreds of names with corresponding book volume numbers.

Dr. Kirkland suddenly takes on a serious demeanor. His eyes scan down the page, seeing random names and numbers.

He whispers softly, "Maria Conchita Chavez...Volume 149."

He gets up and goes to the bookshelf. All the volumes are in chronological order. He finds Volume 149. The cover says Maria Conchita Chavez 2003. He takes the book off the shelf, sits back down and opens it.

"Maria Conchita Chavez, aborted September 24, 2003, by Dr. Stephen Kirkland, Planned Parenthood Clinic, Bronx, NY."

The subsequent pages are all about Maria's life—the life she never had. Just like his own book, there are baby photos, childhood photos, school pictures, her prom, dating, her marriage, the birth of her children, her career, etc. The book chronicles it all. Her career page shows she would have been an advocate for handicapped children, fighting for various legislation on their behalf. The details go on and on.

A grave look comes over Kirkland's face. He looks back at the list and finds another name: Randall James White...Volume 188.

Again, he gets up and looks on the shelves for the volume. He finds it. This time he opens it up standing in front of the bookshelf.

"Randall James White, aborted on November 28, 2004, by Dr. Stephen Kirkland, Planned Parenthood Clinic, Bronx, NY."

The story of Randall details the life of his unwed mother, Latisha, and her struggle with drug addiction. With an addiction problem, Latisha opted not to bring her child into this world, so she went to Planned Parenthood and had an abortion. What no one knew was that the abortion left Latisha in a deeper state of depression, making her spiral deeper into her addiction and drug use. She eventually would die from an overdose.

If Randall had been born, Latisha would have had her parents' help in raising Randall. Her mother would have helped her finally get clean while making sure Randall stayed out of trouble and went to school regularly. As Randall got older, his grandparents would have taken him and his mother and moved south to Florida. This would give them both a new start in life, away from the troubles of their Bronx neighborhood. Randall would have excelled in the warmer climate and the change of scenery from New York. He would have had a deep love for sports. He would have been a star in both basketball and football. His coaches would have made sure he studied hard and got good grades in order to be able to stay on the team. He would have also excelled academically, eventually receiving a full scholarship to the University of Georgia, where he would have pursued and ultimately earned a law degree. Latisha would have finished community college to eventually become a paralegal and wind up in a career she could be proud of.

Latisha would have been the proudest of mothers, watching Randall graduate from a fine university and go on to achieve things she never dreamed possible.

As Kirkland reads more details of the life Randall never got to live, a deep sorrow fills his heart. He is overcome with sadness as tears fill his eyes. He closes Randall's book. He looks around the room and sees the hundreds and hundreds of volumes he is required to read, per Phillip's initial instructions. Kirkland sits down. He is visibly upset and begins to cry.

Just then, the door opens. In walks a man dressed as a doctor. He walks in and sits across from Kirkland.

Kirkland looks at him. "Who are you?"

"I'm Dr. James Rockleigh. I'm a well-known oncologist...or at least I would have been."

"What?"

"James Arthur Rockleigh, Volume 53."

Shock overtakes Dr. Kirkland's face. "You were in one of these books?"

"Yes. My parents were Ann Cooper and Dr. Mark Rockleigh. A long time ago, they were dating and talked about getting engaged. Both came from well-to-do families in Massachusetts. My father was a pre-med student at Harvard and my mother was the daughter of a wealthy industrialist. They had everything life could offer: money, cars, a vacation home on the Cape. They had it all. But one drunken night, Mark got Ann pregnant. They were so young. They could have easily had me; God knows they could afford it. Yet I didn't fit their lifestyle at the time. Mark was still pursuing his undergraduate degree, and Ann was headed to Salve Regina College in Newport, Rhode Island, to study music. Having me would have brought scandal and embarrassment to the families, not to mention putting their career plans on hold. They made a connection through a discreet family friend. That person knew the head of Planned Parenthood in Boston. They felt it was best to go out of town, so a connection was made to your office in New York. You were at a clinic in the Bronx. Not exactly the type of place two affluent young adults from New England would go, but it actually better served their secrecy."

"Look, I'm sorry. These are not things people think about when having an abortion."

"What things?"

"Thinking about a hypothetical scenario of what the child would turn out to be."

"And that's exactly the point of why I'm here. Back then, to you, it was just a medical procedure, not a life. You never had to know anything about me—who I was or what I'd become…until now."

Dr. Kirkland shakes his head. "Look, I'm sorry. I never realized…"

"You never realized? A smart guy like you? You're a doctor. You've seen and performed abortions in all stages. Maybe you chose not to realize. The culture has a way of changing people's priorities, doesn't it? You have recently saved children from death in the ER. You've done amazing things in that ER. Yet, I wasn't a child to you. Nor were the others."

"Look, I gave up that practice. The ER allowed me to try and save people. I was a different person back then. We are trained to be doctors, not priests. I'm making a difference now…or at least I was until the accident."

"That's true. The purpose of me being here is to put a little more depth into what you thought was a medical procedure. You can't run from the past. It's yours."

"I'm so sorry. I was a fool."

"Well, let me fill in a few more blanks before I go, then I'll leave you to contemplate. After all, this place is part of revealing your life. So, my mother, Ann, never got over the abortion. It always haunted her. My father broke up with her because she couldn't get over it. He went on to become an excellent doctor. Ann graduated college and became a music teacher. She never felt whole again until recently. She finally met a spiritual man who helped her heal and repent. Not a day goes by where she doesn't wonder about me. I would have gone on to the best private school in Boston. I would have been captain of the rugby team and graduated near the top of my class. I would have gone to Harvard Medical School. I truly wanted to be an oncologist, after watching some beloved relatives pass from cancer. I would have dedicated my life to finding a cure for cancer. I'd still be a doctor today, making great strides in cancer research throughout the world. But as you know, none of this ever happened."

Kirkland sits quietly. He has nothing left to say. James stands up to leave. He says, "I know you have much more to read and more lives like mine to examine. As you read through these books, others like me will periodically come to see you in person to tell their stories."

James walks out the door and closes it behind him. The room is solemn. Not a sound can be heard. Kirkland looks around the room at the volumes of books he still must go through. He begins to sob.

"What have I done? What have I done?"

CHAPTER 15

Protocols, Probes and Progress

t's Monday evening and the streets outside Lenox Hill Hospital are busy. Inside the hospital, nurses and doctors are tending to patients. The day Officers Benuti and O'Connell were shot, the story obviously became major news in New York, which caused a media frenzy. With the nonstop commotion, the media turned the emergency room, cafeteria and the front of the hospital building into hot spots for TV news personnel to report their stories, capturing the attention of onlookers. The police eventually took control of the hospital entrances and began restricting access.

Some time has passed and the media is still buzzing about the hospital, looking to get any update on the condition of the two officers. The police are still controlling media access to the main entrance and to certain parts of the hospital. As both Benuti and O'Connell remain in serious condition, the media has now been restricted to report and film near the front entrance, but not inside. The police are still on the lookout for anyone who belongs to the Rojos gang.

In the intensive care unit lies Officer O'Connell. He is hooked up to various types of hospital equipment, from EKG machines to suction pumps to infusion pumps. Sergeant Dennis Combs is just arriving to visit O'Connell. Combs is a twenty-year veteran of the police department. He's in his late fifties, physically fit with graying hair. He is a hard-nosed detective who made his way up the ranks. As he stands outside the room, the elevator door opens. It's Officer Moran. Moran walks over to Combs and quietly shakes his hand. They both glance through the glass window of the ICU and quietly look at O'Connell. A nurse comes over and closes the window's curtain as they change the PICC line on O'Connell.

A doctor walks out of the room and Combs quickly grabs him before he can walk down the hospital corridor.

"Hey, Doc, how's he doing?"

The doctor inhales deeply. "After two surgeries, we've finally got him stabilized. But he's not out of the woods yet. His vest stopped some of the bullets, but one hit his shoulder, his subclavian artery. Honestly, he's lucky to be alive."

Moran looks on, perplexed.

"What exactly does that mean in layman's terms, Doc?"

"Basically, it's the main artery of the arm, but we're watching it closely."

Combs interrupts before the doctor walks away. "How about Officer Benuti?"

The doctor's expression changes. "Unfortunately, he's still in a coma. He's in worse shape. He took a bullet just below his neck. He had a ton of internal bleeding."

"Thanks, Doc. Take good care of my guys," says Combs.

"Believe me, we're doing everything we can," responds the doctor.

Combs extends his hand. The doctor gestures back with a handshake and then walks away. Combs spots an empty room across from the ICU and he signals to Moran. They step inside and close the door behind them, sitting down at a desk.

"Sarge, this is crazy. Benuti's in a coma and Kevin is barely hanging on."

Sergeant Combs looks over at Moran. "We both know it's part of the job, and I'm pretty sure O'Connell and Benuti feel the same way, but nobody saw this one coming."

Moran clasps his hands together, placing his elbows on the desk and leans forward; he then rubs his chin.

"Do we have any kind of an update on the Rojos? I got a feeling they'll be looking for me. I'm the one who shot Medina. They'll want revenge after the grand jury ruled in my favor."

"We're still investigating, but as far as we know, that coward Valles acted alone, and he's dead. Plus, Medina wasn't a Rojos, so I don't see them coming after you. Valles was the head of the Rojos. You know the old saying, 'remove the head and the body will fall.'"

"Yeah, but that kid Castilla, he's shooting off his mouth about us setting them up. I'm sure he's got the rest of the crew riled up. They may come looking for me. Every day that goes by still feels like this is a never-ending nightmare," he exclaims as he gets up and paces across the empty room.

Combs replies, "Valles shot two cops and killed an innocent bystander. Trust me, the Rojos will be in hiding for a while. I don't think you have anything to worry about. As soon as we get the chance, we'll take care of our biker friends. They'll go down for this. No one shoots our guys. They'll pay the price. We've got to send a message to every dirtbag out there that they'll pay a heavy price if they shoot one of ours."

"How long do you think?" Moran asks.

"For what?"

"For us to go after the Rojos?"

Combs gets up and walks over to Moran. "Look, just keep a low profile for now. Let's just worry about O'Connell and Benuti coming out of this alive. In time, everything else will be taken care of," Combs answers with assurance.

"Okay, Sarge."

Combs pats Moran on his shoulder. He opens the door and walks out of the room and heads for the elevator.

"I'm going to hit the head, Sarge, then I'm outta here. I'll see you back at the station."

Moran proceeds to the men's room. He looks at himself in the mirror while washing his hands, replaying everything that happened, from the incident with Ruben and Manny to the shooting of his fellow cops. He feels uncomfortable about the whole situation and how it all played out.

He whispers to himself, "What do I do?"

As he steps out, there's a woman standing outside. He catches her by surprise and she quickly acts somewhat confused.

"Hi, I was wondering if you could steer me in the right direction. I was looking for the cafeteria," she queries, batting her eyes.

Moran looks perplexed. "Sure, I believe it's on the first floor."

He starts to walk away, but she grabs his arm. He is a bit surprised by her boldness.

"I'm sorry. Do you know how those cops are doing? You know, the ones that got shot by the bikers," she inquires.

Moran looks at her. "I guess you're really not interested in where the cafeteria is. Who are you?"

She smiles as if she's flirting with him, but Moran's not having it.

"Just a girl looking for a little bit of information."

He knows she's a reporter.

"Look, I don't know how you got up here, but I suggest you find your way downstairs. Otherwise, you're going to be in big trouble… with me."

"What's the big deal? You can at least tell me how they're doing. Wait a minute, aren't you Officer Moran? The one that was acquitted?"

"No. I'm a detective. Time for you to leave."

Officer Moran grabs her arm strongly.

"Hey, that's not necessary!" she shouts.

He hurriedly escorts her down the corridor. There's a cop in uniform standing by the elevator. He calls him over to see to it that the reporter is led out of the building.

"Get her out of here now and make sure security knows that no reporters are allowed on this floor!" he barks.

Moran heads for the stairs as the woman goes down on the elevator, feverishly writing in her pad.

Suddenly, back on the floor, Officer Benuti goes into distress. Monitors are flashing and alarms are sounding. Doctors and nurses run to his room. The ICU doctor moves quickly and grabs the defibrillator paddles.

"We've got ventricular fibrillation. He's going into V-fib arrest. Stand clear."

With that, he jolts Benuti not once or twice but three times, delivering doses of electric current to Benuti's heart. After a few jolts with the defibrillator, Benuti's heart returns to normal. The doctor turns to the nurse. "That was close. Keep a closer watch on him for the next hour."

ON THE OTHER SIDE OF TOWN IN HER SMALL APARTMENT, Maggie is sitting on her couch. She is dressed in a black pantsuit and black platform heels. She's ready for her first day of teaching at FIT. She is a little nervous. She doesn't know why. After all, it's an entry-level college course, yet she has anxiety nonetheless. In her hand, she's holding a business card that's been sitting on her coffee table since she found it in a folder. It's the business card of a private investigator, Mark Hatcher.

She stares at the card ponderingly. In the back of her mind, she can hear her sister Kate's voice compelling her to take her life back. Today is a new beginning for her. Maybe she needs to finally pursue what she left behind in LA. Maggie inhales deeply at the thought of making the call. She nervously picks up her cell phone and dials the number. The phone rings on the other end.

A man picks up.

"Hello, Mark Hatcher here," he answers.

"Hello, Mark, this is Maggie Hargrove. I worked with you a while back when I was with Text Styles Inc. Do you remember me?"

Mark seems happy to hear from her.

"Sure, yes, Maggie. I remember you. We worked on catching that company that was selling knockoffs of your designs. They were running that sweatshop operation in the Bronx. How are you?"

"I'm good. Great memory, by the way, and yes, you did great work on that case."

He retorts, "As I recall, that was a five-million-dollar trademark infringement deal. So, how can I help you?"

Maggie leans back on the couch. "This is personal business. I want to hire you to dig into my former firm. In a nutshell, they set me up, destroyed my career and my reputation. I think it's time that I reclaim what's mine."

"Yeah, I read about that. If I recall, they made some strong claims about you embezzling money. Serious stuff. Didn't you resign?"

Maggie gets up and walks around her small apartment. The memories of everything that happened come rushing back, only now, she's getting angry and fired up.

"Well, it's all bullshit. They set me up and forced me out. I just need to prove it. My ex-husband, Brad Collins, was screwing my partner and they wanted me out of the picture. That's how that whole embezzlement angle came into play."

"Collins? He's that hotshot venture capitalist, right?"

"That would be him."

"He has an interesting reputation in LA, to say the least."

Maggie looks out the window onto the fire escape and sees flashing red lights, which are lighting up her apartment.

"That's an understatement."

"So, what do you want me to do?"

"I want you to dig into Brad, my old firm, Text Styles Inc., and their CEO, Kara Kline. I need to find proof that they set me up, something that'll hold up in court."

Mark Hatcher perches in his chair, absorbed. "Another familiar name, Kara Kline. She's a big deal in LA in the fashion industry. I heard you two were quite the team."

Maggie replies sarcastically, "Yeah, until my 'teammate' wanted my spot in the starting lineup. I found out the bitch was screwing my ex-husband. I carried her ass in that company. She clearly wanted me out of the way."

"Interesting. Well, they're both in LA, so we'll need someone who is out there. My brother Dennis is my partner, and he runs our West Coast office. He's a retired LAPD detective, well respected with a great reputation. Will that work for you?"

Maggie smiles subtly. "That will be perfect."

"You realize, Collins and Kline are well connected, with a lot of resources. You sure you wanna do this?"

Maggie sits back on her couch with a look of confidence. "Very sure. They're lying dirtbags who destroyed my reputation. I'm aware how connected they are, but I didn't steal any money. They framed me. The truth is out there and it's time to find it. I've waited long enough. As I said, I want my life back."

"Okay, I hear you loud and clear. Why don't we meet next week at my office and we'll start the process? Our fees will be one hundred and fifty dollars per hour, plus expenses. We usually get double that. Seeing as you're an old client and I know this is personal, I'll give you a break. Does that work for you?"

"I'll make it work."

"Perfect. I'll check my schedule and text you back with some open dates when we can get together. That okay?"

"Sounds good. Thanks again," Maggie responds.

"Looking forward to it."

Maggie hangs up the phone. She doesn't fully realize it, but she just had a defining moment in her life. For the first time in a very long time, she decided to step up and fight. She knows she's about to make some difficult moves, but it's time to get out of her funk and take back what's hers. She reaches for a cigarette in her purse. She lights it, takes a long inhale and blows out the smoke, which creates a smoky ring. She looks at the cigarette, pauses for another moment and puts it out in the ashtray on the table. She looks at her watch. Realizing it's getting late, she grabs her briefcase and heads out the door for the subway station.

While riding on the subway, Maggie reflects on her life, thinking back to when she first started college. She always dreamed of making a difference in the design world. Not just for herself, but for others as well. Despite her successes, she made mistakes along the way, costly ones. They have haunted her, even though she felt justified at the time. With her renewed confidence in hiring the private investigators, maybe this teaching job came along at the perfect time to help her get back on track. It's time to put the bad parts of her life behind her. She knows she can make a difference for these students.

Across from Maggie on the subway is a family with two young girls. They are carrying lighted toy wands from a Disney Live show they just came from at Madison Square Garden. The girls are fooling with each other as the parents converse quietly. They are teasing each other, back and forth, laughing all the while. Maggie looks at the girls and fondly remembers those types of outings with her family as a young girl. She can easily picture herself and Kate as those two little girls. She remembers a family trip to see the circus in Chicago. Kate was afraid of the lions and tigers. Maggie would growl at her suddenly to scare her. They both loved the parade of elephants and the crazy antics of the clowns. The high-wire acts always made them gasp in amazement. Maggie can almost smell the popcorn as she sits on the subway. How she misses those days. As her mind wanders, the subway pulls into the station. She snaps out of her daydream and quickly exits the train.

Maggie comes up from the subway stairs and walks out onto Seventh Avenue. She walks a few blocks south to Twenty-Seventh Street, and as she rounds the corner, she sees the Fashion Institute of Technology. Memories of her college years fill her mind again, bringing a smile to her face. Even though there is a familiarity with the surroundings, Maggie is a bit apprehensive. This is a new start, a real chance at regaining her former self.

Don Phillips is waiting for Maggie in front of the school. He sees her and waves. She seems surprised to see him. He runs up and gives her a big hug.

"So good to see you! I'm so glad you agreed to take this job."

Maggie returns the enthusiastic embrace.

"Well, I must admit, it's a much better view than my day job. How did you know?" she jokes.

"The dean of the school told me you accepted. I wanted to be here to congratulate you in person."

Maggie steps back and wipes a tear away, looking up at the building and then at Don.

"I'm surprised I said yes. Thanks again, Don. You've always looked out for me."

"These students don't realize that it is the 'great Maggie Hargrove' who will be taking them under her wing."

"You're too sweet. I must admit, I was a bit nervous earlier today. Imagine that."

"And now?" Don asks.

"Now, I'm good. I always gain some extra courage after riding on the subway," she laughs. "I guess I'd better get my 'wings' upstairs to class."

"Congrats again. I'll text you after you settle in. We'll get together and have a few drinks to celebrate."

Maggie heads toward the glass doors of the front of the building. "I'd like that, Don. Thanks for believing in me!" she shouts.

"Believing in you is the easy part."

Maggie heads into the building's lobby, which, she realizes, has an even better view. A large horseshoe-shaped security desk sits up front. Maggie checks in and admires the glazed floors with their detail of marble and the huge pillars that stand firm throughout. The heels of her shoes echo as she walks over to the elevator.

The doors to the elevator open suddenly. There's an elevator operator on the other side, unbeknownst to Maggie. It's Dante in human form.

"Going down?" he utters.

Maggie looks at him but doesn't step inside.

"No, thank you, I'm going up."

"Are you sure about that?" he asks.

Maggie looks at him, confused. "Sorry?"

She has an uneasy feeling about him. Unexpectedly, the elevator directly across opens. There's another elevator operator inside. It's Matthias.

"This elevator will take you up to where you want to go, ma'am."

"Uh, yes, thank you," she responds.

Maggie hastily leaves the elevator with Dante and walks across to Matthias. She now feels at ease and gets on the elevator that is going up. Matthias stares across at Dante, who vanishes with a look of disgust as his elevator door closes. While Maggie is in the elevator, she nervously fixes her clothes. It's obvious that she's anxious. Matthias looks over at her and gives her a gentle, reassuring smile. She immediately stops and smiles back at him.

"First evening of a new class tonight?" Matthias asks.

"Why, yes."

"These are great kids in this school. They are so creative with so much God given talent."

"Yes, the best."

"Well I'm sure if you're their instructor, you must be pretty talented yourself."

"Thank you. You're too kind."

"You're welcome. Have a great evening."

The elevator reaches Maggie's floor. Matthias smiles again and gestures with his hand as she has reached her floor.

She steps off.

"Have a wonderful evening, ma'am."

Maggie looks back at him. "You too."

The elevator door closes slowly.

Maggie hastily walks down the corridor to the classroom. She sighs heavily as she reaches the door, places her hand on the knob and opens it. The classroom is large with two huge, long wooden tables in the center, surrounded by high round stools. The walls are a bright orange and the windows are covered with light wood-colored shades that are open, letting in the moonlight.

There are twenty students in the freshman textile design class, Studio Practices. All seem eager as they watch her gather her thoughts behind a large dark wooden desk while seated in a swivel chair.

She takes in another deep breath. A sense of sureness takes over Maggie. She's ready.

"Good evening, class. I'm Miss Hargrove. Welcome to Studio Practices. We will focus on studying the practice of good design and color as they apply to the print apparel field, with special emphasis on the use of gouache."

Maggie feels empowered as she looks around the room at the twenty enthusiastic young minds.

"The projects you complete in this course will help you develop your portfolios that you will need for your design career. Am I correct to assume that you all have your current portfolios with you?"

All the students nod yes.

"Great, I'd like to spend some time with each of you. Show me something you've done and tell me a little about it as I walk around."

Maggie steps from behind the desk and begins to walk around the room, going from student to student to observe their work. She takes her time going through each of their portfolio briefs as the time passes by, making minor small talk and becoming more familiar with each of her students and their creations. She stops beside one of her students, a young woman somewhere in her late teens with long stringy dark brown hair and a slightly pale complexion, dressed rather artsy in a long skirt with polka dots and a bright yellow flower-patterned shirt. Her name is Alice. Alice looks up at Maggie and smiles; she is extremely nervous, though. Maggie opens her portfolio brief and begins to look through it. Alice seems somewhat shy in sharing her work. Inside her portfolio brief, mixed in with her work, is a copy of one of Maggie's award-winning designs that was done for a top designer in LA.

Maggie sees it and points to the design, looking down at Alice. "You like that?"

Alice perks up. "I love it. It's one of my favorites, Miss Hargrove. It inspired me to be a designer. I only found out tonight that you were teaching this class. They hadn't told us anything. I can't believe it. I'm so excited you're here, you have no idea!" Alice exclaims.

Maggie grins humbly and flips through to another piece of Alice's work.

"Well, Alice, I'm glad to be here too. I look forward to working with you. So, tell me about this piece?"

It is a drawing of multiple faces—a very intense drawing.

"I call it 'The Faces of Addiction.'"

It piques Maggie's interest. "Hmm… 'The Faces of Addiction.' What inspired you?"

"My parents. They were both drug addicts. My dad died a few years back, but my mom is clean now. The faces represent the despair, depression and loneliness of addiction."

Maggie can see the depth of feeling in Alice's work. It's something she has not seen in quite some time, especially from such a young woman. But it is apparent that Alice has experienced a lot of pain in her life.

"I love it. I can see the intensity and emotion in the faces. Excellent. I'm glad to have you in this class."

Alice smiles. Her nervousness subsides.

Maggie pats Alice on the shoulder, offering her approval. She strolls back to the front and addresses the rest of the class.

"Okay, class. I see some great stuff in your portfolios and I must say, I'm impressed. Over the semester, we'll be working to bring what's in your head and your heart to paper. As you leave, grab an assignment sheet and syllabus from the desk. I'll see you all on Thursday."

There's chatter as the students gather their materials and exit the classroom. Maggie smiles as they walk out and takes the time to shake a few of their hands. She then begins to pack up her briefcase and exits the classroom. She heads for the elevator, looking around the empty corridor, and taps the button to go down. It's the same elevator she rode up in, only this time there's a tall, friendly black man inside.

"Good evening, ma'am. Lobby?"

"Yes. Wasn't there a different operator earlier this evening?" Maggie inquires.

He looks back at her as she steps inside the elevator.

"A different one? I don't think so. It's pretty much me or Donald, and he's off today. When Donald or I aren't here, the elevators are self-operated. By the way, I'm Louis," he says, extending a grand smile.

Maggie's silent for a moment, peering out of the open elevator. "Ma'am...? Lobby?"

Maggie snaps out of her thoughts. "Yes, I'm so sorry. I guess I'm just a little tired."

The elevator reaches the lobby. The doors open and she steps out.

"Have a nice evening."

"You too," Maggie responds.

Maggie walks out the front glass doors of the Fashion Institute. She walks east on Twenty-Seventh Street, rounds the corner and heads up Seventh Avenue, back towards the subway. Standing on the corner, unseen to Maggie, are Dante and one of his demons.

He points to her.

"Don't let that bitch out of your sight. We're heavily invested in destroying her soul. I thought shooting those cops in front of her would do the trick, but she had to stop in that damn church. We need to derail her newly found self-confidence. Follow her and look for any opportunity to trip her up."

CHAPTER 16

Wheels in Motion

Officer Moran returns to the hospital and greets the nurses at the front desk. He seems to have developed a friendly rapport, especially since he and his fellow officers have been in and out of the hospital on a regular basis ever since the shooting. He jumps on the elevator, headed for the top floor. As the elevator door opens, he spots Sergeant Combs outside Officer O'Connell's room, speaking with the doctor. He walks over to Combs as the doctor walks away.

"Hey, Sarge, what's the latest?"

"Benuti is still in bad shape," Combs replies.

Moran looks down in distress.

"But O'Connell regained consciousness. He's going to be okay."

"Well, that's great to hear. Can I see Kevin?"

"Sure, but the doctor said to keep the visits brief. They're still monitoring him very closely."

"Got you, Sarge."

Moran walks into O'Connell's room. The drapes are drawn and it's silent other than a beeping monitor. Moran draws back the curtain and is happy to see that O'Connell is alert. O'Connell looks over at him.

"Hey, Kev, how ya feeling?'"

"Like hell. Feels like a Mack truck rolled over me, but the doc says I can get out of here in a few days."

Moran grabs a chair by the window. "That's great. We were really worried about you. Yeah, now you've got to rest up. Thank God you're okay."

Kevin struggles to sit up. Moran helps him.

"Hey, be easy, remember you got shot pretty bad. You don't want to do more damage."

"Yeah, I know. This hole in my shoulder is a reminder. Look—Kevin peeks over at the door to make sure no one is there— "I got the lowdown from Combs on the whole thing. That effin' Rojos gang. I knew it was that slime ball Valles that shot me. I recognized him. Sarge said Benuti's in rough shape?"

"Pretty much, still in a coma," Moran replies.

"At least that piece of shit Valles is dead. If not, he wouldn't be alive for long. Between you and me, the rest of the Rojos need to go."

"What do you mean?" asks Moran.

"I mean it's time we rid our precinct of these dirtbags once and for all."

"What are you going to do?"

O'Connell looks at Moran intensely. "Leave that to me. I have friends in low places."

"Come on, Kev, Valles is dead. Just leave well enough alone."

"Are you kidding me? They almost killed me, and Benuti might not make it. Did you forget Castilla knows we planted that knife on Medina? That's why that asshole Valles decided to shoot us. He wanted us dead. These are *my* streets. I'm not letting the scum make the rules. Listen, don't worry about anything. I just need to know you've got my back. After all, I have yours."

"Yeah, sure. You know I've got your back."

"Good. After I get out of here, I'll take care of it," Kevin retorts cunningly.

"No problem, but in the meantime, you need to get some rest."

"I will. Thanks, man."

Moran gets up and starts to walk out of the room.

"Hey, Moran?"

Moran looks back at Kevin.

"I told you to stick to the plan. Now you're acquitted. If we stick together we'll be fine."

"I know Kev, I'm on board."

"Remember, this stays between you and me."

Moran nods and walks out of the room, feeling uneasy about the conversation. He doesn't even stop to say anything to Combs. He gets on the elevator and heads down and walks out of the building.

FURTHER DOWNTOWN, MAGGIE IS WALKING ON PARK AVENUE, preoccupied, looking at a piece of paper in her hand. She is checking numbers on the buildings as she continues to walk. She mumbles to herself, "That's it. Hatcher's office, 215 Park Avenue South, tenth floor." She crosses the street and heads inside the building.

The hallway is narrow with a few paintings and a large mirror on the wall. There are two elevators. The elevator to the left arrives and Maggie gets on. Just as the door is about to close, someone puts their hand in, prompting the elevator door to open. A handsome man in a tailored suit gets on. It's Matthias. He looks at Maggie.

"How are you today? Beautiful day, isn't it?"

"Yes, it is. What floor are you going to?"

He sees she is going to ten. "I'm going to nine. Today's a big day. I have a second interview for a new job. It looks promising. You know what they say, it's never too late for a fresh start."

"No, it's not. What kind of job is it?"

"Working for a nonprofit company that helps unwed mothers get on their feet. I have a soft spot for helping people in need."

"That's beautiful. The world needs more people like you."

"Thank you. There's something about helping others that just makes you feel good, right?"

"Yes, it does. Best of luck. I'm sure you'll get it. They'd be lucky to have you."

"Thank you. You know, my life has been blessed in so many ways. I always need to remember to be grateful for all I have."

Maggie smiles, thinking about her own circumstances. "Yes, we all do."

"Sometimes life gets so crazy, we forget how blessed we truly are."

"You are so right!" Maggie responds.

With that, the elevator stops and Matthias goes to get off. "Well, you enjoy the rest of your day."

"Thank you so much. You too. Good luck again!"

Matthias's voice resonates with his last few words. "Good luck to you as well."

With that, Matthias departs. Maggie again has a sudden feeling of calm and confidence. She knows she is doing the right thing.

Maggie steps off the elevator. She sees the door marked "Mark Hatcher, Private Investigator." She goes in.

She's surprised to see that the office is modest. There's nothing bold about its appearance. There's no receptionist on duty nor a large wooden desk with all the bells and whistles inside. Just an individual desk, medium in size, a small waiting area, a water dispenser in the corner and a door leading into Mark Hatcher's office.

Mark steps out to greet her.

"Maggie Hargrove. Nice to see you again. Come in and have a seat."

They walk into Hatcher's office and its appearance is the same as the outer office, nothing extravagant and rather small. He sits behind his desk with a few brown filing cabinets behind him. Maggie sits opposite him.

He moves some papers around on his desk. "Any trouble finding the place?"

"No, not at all. Once I got my bearings, I realized it's not that far from the school I work at. Thanks for seeing me."

"Of course. Let me get my brother Dennis on the phone out in LA and we'll conference him in."

He dials the phone and puts it on speaker. A man picks up.

"Hey, Mark, what's up?"

"Dennis, I'm here with our client Maggie Hargrove."

"Hello, Maggie, nice to be speaking with you. I look forward to helping you."

"Thank you. I appreciate you taking the time out of your schedule. As I've told Mark, it's time to prove they set me up. I want my life back."

"Well, that's our goal," Dennis responds.

"Do you have any updates?" Mark inquires.

"I do. Based on our initial discussion, I've done some digging into Brad Collins and it seems he has other clients with accounts at the same offshore bank you were accused of wiring money to. Those accounts have wired money to Brad in a corporate account he has in Europe. That doesn't prove anything for you yet, Maggie, but it sure makes me very, very curious. That's a big red flag in my book."

"Nice. What else have you got, Dennis?"

"I'm not coming up with much on Kara Kline, other than she's been reassuring her clients that she will step in and handle your projects."

Maggie sucks her teeth. "How nice. Clients don't like her. Her ego gets in the way. They see right through her."

Dennis continues, "She is also introducing them to a Valerie Simonetti, who she says will work with her on their accounts."

"Valerie Simonetti, seriously? She was an intern. The clients go from having me directly involved in their business to someone who has no clue what she's doing? She was always kissing Kara's ass. She's Kara's errand girl. Brad was always hitting on her. How ironic. Kara's banging Brad and he's probably banging her protégé too."

"Well, I'm digging deeper into her. She always seems to be around Kara, and I've seen her with Kara and Brad on multiple occasions having cocktails at a bar in LA."

"Dennis, I'm pretty sure she would do anything they asked her to do," Maggie interjects.

"What kind of involvement did she have with you? Did she ever have you sign any paperwork, etc.?"

"Not really. Everything went through my assistant, Crystal."

Mark looks over at Maggie curiously. "What about her? She trustworthy?"

"I've known her for ten years. She's extremely loyal. She wasn't a fan of Kara, but she was always respectful. She thought Valerie was too eager."

"Have you kept in touch with Crystal? Can I contact her?" Dennis chimes in.

"She texts me all the time to let me know how worried she is about me. She would help if she could."

"Dennis, maybe you should contact Crystal. She might be a good path to venture down," Mark suggests.

"I agree. Maggie, give me her contact information and I'll get ahold of her and do some more digging."

"Somehow, Dennis, they found a way to get Maggie to sign the bank documents. Either that or it's a perfect forgery. We just have to figure out who did it and how."

"And we will, Mark. Maggie, we'll get to the bottom of it. We know you got screwed over. We'll catch them. The Hatcher boys don't like losing or having our good clients' names dragged through the mud."

"Okay, Denny, I'll email you. Talk to you later."

Mark hangs up the phone and looks over at Maggie. He seems pretty sure about himself. His confidence encourages Maggie. Mark accompanies her out of the office down the small hallway and toward the elevator.

"What my brother said was true. We will find out who did this to you. I'll keep you updated. Thanks for coming by."

"Thank you, Mark. I'll be in touch."

Maggie gets on the elevator. The door closes.

WEEKS HAVE NOW GONE BY SINCE THE SHOOTING INCIDENT AND Maggie's initial meeting with Mark Hatcher. Time is passing, but for Maggie, it sometimes feels like it's standing still, especially when she's back at the diner. Now that the FIT job has started, she is contemplating quitting the waitress job in the next few weeks. It's time to move on and put the shooting behind her.

Maggie is at the diner. It's just about dusk and she's finishing her shift. She goes to the back room to get more sugar packets for the counter. When she returns, she sees someone enter the diner, walking very slowly with a pronounced limp, leaning on a cane. It's Kevin O'Connell. She is shocked and overwhelmed, to say the least.

Kevin O'Connell takes a seat at the counter. He's obviously moving very gingerly.

"What's a guy gotta do to get a cup of coffee around here?"

Maggie has a stunned look on her face and remains silent for a moment.

"What, no snappy comeback?" Kevin probes.

"Officer O'Connell. You're…you're…okay." Maggie has a tear in her eye.

"Oh geez. You see a little blood and you go soft on me?"

"A little? I thought my uniform was red. I thought you died. It was horrible," Maggie expresses with emotion. She quickly grabs a cup and pours coffee into it and sets it in front of Kevin.

O'Connell responds, "I tried to stop by yesterday, but it looks like they closed early. I just got released from the hospital. I'm still not moving too well."

"Yes, Stavros's wife passed away suddenly. The family is taking it hard, so the hours have been a little staggered."

"Oh no. How did it happen? I saw her here not long ago. She looked okay."

"She had a massive heart attack. Right in front of their house. It was awful. Stavros was with her when it happened."

"Please give my condolences to Earl and Stavros."

"They're both not back yet. Their cousin from Astoria is handling things for the next few days."

"I'll swing by at the end of the week to pay my respects. They're good people. A nice family."

Maggie grabs a Danish pastry and puts it in front of O'Connell. "How's Officer Benuti?"

"He's in bad shape. Not good at all."

"I'm sorry to hear that. I just stopped watching the news after a while. It just got to be too much. I didn't even know. That poor man. How 'bout you, are you okay now? I can't believe you're up and about. After everything I saw…I just thought…"

"I'm okay. I'm actually supposed to be home resting, but hey, I can't stop living. I've got a few holes in me. I'll be out of action for a while. I wanted to come by and check on you. To see how you were holding up."

"I'm okay…I guess," Maggie replies.

"Must have been a mess. Anybody get hurt when the window was shot out?"

"No, thank God. There was glass everywhere, though. Honestly, I try not to think about it."

"Well, we're gonna clean up all the scum from the gang that was responsible for this. This is my town and my precinct. They screwed with the wrong cop."

Just then, O'Connell's phone rings. He looks at the number.

"Hey, I gotta run. Can I get this to go, Maggie?"

"Sure thing."

"I really wanted to come by to thank you. The guys told me you kept pressure on one of my arteries. If it wasn't for you, I might have died."

"I tried my best to keep you calm. It all happened so fast."

"You did great. I owe you."

Maggie blushes. She turns and gets a to-go cup for Kevin and pours the coffee into it. She hands it to Kevin and comes around the counter to give him a hug.

"The coffee and Danish are on me, Officer O'Connell."

"Wow, if I'd known you'd be this nice to me, I'd have gotten shot sooner."

"That's not funny, you ass."

"Oops. Spoke too soon. What's that song say? 'Look out, old Maggie's back,' or something like that?"

Maggie shakes her head and smiles.

"I gotta run, Maggie. I'll see ya again soon."

"You take care of yourself and stop trying to be a hero. It doesn't suit you."

O'Connell replies, "Telling me what to do—now that's the Maggie I know. Hey, after all this, maybe now I've got a shot to take you out? You did save my life. The least you could do is let me buy you dinner."

Maggie shakes her head and rolls her eyes. "Some things never change," she whispers under her breath.

Kevin gets up, leaving Maggie a fifty-dollar tip, and heads out the door.

"Catch ya later, Maggie. I'll keep you updated on Tony."

Maggie smiles for a moment and watches Kevin leave. She thought she'd never see him again.

Later that night, Kevin O'Connell pulls up to a secluded spot under the Fifty-Ninth Street Bridge. The moon is lit up brightly as he looks up to admire the night sky. He gets out of his car, leans against his trunk and lights a cigarette. A few minutes go by. Two black Chevy Tahoe SUV's pull up behind his car. The doors open and six men get out. A seventh figure, the last man out of the first car, is Diego Jimenez, head of the NYC Colombian drug cartel.

Diego is dressed in black slacks, a black collared shirt, a black leather jacket and a dark brown fedora. He's a rough-looking sixty-something-year-old man with a slightly protruding belly. He approaches O'Connell as the six other men stand near the SUV, as per Diego's instructions.

"How are you feeling, Officer O'Connell?"

"I've been better."

"Foolish move by Valles trying to gun you down. He was always a hot-headed idiot. If he wasn't shot by the police, we would have done it for them. How's your partner? Word is he's in critical condition."

"He's in bad shape. Thanks for asking. Now let's get down to business. Bottom line—I want the Rojos gang gone. Valles tried to kill me and my partner. I know the Rojos mule your drugs. It's time for you to find new mules."

Diego smiles subtly. "What happened was unfortunate, but now you want me to change my business? That complicates things for me."

"I don't care how complicated it is."

Diego's men begin to approach as O'Connell's voice gets loud. Diego puts his hand up, letting them know it's okay.

"Hey, I protect you from the narcs, keeping them from finding out more about your operation than the little bit they already know. I need you to do this for me."

"And you're well compensated for the things you do for us, Officer O'Connell."

"This is different. That asshole tried to kill me. The Rojos are going down, one way or the other, with you or without you. If it's without you, I'd hate for them to get busted moving your drugs and it leads back to you. That would be unfortunate. Wouldn't it?"

"Now, now, no need to make such implications. I'm sure we can work something out."

"Well, make it work and make it work soon. The Rojos are under extremely tight surveillance. You don't shoot two cops and get a pass in this town. I'd rather see them dead than in jail."

"We will take care of this. You have my word," Diego promises Kevin.

"Let me know when it's going down."

Diego nods. "I hope your partner pulls through. We'll be in touch."

O'Connell drops his cigarette to the ground and stamps it out as Diego walks back to his awaiting vehicle and men. O'Connell gets in his car, looks back and drives off. Diego stands by his vehicle, watching O'Connell's car drive around the corner. One of his men, Hector, approaches Diego.

"We gonna wipe out the Rojos for this cop?"

"The Rojos are no good to us anymore now that they did this. These cops won't let up. We don't need the heat. The Chinese will move our drugs through their businesses. It's cleaner and safer anyway."

"You trust this cop? I heard him—he implied they could take us down as well."

"He's been useful, but he's becoming a liability. Besides, if we work with the Chinese, we will be far more under the radar and he becomes a lot less useful. Let's take care of business and then we'll see about our arrangement with Officer O'Connell."

Hector opens the door of one of the SUVs for Diego and he gets inside. He reaches for his cell phone and dials a number.

"Ruben, we need to meet. Our situation needs to be adjusted. There is too much heat on your group now after the shooting."

"Agreed. These cops are all over us. We're all laying low right now. What do you have in mind?" Ruben queries.

A grimace appears on Diego's face. "I have a plan. It'll let you stay under the radar and still move our merchandise. We need to meet to discuss it in detail. Bring Ramon and your crew to the old maintenance shack at Calvary Cemetery in Queens on Thursday after midnight, say twelve thirty. I've got friends who oversee the gravediggers at the cemetery. I'll make sure the gate at Queens Boulevard and Fifty-Second Street is left unlocked. There is a key to the maintenance shack hidden in an old yellow Chock Full o' Nuts coffee can, behind the building. If you get there before we do, let yourselves in."

"Chock Full o' Nuts? Didn't they used to call that 'the heavenly coffee?' How appropriate for a cemetery building. Yeah. Okay, Diego. We'll be there."

Diego is not amused by Ruben's subtle joke. He hangs up and taps the driver's shoulder. His car pulls off first with the other following behind him.

It's late and the lights to the diner are still on. Maggie's inside wiping down the counter. She rinses out the coffeepot and then grabs her purse off one of the tables by the door. She offered to stay late with their cousin Pete at the diner, with Earl and Stavros still out since Lexi's death. She shuts the lights and Pete locks the door. Pete thanks Maggie for helping. He hands her a bag with some leftover food from the kitchen. Maggie is appreciative as she takes the bag and heads up the street.

Maggie is happy Kevin stopped in and that he's doing well. The fact that he's okay somehow relieved the horror of the shooting for her, although she's still concerned about Benuti and hopes he can recover. It's a rather warm night as she walks along the sidewalk, admiring a couple in front of her holding hands. Her phone rings and she reaches for it in her pocketbook. She sees its Hatcher's number. She quickly picks up.

"Hello, Mark."

"Hey, Maggie. Sorry to call you so late. Are you free to talk?"

"Yes, of course, I just left work. Do you have news for me?"

"Yes, Dennis is meeting with Crystal in the morning. He also found out some interesting stuff about the intern Valerie."

"Like what?" Maggie stops in front of a brownstone to focus on the conversation.

"She's having an affair with Brad behind Kara's back. We've tailed the two of them to multiple places throughout the LA area. Also, Valerie's sister Donna works at the LA office of the bank that the offshore account is connected to. It's just too much of a coincidence. Your boy Brad is behind this. The pieces of the puzzle are starting to fit nicely. Now we must figure out how they did it. Also, Dennis has been following Valerie to a few clubs. We may have her on some illegal activity. We're watching her very closely."

"Are you serious? I would have bet money they were having an affair," Maggie responds.

"Very serious."

"My ex never ceases to amaze me. What a sleaze ball. If Kara caught him with Valerie, she'd cut his balls off."

Hatcher laughs. "That sounds pretty painful. He might prefer that, especially if this all pans out the way it's coming together."

Maggie thinks for a moment and then continues to walk down the street.

"Look, I'll let you know how Dennis makes out with Crystal."

"Thanks, Mark."

Maggie hangs up the phone and hails a cab. One pulls over and she jumps in.

THE NEXT MORNING IN LA, DENNIS HATCHER SITS IN A STAR-bucks at a table near the front window. The Los Angeles sun is beaming brightly as he looks outside and away from the paper he's reading. A few moments later, an attractive woman walks in. She's pretty, with golden brown skin, long lanky legs and natural sandy-colored hair that perfectly frames her face.

Dennis looks up from the paper as she strolls over to him.

"Are you Mr. Hatcher?"

Dennis quickly puts the paper down on the chair next to him and stands up to shake her hand.

"Yes…Crystal?" he asks.

"Yes," she replies and takes a seat across from him.

"Can I get you something, coffee or water?"

"No, but thank you."

"It's nice to meet you. By the way, call me Dennis. Thanks for coming by."

"No problem. Anything I can do to help Maggie, I will."

"Let me jump right in from where we left off on our phone conversation. Would Valerie have had access to Maggie to have her sign a document of any kind?"

"No. Everything needing Maggie's signature would have to go through me."

"So, there are no circumstances you can recall where she would go straight to Maggie?"

"No. Not that I can recall." Crystal perks up suddenly, as if remembering something pertinent. "Wait. There was one time she had given me some contracts from a client that needed Maggie's signature. She left them for Maggie to sign, but then she came back a little later and said Kara needed to check some type of clause in the agreement. She said that Maggie was in with Kara and once she checked them, she'd have Kara give them to Maggie. So, I gave them back to her."

"That doesn't seem too out of the ordinary," Dennis replies.

"No, but I always kept copies of whatever Maggie signed. When I asked her for it later, she told me that Kara said there was a problem with it, and they needed to have the attorneys look at it and that she would get me a copy later. I thought nothing of it at the time, but I never got a copy."

"Interesting. What do you think of Valerie?"

Crystal makes a suggestive frown. "Off the record?"

"Yes, of course."

"She acted like she was more important than she was, working with Kara and all. I don't think she respected me. She didn't seem to care that I'd worked with Maggie for many years."

"How was she with Maggie?"

"A bit of a phony. Her compliments weren't genuine. You could tell they were transparent. It's almost as if she only respected Maggie because she had to."

"Crystal, did you ever see her around Brad?"

"Oh, yes. She thought he was gorgeous. She flirted with him every chance she got. Didn't seem like he minded it either."

"Did Maggie sense that?"

"No. She never did it when Maggie was around. I never said anything to Maggie. I didn't think it was my place to make an accusation or stir up trouble."

"You did the right thing. Anything else?"

Crystal leans in and looks around before responding. She whispers, "I've heard rumors from the other girls that she parties a lot—into ecstasy. She's always hanging at trendy clubs in LA. Her ex-boyfriend got busted for dealing a while back."

Crystal's comment confirms what some of his sources have been telling him about Valerie and her boyfriend.

"Interesting. What's his name?"

"Alfonse. Alfonse King. He's seems sleazy. I haven't seen him around since she started taking on more responsibility with Kara. She acts like she's an executive, but she hangs out with characters like Alfonse, which is truer to who she really is."

"Great. I think I have enough for now. Thanks again for coming. Please keep this conversation confidential."

"I will. Like I said, anything to help Maggie. She got a raw deal."

Dennis gets up and shakes Crystal's hand and watches her leave. He picks up his phone and dials Bill Stevens, a friend and an undercover LAPD detective. He leaves a message.

"Bill, it's Dennis. Let me know what you've got on an Alfonse King. Thanks."

Dennis hangs up and goes back to reading the *LA Times*.

CHAPTER 17

A Deadly Night

t's just past midnight. The night air is warm, but a light breeze brings about a feeling of rawness. Out in the distance, you can hear the loud tremors of motorcycles approaching. The Rojos bikers are headed to Calvary Cemetery in Queens, not far from their clubhouse in Manhattan. With over three million burial plots, Calvary has the largest number of interments of any cemetery in the United States. Although some of its rolling hills offer impressive views of the New York City skyline, it's bordered by the busy Brooklyn-Queens Expressway, making this overcrowded cemetery never a peaceful place. The noise of the highway poses a real challenge to the phrase "Rest in Peace."

The Rojos pull up to the cemetery gate from Queens Boulevard, and, as promised by Diego, the gate is not locked. Ramon jumps off his bike and opens the gate wide enough for all the bikers to drive through. He pulls his bike in last and closes the gate behind him, making it look as if it were locked. The Rojos drive about one hundred yards to the maintenance shack. They park their motorcycles around the side of the building. As one might expect, the cemetery is quiet, dark and eerie.

Ruben says to Jose, "Get the key in the coffee can as Diego told us, then go inside and check this place out."

Jose looks behind the building and finds the old Choc Full O Nuts coffee can and gets the key. He opens the door and goes inside. He walks through the room to see if everything is as it should be. It's dark and quiet. He comes out after a few minutes.

Jose yells out, "Nothing but tools and two riding mowers. All clear!"

Each of the members jumps off their bikes and goes inside the dingy, dark building.

"Where's Jimenez? This is bullshit," Ramon probes.

Ruben looks around. "He'll be here. Chill, bro." Ruben continues to search around the building. His phone rings. He steps outside to answer it. He recognizes Diego's number. "Diego, we're here."

"We're two blocks away. Be there in a few minutes."

"Okay."

Ruben heads back inside and tells the guys that Diego is on his way. He looks over at Ramon and asks for a cigarette.

"This is my last one, bro."

"I got you. I got a few more packs on my bike."

"If you've got extra, bring me a pack too."

Ruben gestures to Ramon with his middle finger and walks out to his motorcycle. He reaches into a saddlebag for the cigarettes. Diego is sitting in his car outside the cemetery walls on the street.

"*Adiós, Los Rojos*," he whispers as he blows his breath into his closed fingers.

He reaches for a remote control on the seat beside him and presses a button…BOOM!!! The building with the Rojos crew inside blows up instantly! The explosion blows out the windows entirely and the building is quickly engulfed in flames. Ruben, still standing by his bike, is thrown by the blast. He looks on in horror. He's terrified. He looks down at his leg, which is badly injured. He tries to get close to the building to save some of his brothers, but the flames hold him back. With all the gasoline and chemicals in the building, the inferno is extremely intense. He is helpless to save anyone. He tries to get close one more time, but the flames are shooting through where the windows used to be. His Rojos brothers were killed instantly by the explosion. Now what's left of their bodies is being quickly incinerated.

Ruben is horrified and panicked. He knows he has to get out of there. He limps away from the building and watches the raging flames from a distance. The fire is so intense the flames and sparks can be seen from the expressway. If he hadn't gone out for the cigarettes, he'd be dead too, burnt beyond recognition. He realizes this was no accident. It was planned. Diego set them up for Victor's shooting of the cops. He suddenly realizes it won't be long until the fire department and the police show up and he wants no part of that, so he best be leaving. He gets on his bike and rides to the front gate. He's able to pull it open just enough to ride his bike through and out onto Queens Blvd and speeds off into the night.

Standing in the flames, smiling, are Dante and his demons. They are amused by the horror that is taking place.

"Tonight, the victory is ours and ours alone. Go get their souls. They're all ours," he commands his demons.

The demons swoop inside the burning building. Loud, terrible screams fill the air momentarily. Even though the Rojos members are dead, part of Dante's torment is to awaken their spirits and let them feel the horror of being dragged to hell. Each demon leaves with a burning figure under their arms as they swoop into the ground and vanish. Dante stands atop the burning structure, looking towards the heavens. He mockingly yells out, "Curse you and your God. These pathetic humans are your creations? How easily we led them to evil. Now their souls join the ranks of the damned. We'll fight you for every last soul. All honor to the ruler of the dark world, mighty Satan."

As Dante finishes his victory exaltation, an army of Matthias's most powerful angels swoop down and, with a tremendous thrust, knock Dante off his perch and into the smoldering building down below. Dante hits the ground with such force, his body creates a hole ten feet deep. He is covered in debris. He springs forward, shakes off the debris, and flies away in anger, above the dark cemetery and into the night sky.

ACROSS TOWN, KEVIN O'CONNELL SITS IN HIS APARTMENT IN A HIGH-back red leather chair, watching the ball game. He lives on the Upper

East Side of Manhattan in a gorgeous, old brownstone. For someone on a police officer's salary, his place is rather lavish. It's adorned in leather furniture, sectional couch with red accent pillows and gray walls. Near the door is a nice-size dining room with a large mahogany table, white chairs and a large decorative vase that rests near the entrance. Adjacent to the door is a spiral staircase, leading to his bedroom. His long hallway is covered in pictures, the expensive type, something you'd see in a gallery. By the appearance of his place and its extravagance, it's easy to ascertain where some of those kickback dollars went to. This was not your typical bachelor pad for a city cop. Kevin had expensive taste.

His phone rings. The voice on the other end is Diego. "It's done."

Kevin responds with an attitude. "I thought you were going to let me know when it was going down?"

"Sorry, there just wasn't enough time. We had to move at the first opportunity we had. Tonight, the opportunity presented itself, so we took care of your problem."

"You mean our problem, don't you?"

"Yeah, our problem. Now we move forward. I suggest you rest up, Officer O'Connell, and we'll discuss our new arrangement with you tomorrow to move our product."

"This time, it'll be on my terms. I can't afford any more screwups like the Rojos. You get me, Diego?"

"I got you. I'm sure we can come to a mutual understanding. I am certain you will be happy with what I will propose. Just rest. We'll discuss the details later."

"Where did it go down?"

"The Calvary Cemetery maintenance building. It blew up with the Rojos inside. I'm sure you'll be hearing about it shortly."

Another call is coming in, from Officer Moran.

"I gotta go. I'll be in touch, Diego."

O'Connell disconnects Diego and answers Moran's call.

"What's up, Mo?"

"Hey, good news! Tony came out of his coma! He's still in rough shape, but he's awake."

"Hell, that's great news. Thank God. I'll get down there first thing in the morning to see him. Hey, are you by yourself?"

"Yeah, about to get into the car, what's up?"

"I thought you should know… the Rojos are dead."

"The Rojos are dead? What? How?"

"A maintenance shack at the cemetery blew up. They were inside."

"How do you know this, Kevin?"

O'Connell remains silent for a second or two. "Don't worry about that, but it solves our issue. Screw those slime bags anyway. They got what they deserved. Listen, I need you to confirm how many of those dirtbags were killed. There are at least ten members. You should know by how many of their motorcycles were parked at the scene."

"I'll call in to find out about the explosion. I'm sure there's a team en route already, but it will take them a while to sift through the rubble and get a count of what's left of the burnt bodies," says Moran.

"Contact the crew on the scene now and get a count of the bikes. That's all we need."

Moran has his police scanner on in the background.

"Hold on, Kevin, the call is coming over the scanner now."

Moran pauses a few moments to listen to the scanner. He says to Kevin, "Hey, I just heard the report. There are nine motorcycles parked outside. They presume at least nine are dead, but they won't know until they sift through the site."

O'Connell sits up from his slouched posture on the chair and says, "Ah, shit! I know for a fact there are at least ten of them. That effin' asshole! Someone's missing. We need to confirm that Ruben Castilla is dead. Hey, he has a Harley with a large chrome skull with red glass eyes mounted on his front fender, with his initials, RC, etched on it in gold letters. You can't miss it. Check to see if his bike is there."

"Okay, I'll radio the crew on the scene and ask them to look for that particular bike. Hold on a few minutes."

O'Connell waits again as Moran calls the crew and has them check the bikes. A few minutes later, Moran gets back on the phone. "Hey, Kev, they said it's not there. Castilla's bike, it's not there."

177

"Damn! Those stupid morons. How did they screw this up and not kill Castilla? You and I need to find Castilla ourselves now, and fast. Get your ass over to the Rojos' clubhouse and see if Castilla went there. I'll meet you across the street from the building. Wait for me. I'm getting dressed and I'll be on the way in a few minutes."

"Okay, Kevin, I'm heading there now."

Kevin hangs up the phone. He jumps up to change his clothes, heading toward the spiral staircase. Just at that moment, the doorbell of O'Connell's apartment rings once, then twice.

O'Connell walks over to the door and looks through his peephole. He doesn't see anyone. He steps away and the bell rings again. This time he opens the front door to his apartment. He sees flowers and a wrapped box outside his door. A card attached to the flowers says, "Get well soon." He takes the box and flowers inside.

He whispers to himself, "I wonder who this could be from?"

O'Connell sets the box on the dining room table. He rips open the paper, lifts the lid… BOOM! The box explodes. Part of Kevin's face is blown off. The carpeting, drapes and furniture catch fire. Within minutes, the room erupts into flames. O'Connell lies on the floor, burnt to a crisp. He's dead.

CHAPTER 18

Actions Have Consequences

Kevin O'Connell awakens and finds himself seated at the bar of a dingy club. He glances around the room and notices that there are no other patrons. The bartender is a dark, menacing-looking character. It's Dante. For the moment, he looks disinterested in anything going on around him. He is quietly washing and drying drink glasses.

Kevin, not really knowing where he is, says, "Hey, bartender, can I get a shot of Jameson's and a beer?"

Dante looks at him briefly and then ignores him.

"Hey, bartender, can't you hear? I said I want a shot of Jameson's and a beer."

Dante still ignores Kevin. In the background, Kevin starts to hear the muffled sounds of groans and cries. The noises gradually get louder.

Kevin again addresses Dante. "What the hell is that sound? As matter of fact, where the hell am I? Why won't you answer me, asshole?"

Dante looks at Kevin and laughs. "You're exactly where you belong, you pitiful fool. Don't you remember anything, Kevin? Or should I call you Officer O'Connell?"

Kevin begins to recall being in his apartment while there was some type of explosion.

"Yeah, come to think of it, I do remember a little. Something exploded in my apartment. I took in a package. It must have been the package. Yeah, it must have exploded and then... nothing. For some reason, I keep reliving that moment, though. Who the hell would send me a bomb? I thought the flowers were from the diner.

No wait...*Diego!* That bastard tried to kill me. He double-crossed me. But how the hell did I get here?"

Dante looks him in the eye. "Tried to kill you? You're dead, asshole. He did kill you."

Kevin's face turns white. Before he can say anything, the cries and groans get louder and louder, now a piercing sound that becomes almost unbearable. Kevin puts his hands up to cover his ears. He screams out, "What the hell is that?"

Suddenly, the sound stops. Kevin looks confused. He turns around and now sees a sexy, seductive redheaded woman seated at a table not far from him. The woman looks at Kevin. "Oh, those are the cries of tortured souls, Kevin O'Connell."

"Tortured souls? What the hell are you talking about? Who are you and how do you know my name?"

"We all know you, Kevin. We've been waiting for you."

The woman gets up and comes closer to Kevin. She is the ultimate temptress, irresistibly beautiful and seductive. Kevin, forgetting what is happening for a moment, resorts in typical fashion to his charming ways. He can't resist the woman's beauty.

"Well, if you've been waiting for me, why don't you come sit next to me and have a drink, babe?"

Suddenly, the groans and cries of the tortured souls start up again; this time it's even louder than before. Kevin again covers his ears. The sound is deafening. Now he looks frightened. Kevin quickly drops his charming act with the woman and realizes something is deeply wrong. The sound suddenly stops again.

"What's the matter, Mr. Macho Cop, are you scared? You want to know who I am? Well, let's just say I represent every person you ever abused, screwed over or shit on in your life, especially as a crooked cop."

"What are you talking about? I'm a damn good cop."

The woman gets closer and looks Kevin directly in the eyes. "No, you're not a 'damn good cop,' you're a *damned* cop."

Kevin's jaw drops. He is stunned and speechless with a blank look on his face. She continues, saying, "You screwed over so many people, we started to lose count. The list of people is enough to shock even some of the other residents here. But not only were you a prick as a cop, you had a long track record of abusing women. You think you're charming, some type of stud, don't you? You're really just an evil asshole. Remember that girl Kelly, the shy girl in high school, who you seduced with your phony macho charm? You stole her virginity, didn't you? Got her pregnant. Now that was inconvenient, wasn't it? She wanted to have the baby, but you convinced her it would ruin her chances at going to college. You turned on your BS charm and you convinced her to have an abortion, because it was the right thing for the both of you. No, Kevin, it was the right thing for you. You told her you would support her through it, but afterwards, you ignored her. You wanted no part of being responsible. You didn't give a crap about her. That abortion destroyed her emotionally, ruined her life. Yet, you wouldn't know it, because you ignored her whenever you saw her."

Kevin says meekly in defense, "Wait, what is this shit? Who told you that?"

He starts to get up from his barstool. Just then, Dante grabs Kevin's shoulder and shoves him back down so forcefully that Kevin feels almost as if he's being pushed through his barstool. He looks in fear at Dante, who says, "Keep your damn mouth shut while the lady is speaking."

Kevin is now petrified. The woman continues, "How about all those hookers you forced to have oral sex with you so you wouldn't arrest them? What a guy. Who cares about them? They're just hookers, right? How about that girl on your vacation down in Mexico? You know, the one you raped when you were both drunk? But she wanted it, right, Kevin? Saddle up, babe, it's vacation! You were just having a good time, weren't you? Her name was Jessica, by the way—but that doesn't matter, right? Poor girl. She was never the same. After you, she was an emotional wreck. Nothing but broken relationships and a failed marriage. Wow, you did some number on her. But at least you got laid, right? Should

I keep going? Nah. That could take forever. Although we do have all the time we need."

She pauses briefly and continues, "But you're starting to bore me, Kevin. Do you realize where you are yet? So many wrongs you've done in your life, Kevin, so many wrongs. It's hard to believe we didn't snatch you up before now. After all, you've been a self-centered, egotistical prick your whole life. But here you are, with us. By the way, nice touch having the Rojos boys killed. That really got your ticket punched to get you straight here, for sure."

Kevin is now deathly afraid. The woman walks in slow motion towards him, her eyes fiery red. She starts to look more sinister. Kevin stands up and slowly tries to back away from the woman. He says to her, "Snatch me up? I don't have to listen to this. I'm getting out of here."

He turns and tries to run to the door, or what he thinks is a door. The door vanishes. There are no exits. Kevin turns back around. The woman is now surrounded by multiple thugs and criminals, men Kevin either framed, tortured, beat or killed as a cop, including members of the Rojos gang he just had killed.

The woman looks at him. "These are some of your old friends. You know, all the lowlife scum you so hated. We thought you'd love to get reacquainted. They've been anxiously waiting for you after we told them about your pending arrival. Well, I think I'm done here. Too bad. What a waste of such a handsome face, at least before it blew off. He's all yours, boys…"

She winks at Kevin and blows him a kiss. The thugs quickly grab Kevin. As he starts to scream and struggle, they beat him severely.

"Your old friends will be escorting you out now."

The woman turns to walk to the bar. She pauses, turns around and walks back towards Kevin.

"Oh, I almost forgot. One more thing. Since none of those women you abused are available to meet you here…and I'm just not in the mood"—she moves in to whisper softly in his ear— "these obliging gentlemen, after they finish giving you a well-deserved beating, they will be having their way with you—entirely. So, buckle up, Kevin! You don't have to worry about ever being lonely again."

Kevin shrieks in horror as the thugs drag him through a black opening that suddenly appears in the wall. Kevin screams, "Help me! Help me! This is a mistake, I don't belong here. Nooooooooooooooooooooooo!"

Kevin screams as they drag him away. As quickly as it appeared, the black hole in the wall disappears. The muffled sound of Kevin's screaming fades into the distance. The woman walks away and sits at the bar across from Dante. "Let me have, um…let's see…a shot of Jameson's… and a beer, please," she says coyly, ordering the same drinks Kevin asked for.

As Dante pours her drinks, he and the woman look at each other and suddenly burst into sinister laughter.

"In flaming fire, He will inflict vengeance on them that know not God."

2 Thessalonians 1:8

CHAPTER 19

What Happens in the Dark Comes to Light

Back on the West Coast, private investigator Dennis Hatcher and LAPD detective Bill Stevens are getting ready for their sting operation. Their investigation and surveillance of Valerie has shown that she and her boyfriend, Alfonse, have been selling ecstasy in multiple clubs throughout LA. Now it's time to set up an undercover buy at a club. Bill will be involved inside the club, as he's is in his late thirties, with blond hair and blue eyes. As one of LAPD's top undercover detectives, his youthful looks allow him to fit in easily with the nightclub crowd.

Dennis and Bill meet outside of Sparkle nightclub, located on Santa Monica Boulevard in Los Angeles. Dennis knows the manager there and chats with him briefly. He comes back outside to meet with Bill.

"I have a few of my guys inside. They contacted Valerie at another club to set up the buy. They'll make the purchase and let her leave. As we discussed, you'll be by the bar, watch the transaction and follow her out to make the bust."

"Sounds great, Dennis. So, when is this girl Valerie showing up?" says Bill.

"She should be here shortly. We've watched her movements the past few weeks and she comes in here to sell ecstasy to a few select clients on Fridays. She shows up early and leaves early. She makes the rounds at a few other clubs with her boyfriend driving her. They're making some nice money. She handles mostly small transactions with only well-known customers. She sets up large deals in advance and takes off quickly once they're completed. She prefers to sell to middlemen, who then sell directly to their customers. It's much cleaner that way and involves far less interaction. My guys bought smaller amounts from her on multiple occasions after they gained her trust through some of our informants. Now that they've gained her confidence, they're setting up a much bigger buy. Only she doesn't know these particular clients are my guys."

"Nice. So, the plan is to put a little fear of God in her and get her to implicate your client's partner and husband in that Text Styles Inc. deal, right?"

"More like give her only one real choice. Hey, here she comes now. You better head inside."

With that, Bill goes inside and orders a drink by the bar, near the area of the club where Dennis's guys are waiting for Valerie. Valerie and her boyfriend, Alfonse, pull up to the club in a late-model black Camaro convertible. Alfonse waits in the car as Valerie heads inside.

Valerie is a very attractive girl, long dark hair and curves in all the right places. She's not the smartest, but she more than gets by on her good looks and cunning. She figures sleeping with Brad is her ticket to a better life. At that point, Alfonse will most likely get kicked to the curb. For now, she's playing the game. Little does she realize that Brad is only interested in her for sex, yet he convinced her to be involved in their plot to push Maggie out.

Dennis waits patiently while she goes into the club. Their undercover contact will signal them when the transaction goes down without a hitch. Dennis radios in to his undercover guys. "She'll be walking in any minute. She's wearing a yellow jacket and white slacks. Make the deal with her. Once she makes the sale, we'll grab her outside."

Dennis instructs two other detectives to stay near the Camaro, so the moment they nab Valerie, they'll grab Alfonse as well.

Valerie heads to the back corner of the club, to the VIP bottle service area. She takes a seat across from two Russian men who are waiting for her. They chat for a bit. Valerie reaches into her purse and slips them a small bag under the table. In return, they slip her a roll of cash, which she quickly puts in her purse. Dennis has another associate nearby, recording the transaction on his phone.

After a few minutes, Valerie gets up, gives them a superficial hug, and walks out the door. As she walks to her car, Stevens follows her. He lets her walk outside the club as she heads toward Alfonse, waiting in his car. Bill hurries up and walks directly in front of her. Dennis walks over to both of them.

"Excuse me, ma'am. LAPD."

He flashes his badge. Valerie turns around, realizing she's in trouble.

"I'll need that purse. You're under arrest for selling narcotics."

Valerie stands there, stunned. Alfonse, seeing what's happening, is about to pull away when the two undercover cops surround his car. They tell him to shut off the engine and step out of the car.

"Valerie, right?" says Hatcher.

"How do you know my name? Who are you?"

"You work at Text Styles Inc., for Kara Kline, correct?"

"Yeah, why?"

"Well, as I see it, you've got a big problem. Selling ecstasy. Not good. That's a felony in this town. Maybe I can get this nice detective to look the other way if you agree to help me."

"I don't know what you're talking about."

"Let's just say I know you helped Kara and Brad set up Maggie Hargrove. I need you to give me the proof. So, here's the deal. We'll let you walk on this drug deal and we'll get you immunity from prosecution if you give up Kara and Brad. Otherwise, you go down for both."

Valerie is scared and tries to bluff her way out.

"I don't know what you're talking about. I didn't sell anything. Those were friends of mine."

"Really? Well, those two Russian guys you call 'friends,' they work for me. I have every ecstasy pill you've sold them from the other clubs and phone video of you doing it. I got enough drug sale exchanges to make you do serious time. But I'm more interested in taking down Kara and Brad than busting you for your little side job. So, what's it gonna be?"

Detective Stevens opens her purse and pulls out the wad of cash. Dennis's undercover buyers walk out and hand Dennis their current purchase. Another associate walks over and hands him a phone, which Dennis holds up, showing Valerie the video.

"Well, isn't this nice? You're selling some ecstasy to these two gentlemen. So, let's cut the crap."

Valerie looks over at the two Russian men that set her up. She turns away and pauses for a moment. She realizes they caught her red-handed.

"I'm off the hook for the drugs and I get immunity if I give up Kara and Brad, right?"

"Yep. Sounds like an obvious choice to me."

"You've got a deal. I didn't want to be part of their scheme anyway. Brad made me do it."

"Yeah, I'm sure he twisted your arm. Did he twist it while you were screwing him, or after? Boy, that bit of info would really piss off Kara, wouldn't it?"

"Okay. I said I'll talk."

"But I'll need to know how you got Maggie to sign the bank papers."

"That was easy. I gave Crystal a contract that needed multiple signatures. Kara signed them in advance to make them look official. I went back to Crystal about an hour later and took back the documents, telling her Kara wanted to review something in one of the clauses. Crystal looked through it quickly and saw nothing out of the ordinary, so she gave them back to me. I took them back to my office and slipped the offshore bank transfer documents in among the other papers that needed signatures. I waited about twenty minutes.

"Kara made sure she and Maggie were hurrying out the door. She deliberately made them run late for an appointment as a distraction. When I stopped Maggie to sign them, she told me to give them to

Crystal. I told her Crystal already reviewed them, which she did, but before I altered them. Kara told Maggie to take a moment and sign them as she needed them to go out. So, as they were heading out the door, Maggie stopped and signed eight signatures in haste, two of them for the offshore accounts. After they left, I made copies and gave the originals of the offshore documents to Brad. He took care of getting the papers sent to the offshore banks."

"You have any of the copies?"

"I have a copy at my apartment. Brad told me to hold on to a set."

"Good. Let's swing by there and get it. So, we have a deal, correct? I assume you'd rather not go to jail."

"Yeah, I guess."

Dennis turns to Bill. "Bill, after we get the copies, take her downtown to get her formal statement on Kara and Brad."

Bill turns to Valerie. "We're going to let you and your boyfriend walk for now on the drug charges. I'll keep the drugs and video of the sale, just in case Kara and Brad try to get you to change your mind."

Dennis looks at Bill. "Tell your guys to let the boyfriend go."

With that, Bill gestures to the two cops, who tell Alfonse, "You've got a minute to get lost."

Alfonse jumps in his car, puts it in drive and speeds away.

Valerie gets into the back of Dennis' car. Dennis grabs Bill. "Thanks, Bill. Once we get the statement and proof, you'll get a nice big collar for taking down two embezzlers instead of an ecstasy bust."

"Works for me, Dennis."

The two get into their car and drive away with Valerie.

———

IT'S 3:00 A.M. BACK IN NEW YORK. RUBEN GOES TO HIS MOTHER'S house. His clothes are disheveled, dirty and singed from getting too close to the flames. His mother is lying on the couch with a bottle of pills beside her. He bangs on the door repeatedly. The door isn't locked. He pushes the door open and sees his mother lying on the couch, passed out. He picks up the bottle of pills. Vicodin.

He realizes his mother is probably hooked on the pain meds. He rushes over to her.

"Ma, come on, wake up, wake up! What the hell did you do?"

She's groggy. He shakes her a few times. She opens her eyes and looks at him.

"What is it? What is it? Stop shaking me! What are you doing?" She pushes him away, then looks at him and sees he's all disheveled. "What happened to you, mijo?"

He gets up and walks around, nervously looking out the window. She realizes something is terribly wrong.

"Ruben, tell me what the hell is going on."

He goes over to her and sits next to her on the couch. He is upset and starts to tear up.

"My Rojos brothers…they're all dead. We had a meeting. I went out to my bike to get a pack of smokes…then the next thing… I don't know…it just happened so fast. The building blew up. I got thrown into the air. The building was on fire. I tried to save them, but I couldn't get near it. I couldn't save anyone. I just got on my bike and rode. If I was in that building, I'd be dead too."

He gets up from the couch and starts to pace. He continues, "Look, I've gotta get out of here. I can't stay. It's too dangerous for me."

Rita, though drowsy from the Vicodin, is more alert now, simply from pure adrenaline.

"What are you talking about, mijo? What do you mean they blew up the Rojos? Who's they? A building blew up? Where? The clubhouse?"

"No, at the cemetery. We were there for a meeting—"

"The cemetery?"

"Ma, I don't have time to explain. I can't stay here. I've got to go. I need to leave now. They're gonna come looking for me. Whoever placed that bomb wanted all of us dead. Don't you understand? I was only outside to get a pack of cigarettes. I should be dead too. Just trust me. Please, trust me, for once, okay?"

Between the effect of the meds and the sudden shock of the news, Rita is distraught. She says, "Get out of here and go where? Where can you go?"

She puts her hands to her head and momentarily covers her face. She tries to compose herself. She looks at Ruben. "What do you want me to do?"

"Give me your car. I'll leave my bike here in the garage. I'll have someone come by in an hour with a truck and they'll get rid of it for me."

"Where are you going?"

"I've got a friend in Pennsylvania, in the Poconos. I can hide out at his place for a day or two. First, I'll head to Staten Island. My friend Rico has a place I can hide out till I take off for PA. I'll probably head west from there once I can get some stuff together. I gotta stay one step ahead of everyone and keep moving. I'll have my friend bring your car back in a few days. I'll call you when I get there."

"I can't believe this. I told you this gang would ruin your life."

"Ma, I don't need a lecture right now. I'll be all right, if I can get out of here. I'm still alive. If I get out, I can start over, I promise you, but I gotta go…now!"

"I love you, Ruben. Go."

She gets up, grabs her keys and hands them to him. She has a spare burner phone, which she gives to him.

"Give me your phone. Put whatever info you need in the burner now before you go. Here's a number you can reach me on."

Ruben kisses and hugs his mother, not knowing if this will be the last time he ever sees her. He heads out the door.

Rita watches him leave. She sits on the couch and starts to cry. She wipes her eyes and tries to compose herself. She knows she must stay alert, as someone could come knocking on her door looking for Ruben. She opens a drawer in the lamp table and pulls out a handgun, setting it on the couch cushion next to her as she blankly stares into space.

CHAPTER 20

Evil Versus Good

Maggie wakes up and heads to the kitchen of her apartment and brews a quick cup of coffee. As she waits for her coffee mug to fill, she turns and clicks on the TV. She grabs her coffee, sits on the couch and lights a cigarette. There's a reporter on the screen detailing the scene of a fire. In the background, what's left of a burning building is viewed behind him. She turns up the volume. The reporter is discussing the killing of the Rojos motorcycle gang at the cemetery last evening. Suddenly, a photo of Officer O'Connell appears on the screen. The commentator says, "In what may seem to be a related incident, Officer Kevin O'Connell was killed in his apartment by a bomb. He was killed instantly. Police are still investigating…". Maggie's face is overcome by shock. She drops her coffee mug, which shatters as it hits the floor.

Across town, Grace Williams glances at a newspaper headline that reads "Motorcycle Gang Killed in Explosion." Grace is walking along the street, and from a distance, she can see the Rojos clubhouse building. The building is roped off with yellow police tape. She's curious and encouraged to get a better view. She walks closer, standing across the street, watching the activity taking place and the investigators closely surveying the exterior of the scene at the Rojos clubhouse. The building is surrounded by police, who are awaiting a search warrant to enter the premises. Now that Officer O'Connell has been found dead, the police are scouring the city for any evidence of the bombing, the Rojos' involvement and anyone who could have been involved in killing O'Connell.

Yolanda Fauci is coincidently walking by. She sees Grace watching the police activity and strikes up a casual conversation. "Such a tragedy. Those men lived rough lives."

Grace looks over at Yolanda. "What a shame. It's not my place to stand in judgment of them. That's for my God. I hope and pray God has mercy on their souls."

"Yes, I hope so too, but some souls just renounce God and turn to darkness."

"I suppose, but God is merciful."

"Yes, He is, but He is also just. Some choose to stay in the darkness and ignore the light."

Yolanda looks at Grace. "I can sense you see things—things that sometimes puzzle you, right?"

"I do. How would you know that?"

"I can feel it all around you. Don't worry, child. It's a gift...from God."

"You may think I'm a little crazy, but sometimes... I see angels and demons."

"You're not crazy, you're blessed. You've been chosen by God. Your heart is pure, and your gift is meant to help others."

"I hope so. Sometimes the things I see are terrifying. Other times, the beauty is so intense, I can't even describe it. By the way, I'm Grace. What's your name?"

"I'm Yolanda. Nice to meet you. Grace... what a beautiful name. It fits you. Well, I better get going. I need to get to mass on time. Bless you, Grace."

"Thank you and may the good Lord bless you too."

"Oh, He has, in many ways." Yolanda walks away.

Grace seems a little bewildered. She looks across the street as police detectives are given the green light to enter the building and search the Rojos clubhouse. As they open the door, Grace sees demons fly out into the sky, almost as if they have been released from the building. She turns to look for Yolanda, but she's gone.

JUST OUTSIDE LENOX HILL HOSPITAL, CLAIRE ARRIVES FOR HER shift. There is a large scaffold surrounding the front of the hospital as there is extensive renovation work being done. Painters are on the scaffold, about two stories above the ground, near the employee entrance. The area beneath the scaffold is clearly roped off, but Claire ducks under the rope anyway to avoid walking further away to another entrance.

Dante is watching ever so closely.

"Time to claim my mercy killer's soul."

He creates a sudden gust of wind that violently shakes the entire scaffold. Workers are startled. The force of the wind knocks them over, and their bodies tumble towards the edge. They are literally hanging on to avoid falling off. If not for their safety harnesses, they'd have certainly plummeted to the ground. As the scaffold shakes and shifts, several large paint cans fall. One of the cans strikes Claire directly on her head with tremendous force. Claire is knocked unconscious and crumples to the ground. Witnesses scream. Others rush over to assist Claire. The workers on the scaffold are still hanging on.

About ten minutes pass before firefighters from FDNY Engine 39/Ladder 16 arrive to get them down safely. Claire is rushed inside to the trauma unit. She has sustained a traumatic brain injury and is in a coma. The doctors work to control the swelling and the internal bleeding.

A few days later, Claire is still in a coma with no signs of improvement. Dr. Walter Killen, who replaced Dr. Kirkland, is the chief trauma doctor who treated Claire the day of the accident. He goes in to check on Claire in the Neuro ICU. Claire's mother, Jane, and her uncle Charles are by her side.

Dr. Killen introduces himself. "Hello, I'm the head of the trauma unit here. I am also a friend of Claire's. She's one of our top nurses. We are all upset over this terrible accident."

Claire's mother says, "Thank you, Doctor. What's the latest prognosis?"

"Well, as you know, Claire suffered a serious traumatic brain injury from the blow of the paint can. The impact fractured her skull. We've done all we can do at this point. We've stopped the bleeding and there's no more swelling, but at this moment there's nothing for us to do but monitor her. We've seen head traumas like this before and they are dangerous. We'll have to just wait and see if she survives this. I'm sorry."

Jane is upset and begins to sob. Her brother consoles her.

Unbeknownst to all of them, Claire is hearing everything they are saying. *What are they saying? What does he mean there's nothing more to do? Hello! Can't you hear me? I'm right here. I can hear you, you know.*

Clare is trying to speak and communicate, but her lips aren't moving. They hear nothing. Her eyes are open with just a blank stare on her face.

"Doctor, what are the chances she won't ever recover? There's got to be something else that can be done," Jane says.

"I cannot say for sure, but her brain injury is very serious. In cases this severe, recovery is rare. All we can do is wait and hope. I'm not sure she'd ever recover fully, if at all. I really can't tell you more than that. I don't want to speculate. We need to just continually monitor her."

I might not recover, Claire thinks. *What are you saying? Do they think I'm going to die? What are you thinking, Mom? I'm still here. You can't be serious?*

Claire's uncle comments, "She's a strong woman, Doc. She'll get through this. This can't be it for her." He turns to look over at Claire. Looking back at Dr. Killen, he says, "There's got to be something else that can be done."

"Again, I'm sorry. There's not much more I can do at this point but wait and monitor her to see if there is any improvement."

With that, Dr. Killen excuses himself and leaves the room. Claire is frantic, but she can't move or speak. *Oh my God, do they think*

I'm going to die? Or do they think I'm in a permanent vegetative state? This can't be happening. God help me! God, please don't let this happen to me, please!

Grace Williams and Reverend Pitts walk into Claire's room. Jane is a member of their congregation. Jane greets them. "Reverend Pitts, Grace, thank you for coming."

Grace walks over to Claire's bed. She gently strokes Claire's hand while Reverend Pitts speaks to Jane. "Of course, Jane, we are here to help in any way we can. So, what are the doctors saying?"

"They're unsure, but it's possible she may never recover. I don't know what to do. Reverend Pitts, what do you think?"

Reverend Pitts looks over at Claire lying in the bed. "Isn't it too early to be thinking the worst? She may come out of it, but I'm not a doctor."

"I'm sorry, Reverend. It's not fair of me to ask you that. I'm so confused. I don't know what to think. If she never comes out of the coma, will we have to decide whether or not to keep her alive?"

"Don't put yourself through that agony," Pitts tries to reassure her. "Let's see what happens. Let's pray for the best outcome."

Grace looks at Claire and can sense she is aware. She looks at Jane. "She can hear you, you know."

"I'm sorry? What did you say?"

"I said she can hear you, every word."

Reverend Pitts, concerned, says, "Now, Grace. Let's not make any kind of diagnosis. That's not what we're here for."

Grace glances up and sees a beautiful angel over the bed. The angel gestures in a reassuring way, as if to signal she'll come out of it. Grace looks back at Claire. She says to Jane, "Oh, trust me, she can hear you. Believe it or not, she's fighting for her life right now. She doesn't want to die. She knows that you've been discussing her condition and she wants you to know she heard it all."

Jane is somewhat surprised at Grace. "What? How could you know this?"

"The angel above her told me. Oh, Claire is in there, trust me, and she wants to live. She doesn't want you to do anything. She's got some things she needs to correct before she leaves this earth and you can't interfere. She's begging you not to."

Grace is referring to Claire's secret mercy killings. Grace can sense that God is giving her a chance to change her ways.

"Angel? What angel?"

"The one that just told me she'd come out of it."

Jane, Charles and Reverend Pitts look shocked at what Grace said.

Charles replies, "But the doctors said—"

Grace cuts him off. "It's not up to the doctors and she's not alone. God is going to revive her. She's getting a second chance. She's going to come out of this. Believe in what I tell you—she is."

Reverend Pitts softly scolds Grace. "Miss Williams, this is highly inappropriate. May I have a word with you, outside?"

Grace strokes Claire's hand. She then grips Claire's hand tight and says a silent prayer. She lets go, and suddenly, Claire's head starts to move, and the blank stare has left her face. Her eyes blink. She lifts her head and looks at her mother.

Everyone looks on in stunned disbelief.

Grace looks at Claire. "Praise the Lord! With God, *all* things are possible."

The angel smiles at Grace and flies away. Claire feels a great sense of peace and starts to further awaken. This is truly miraculous.

Dante is in the room, looking on with another demon. He is furious. "Curse this Grace woman. Now they're using her to help my victims?"

Dante and the demon fly away in anger.

CHAPTER 21

The Police Investigation and the Truth

Following the murder of Officer O'Connell, Sergeant Combs is holding a joint meeting with the detective squad and the uniformed police officers. They are at the local police precinct and the room is packed as Combs addresses the group.

"Gentleman, as you know, Officer O'Connell has been murdered by a bomb that was delivered to his house. As difficult as this is for all of us, we owe it to Kevin to get to the bottom of this and find out who killed him. The Rojos gang was also killed by an explosive device at the cemetery. The crime scene shows this bomb was a well-made explosive device. This wasn't done by an amateur. The explosives used in this bomb match the explosives of the bomb at the cemetery. We have a sophisticated bomber on our hands, gentlemen, and we need to connect the dots immediately. There is strong reason to believe the cartel is involved, as prior investigations show them having the Rojos transport their drugs. We don't know how this connects to O'Connell, but we need to get to the bottom of this. Maybe Officer O'Connell was looking into their dealings and got too close. All I know is, no one, and I mean no one, kills one of our own."

"Don't leave any stone unturned. Shake every tree until something falls out. Come down hard on all your sources and informants. O'Connell is one of us. We need to bring whoever did this to justice. I expect you to provide updates to my staff on a regular basis and we need to know any important information immediately. Let's get out there and catch whoever did this. Officer Moran and Detective Petrizzo, please stop by my office before you head out. That's all for now, team. Let's go to work."

The meeting ends as Combs heads back to his office. Moran and Petrizzo follow closely behind. As they get there, Combs tells Petrizzo, "Give me a minute with Officer Moran."

Petrizzo waits outside as Moran walks in and sits down.

"John, how are you holding up? I know losing Kevin has got to be taking its toll on you."

"I am still pretty shaken up, Sarge. After the trial, the shooting and now this—I'm a wreck."

"Maybe you should take some time off. You know, enough time to get your head together."

"I think I may do just that, Sarge."

"Good. Try and get some rest. I'm gonna need you to help nail whoever killed Kevin."

"You can count on me, Sarge. I'll be okay."

"I know I can count on you. Quick question before you go. You were closest to O'Connell—anything about Castilla or the Rojos you might recall he was working on? The two bombings have got to be related somehow. I recall that Kevin seemed pretty agitated when he was getting released from the hospital after the shooting."

"Nothing concrete that I can think of. I know he sensed the cartel was working with the Rojos, but nothing in particular that he told me about."

Moran is obviously lying. He knows O'Connell wanted the Rojos dead, and he knew about it before the news hit the police scanner. At this point, he isn't saying anything, especially that O'Connell asked him for specific proof that Castilla was killed in the explosion, or the fact that, after he found out he wasn't, he and O'Connell were on their way to track down Castilla.

"Okay. If you think of anything, let me know. Go get some rest."

"Thanks, Sarge."

Moran leaves Combs's office and Petrizzo walks in. Combs motions for him to close the door. Petrizzo says, "How's John holding up?"

"Not too good. I told him to take a few days off."

"That might be the best thing, but this is going to be rough on him, especially after all they've been through together."

"I agree. Hey, Sal, I want you to go and lean on Ruben Castilla's mother. No one knows where Castilla is. For whatever reason, he wasn't killed at the cemetery. That doesn't make any sense. He's the acting head of the motorcycle club after Valles died. It would only make sense he would have been there—unless he was there and somehow was able to get away. Castilla's mother, she's got to know something. She happens to be a nurse at the hospital. She was working there the night of the shooting."

"Interesting. I'll get on that right away."

"Some of the guys have said that while O'Connell was recuperating in the hospital, he was talking about getting revenge on the Rojos for the shooting. We know that during Moran's trial, Castilla claimed O'Connell set them up the night Moran accidentally shot Medina. Moran was exonerated, but there are too many pieces of this puzzle that don't fit. Castilla would obviously have a beef with Moran and O'Connell."

"Makes sense, Sarge. O'Connell was a good cop and a friend, but he always seemed to want to control things his way. Kevin was always a bit of a rebel. I will lean on Castilla's mother."

"Good. Her name is Rita Damaso."

"I'm on it."

"One more thing…Moran. How much do you think he knows about any of Kevin's dealings? He was Kevin's partner and best friend. Kevin seemed to have a handle on the cartel and the Rojos. It would make sense Moran would know a lot of what Kevin was thinking. Moran's gotta know more about O'Connell's dealings with them than he's saying. Maybe there's something there we don't know about."

"They were pretty tight. If Moran does know anything, he's probably keeping it close to the vest. I'm sure he wants to nail whoever killed Kevin as much as the rest of us."

"I agree, but he just doesn't seem right. The rest of the team is really pissed off and he seems reserved and low-key about it. Maybe he's just in shock over O'Connell's death. Moran's a good cop. Keep an eye on him. He's shaken up. See if he tries to do his own investigation."

"You got it, Sarge."

"Whatever you find out stays between us for now."

"No problem."

Petrizzo leaves Combs's office and heads out. Combs heads out the door.

Later that day, Petrizzo heads to Lenox Hill Hospital to talk with Rita Damaso. He parks his car. As he gets out, he sees Officer Moran walking into the ER entrance in plain clothes. He thinks this is odd, since Combs said he was taking some time off. Moran walks in and goes to the main desk. He speaks with the head nurse seated behind the counter.

"Hello. I'm Officer Carlton," he lies. "I'm looking for Nurse Rita Damaso." Officer Carlton is another officer from the precinct who was on duty the night of the shooting, near the hospital.

"Rita is not working tonight. She hasn't been feeling well, so she took a few days off."

"I understand. Would you happen to have her address and phone number? I need to follow up on some information from the night of the shooting." Moran flashes his badge.

"Yes, of course, Officer. Let me get it for you."

The nurse retrieves the information and gives it to Moran, who thanks her and heads out the door. Petrizzo sees Moran leave. He walks inside and goes over to the same nurse behind the counter.

"Good evening, I'm Detective Petrizzo, NYPD. I'm looking for Rita Damaso."

"There was another officer just here asking for her. I told him she was out sick. He asked for her address and phone number, so I gave it to him."

"Oh. Okay. That's great. I didn't realize my fellow officer was also coming by tonight. We must have got our signals crossed. Would you be so kind and to give me her information as well?"

"Sure, Detective. Here you go."

"Thank you. Do remember the other officer's name?"

"Honestly, I don't recall. I think it started with a C... Carlton. He said his name was Carlton."

"Okay, great. You have a pleasant evening."

"You too."

Petrizzo heads out the door. He picks up his cell and calls Combs. "Sarge, Petrizzo here. Moran showed up at the hospital on his own to speak with Rita Damaso. She's not here. She's out sick. He asked for her contact info. Get this—he said he was Officer Carlton. What do you make of that?"

"I don't know, but something's up. Go straight to Rita Damaso's house now. I bet Moran's headed there. Text me the address. I'm going to send a backup patrol car and have them wait for you there."

"You got it. On my way."

Petrizzo texts the address to Combs and then punches Rita Damaso's address into his GPS and drives away.

Sergeant Combs hangs up the phone when another detective, Richard Mahoney, walks into his office.

"Hey, Sarge, I got some info for you."

"What do you have, Richie?"

"The night of the bombing at the cemetery, we had the investigative team at the scene. One of the officers was Eddie Geraci. Geraci just told me that while they were there, Moran radioed them and asked him to count the number of motorcycles that were outside."

"Okay."

"Yeah, but he asked for them to specifically look for a bike with a silver skull with red eyes mounted to the front fender."

"Interesting. Anything else?"

"Yeah, he asked them to check for the initials RC etched on the front fender in gold foil. Turns out that the bike wasn't there."

"RC...Ruben Castilla. Well, we know Castilla wasn't there, but why would Moran go out of his way to ask about his motorcycle?" Combs looks away for a moment. "Thanks, Richie. Keep a lid on this until I can piece it together."

"You got it, Sarge."

Combs realizes that Moran knows a lot more than he's letting on. He decides to call Moran.

"Hey, Sarge. What's up?"

"Aren't you home resting? Sounds like you're driving."

"I couldn't sleep. The doctor gave me a prescription, so I'm running over to CVS to get it filled."

"Sorry. I'm sure the pills will help. Watch those things. They'll knock you out for sure. Don't take it until you get home."

"I won't."

"Hey, I have a quick question for you. Did you know Ruben Castilla's mother was a nurse at the hospital? She was there the night of the shooting."

"I didn't know that. You think she knows where Ruben is?"

"Could be. We're going to investigate that. But don't you worry about that. Go home and get some rest."

"That's the plan, Sarge."

"Talk to you later."

"Okay."

Moran suddenly realizes Combs is digging into all leads. He must find Ruben before Combs does. Ruben can connect the cartel to the Rojos bombing, and the cartel can implicate O'Connell and Moran. He needs to find Ruben and kill him. Combs, meanwhile, calls Petrizzo and tells him Moran just lied to him. He tells him to get to Rita's house as fast as he can.

Moran arrives at Rita Damaso's house. He seems a bit nervous. He sits in his car, thinking about what he's doing. He gets out of the car and approaches the door. He starts banging on it.

"Rita Damaso, open up. This is the NYPD. Your son is in danger. I need to speak with you immediately."

Rita is asleep on her couch and is startled by the banging. She grabs her gun from the side table and puts it behind her back as she approaches the door cautiously. She peeks out through the peephole.

"Rita Damaso, you need to let me in."

Rita is startled and a bit frightened. "Show me your ID," she yells from the other side of the door.

Moran holds up his shield and ID. Rita squints through the peephole and suddenly realizes who Moran is.

"I know who you are. You're the cop who shot Manny. You and that other cop set him up."

"That was an accident. We didn't set him up and I was found innocent. You need to listen to me. Your son is in trouble. The cartel is looking for him. They killed the rest of the Rojos, and they want Ruben dead. We can protect you and your son."

Rita doesn't know what to do. She is now frightened for Ruben, who told her the cartel would come looking for her. Maybe this cop really is trying to help her. She decides to let him in. Moran acts as calm as he can.

Still guarded, Rita opens the door, a crack, holding the gun behind her back.

"Listen, I know you don't trust me, but we need to get your son. His life is in danger. These people killed my partner, Officer O'Connell. They blew him up as well. They won't stop until Ruben is dead. We can protect both of you. Where is he?"

Rita is a bit frantic. She looks past Moran and notices he's by himself.

"Who's we?" she asks.

Moran remains calm and tries to reason with her, tries to get her to feel a bit more comfortable with him, more trusting.

"Look, I'm trying to look out for Ruben. I'm trying to make things right. I need to know where he is before things get out of hand. You don't want the cartel to find him before we do."

Rita is silent for a moment, thinking to herself. "I don't know. He left a few days ago."

"Was he driving his motorcycle? A car?"

"He took my car and left, that's all I know."

"Give me your registration and plate number. I'll wire the plate in and put an APB out on it to see if they can find him. I need to leave. Please give me the info now! I will radio the local police and send someone to come get you and take you to a safe place."

Rita hesitates. After a moment, through the crack of the door, she slips him a piece of paper and gives him the information.

"Keep the door locked. A police unit will be here shortly."

Rita pauses, now deciding to trust Moran.

"I know where he is. He's at a friend's house in Staten Island. He's leaving in the morning for Pennsylvania, then the West Coast. You need to get him before he leaves and take him somewhere safe."

She pulls out a piece of paper and writes down the address.

"Mrs. Damaso, we are going to help you and Ruben. Wait here for the police unit."

Moran leaves and heads out to his car. He sits in his front seat, staring at the paper with the address. This is a crucial moment for him. He knows Combs knows he lied. Is he going to drive to Staten Island and kill Ruben? Then what? How does he explain that? Self-defense? Is he going to set this poor kid up for a second time? Moran starts to sweat.

Just then, Detective Petrizzo shows up. He pulls his car right behind Moran's. He sees Moran and radios Combs.

"Hey, Sarge, I'm at Rita Damaso's house. Moran is here. Something is going on. Send some backup."

"Don't let him leave. They'll be there in five minutes."

Petrizzo gets out and walks over to Moran's car. Moran is sitting there sobbing. Petrizzo walks around to the passenger side and gets in.

"John, what the hell are you doing out here? I thought you were home resting."

At that moment, Moran breaks down. The pressure is just too much for him.

"Sal, I can't take it anymore. I've got to come clean. I can't live like this anymore."

"Talk to me, John. I'm here to help you."

"Kevin arranged for the cartel to kill the Rojos," Moran blurts out. "It was revenge for the shooting. I didn't know about it in advance and I didn't know it was the cartel. He told me after the fact. I assume they killed Kevin, but I don't know for sure. Believe me, if Kevin had anything going on with the cartel, I wasn't involved. Whenever I asked him about anything, he told me to mind my own business."

"Anything else?"

"Kevin was annoyed Ruben wasn't killed in the blast. He must not have been there. He had me radio the guys on site to search for Castilla's bike at the cemetery. It wasn't there. He wanted him killed with the rest of them for what Victor Valles did. He said we needed to get to Ruben first so no one could implicate him."

"Rita Damaso. Is she inside? Is she safe?"

"Yeah, she's fine. I came here to find out where Ruben is. He's in Staten Island at this address. I told her we would protect her and Ruben from the cartel."

"We'll definitely do that. I'm sure he'll want to testify."

Petrizzo dials Combs.

"I'm with Moran. Rita Damaso told him where Ruben is. He's in Staten Island. Here's the address."

Petrizzo gives Combs the address.

"I'll get some detectives over there. Your backup should be arriving."

Within minutes, police sirens can be heard in the distance as they approach Rita's house.

The backup police unit pulls up in front of the house. Petrizzo sends them inside to get Rita Damaso.

Petrizzo looks at Moran, who is clearly shaken.

"Hey, you did the right thing by telling me."

Moran looks at Sal. "Sal, I don't know what I was going to do. The thought crossed my mind to either help Ruben escape or kill him to protect Kevin. I don't know what I was thinking with Kevin being dead and all."

"It's over now. You didn't hurt anyone. We'll get to Ruben and protect him, and we'll put the cartel away for good. We'll get Ruben to implicate the cartel, and we'll get him and his mother into the witness protection program."

"Sal, there's more I need to tell you."

"What's that?"

"The night I shot Medina—it was truly an accident. I thought Medina was pulling a gun and we struggled, and my gun went off. He was only pulling a piece of paper out of his pocket. I panicked. Kevin punched Ruben and knocked him out. Kevin planted the knife on Medina to make it look like I shot him in self-defense. He figured that would keep us from being suspended for harassing Medina. He pulled them over for no reason. He profiled them. When he saw Ruben's Rojos vest in the back seat, he started to harass them. Kevin always liked to let them know that this was his town, not theirs."

"John, you should have told the truth. If it was truly an accident, then you would have been okay."

Moran looks over at Sal. "Kevin didn't want to take that chance. We could have been suspended. I could have been brought up on manslaughter charges, lost my job and my pension. I panicked and Kevin thought that planting a knife made it cleaner. Plus, Ruben had some weed and pills in his pocket, so we did have them on possession of narcotics. That was all legit. Except for the knife. It was in the glove box."

"John, the truth is always better. You've had to carry that guilt around. You also smeared the reputation of Medina, who apparently was known at the church as a good man. It's time to come clean and face whatever punishment you deserve for the coverup."

Just then, Combs calls Petrizzo.

"We got Castilla. He was at the house. We're taking him into protective custody. He's going to cooperate. We told him his mother is okay and that we have her too. Make sure you get Rita Damaso to safety. He's going to tell us all he knows and then we'll issue warrants for Diego Jimenez's arrest. I don't know why Moran was there on his own, but he may have solved this case."

"Yeah, there's more to it, but he's coming back with me and we'll talk to you when we get back to the precinct."

"Okay. I'll see you when you get here."

Petrizzo looks at Moran and puts his hand on his shoulder. "John, you did the right thing. You probably saved Medina from the cartel, and you just let go of a great burden that's been weighing you down. Kevin was our friend and our brother in uniform, but he made his mistakes. He made a bad situation worse and it got people killed. He made his choices, but it's too late for him. You get to wipe your slate clean."

"Thanks, Sal. You've always been a voice of reason. That's one reason why you're a great detective."

"I'm your friend first, John, remember that."

Petrizzo and Moran leave and drive back to the precinct in Manhattan in Petrizzo's car.

Matthias appears with two of his angels. He says to them, "Tonight was another example of how there's always hope that someone will realize the error of their ways, confess and do what is right. Mr. Moran is hopefully back on track. The truth has set him free for now."

With that, Matthias and his angels fly away into the night sky.

It's the next morning at the police station. Moran is sitting in one of the interrogation rooms alone. The door opens. Moran's attorney walks in with the district attorney and the head of Internal Affairs.

Moran's attorney, Phil Gottleib, speaks. "John, based on your confession, here's the deal. We spoke to Ruben and he implicated Diego Jimenez in setting up the meeting with the Rojos at the cemetery. We arrested Jimenez this morning. Phone records show communication between Jimenez and O'Connell, including a call from Jimenez to O'Connell right before O'Connell was killed. Ruben confessed that the Rojos were transporting drugs for the cartel. He also told us they were meeting with Jimenez at the cemetery that night. Cell records show Jimenez calling Ruben from just outside the cemetery gate before the explosion. He is receiving immunity for agreeing to testify against the cartel and will be put into the witness protection program.

"As for you, the DA is going to bring charges against you for obstruction of justice, tampering with evidence and conspiracy to commit a felony with Kevin for planting the knife on Medina. We are considering that Kevin did all of this, but you're a cop and you know better. You could have stopped Kevin from planting the evidence. We interviewed Ruben again about that night and he confirmed you shot Medina by accident. Since the shooting already went to trial and you were found not guilty, and further considering all that has transpired, there will be no new charges for manslaughter."

Moran looks up. "So, what happens to me?"

The DA responds, "If you plead guilty to the charges, you are suspended immediately. If convicted, you will be terminated from the NYPD and you will lose your pension. Because your act of finding Ruben led to us bringing down the Rojos, we'll push for the minimum sentence. You're probably looking at eight to fourteen months in a minimum-security correctional facility. You'll probably do six months with good behavior."

Moran responds, "I understand. I'm good with this. It's time the truth came out. We destroyed Manny Medina's reputation by planting the knife and concocting the story. It was an accident, but he didn't deserve to have his memory smeared so we could save our careers. Kevin's gone. Manny's gone. I need to move on by telling the truth."

The DA tells Moran's attorney that they have a deal and they leave the room. Gottleib, alone in the room with Moran, says, "John, Ruben only implicated the cartel in the bombing of the Rojos. The investigation will link the cartel to Kevin, but not you. You were never connected to the cartel. There is no evidence of you being involved with Kevin on this. You didn't have to confess what you and Kevin did that night to Medina."

"Yes, I did. I couldn't take it anymore. Kevin was getting in too deep. He was pissed off that Ruben wasn't killed in the Rojos bombing. He wanted all the Rojos dead for shooting him. He said that to me in the hospital and I said nothing to anyone else. He was on his way to meet me to go find Ruben when the bomb blew up in his apartment. I assumed he wanted us to kill Ruben. I don't know what I would have done. I can't keep going down the dark road that Kevin was on."

Gottleib says, "During the discussion with Ruben, he stated Valles shot Kevin and Benuti as revenge when you were found not guilty. He said Valles watched the verdict on TV and was enraged."

"Well, there you have it. My little charade with Kevin setting up Medina has caused all this mess. Indirectly, Kevin got himself and poor Tony shot in the process. I deserve what I get for my part in this. Maybe Ruben can start a new life. At least maybe I helped him do that."

Moran's attorney gets up to leave. In walks another man in a blue suit.

"I'm Special Agent James Scofield of the FBI. I'll be processing Ruben Castilla and Rita Damaso into the witness protection program. We have had this cartel under surveillance, and this finally let us bring them down. Thanks for your efforts."

The FBI agent is Matthias.

Moran says, "Don't thank me. I'm a piece of shit. At least Ruben and Rita get a clean start and the cartel is going behind bars where they belong. I'm no hero. I just did the right thing for once."

Matthias looks at him. "It's never too late to do the right thing. You had a choice to keep going down the wrong road and you chose not to take it. That takes courage. Yeah, you'll pay a steep price for your actions, but you cleared your conscience. You did the right thing."

"Thanks for saying that. You sound more like a priest than an FBI agent."

Matthias laughs. "Hey, with all the evil you and I witness, it's good to see some of it come to an end and someone step up for the truth. I'm sure Medina's family will feel a tremendous sense of relief that he didn't try to attack you. He was an amazing young man, you know. He worked hard with the troubled kids through the church. In fact, he was always trying to get Ruben to quit the Rojos and change his life."

Moran looks down in shame. "I'll always regret that night. It was an accident. He was taking a flyer for a sports camp out of his pocket. I thought he was going for a gun. It happened so fast. I made a terrible mistake. I have to live with it for the rest of my life."

"You knew the truth and now you've corrected the story. You ended the lie and gave Medina's family back their son's reputation. Whether you realize it or not, that's a blessing to you as well. Move on and truly change your life. I've got to go. Best of luck to you, Officer Moran."

"Thanks, Agent Scofield, for your encouraging words."

With that, Matthias leaves the room. Moran sits silently alone.

"Anyone who seeks truth seeks God, whether or not he realizes it."
—Saint Teresa Benedicta of the Cross

CHAPTER 22

·········

Clean Slate

t's a brisk Monday morning in Edmonton, Alberta, the outskirts of Canada. Ruben steps out onto the porch of a modest white house, surrounded by lots of land. His appearance is much different. He's dressed in a crisp white shirt, with an emblem attached to the left of his chest that reads "Frank's Mechanic Shop." His worn-out jeans have been replaced by dark blue Levi's, a bit more conservative for a former gang member. His demeanor is much calmer, as he seems more at ease with the world.

Ruben steps back inside the house. Beyond the front door, inside the house, are some boxes stacked on top of each other, some partially unpacked. The inside of the house is a bit mundane, with paisley furniture, a dark wood dining room table with matching brown fabric chairs and a china cabinet situated in the corner of the room. Amidst the chaos of the unorganized room, Ruben looks over at the boxes and begins rummaging through one of them.

"Mijo, what are you looking for?" asks Rita as she enters from the kitchen, holding cleaning supplies and a bucket.

"I was trying to find that book Agent Scofield gave me. You know, the one about Canada?"

Rita goes over to a box next to the cabinet. She pulls out a book and points to it. "This one?"

"Yeah, that's it. He told me about some museum here. I was gonna check it out after work."

Rita laughs. "You, going to check out a museum? Now that's a first."

"I figured we might as well get to know more about our surroundings, get to know Edmonton a little better, other than just work and stay home every day. An idle mind—"

Rita interrupts him quickly. "Ruben, we've only been here a month. Give it time. Before you know it, you'll know all the ins and outs of Edmonton. This is our fresh start, remember that."

Ruben takes the book from his mother and goes over to the couch and slumps down. She follows him and sits beside him.

"What's wrong, Ruben?"

"I'm sorry I got you involved in this. I know you loved your job at the hospital, your house, everything. You had to give up so much in New York."

"It's okay, mijo." She rubs his head. "First and foremost, I'm glad that you're okay. That was always my concern. Plus, I'm getting myself clean here, and working with those unwed mothers is more fulfilling. Maybe that's what I was supposed to do, and look at you, Hector Figueroa, looking all professional," Rita laughs while grabbing the collar of his shirt.

Ruben shakes his head. "I wonder why they picked that name for me. Do I look like a Hector?"

"You know that was my great-grandfather's name. That's a great name. Now Lupe on the other hand, I'm not too sure about that one, but oh well, Lupe I am."

"Tell me the truth, Ma, do you miss New York?"

Rita sighs heavily. "I miss the places I frequented, but other than that, no. You?"

Ruben remains silent and breathes heavily.

"It just takes some getting used to, that's all. Mijo, you didn't belong in that gang life. Even Manny knew it. I'm going to say this and then I'm never going to mention them again. The Rojos gang got exactly what they deserved. You were spared for a reason, and now you get to live your life without them bringing you down."

Ruben nods his head, gets up and heads toward the door. "I'll see you later."

He walks out the door and gets into a jacked-up blue car. He revs up the engine and backs up out of their driveway and out onto the road and speeds off, leaving a cloud of dirt behind him. Rita goes back into the kitchen.

Ruben pulls into his place of employment: Frank's Garage. Frank, the owner, comes out of his office smoking a cigar.

"Hey, Hector, you had a visitor today."

Ruben seems nervous, wondering who could've been looking for him.

"Who was it?"

"Some lady. She said you did a great job on her car and it never worked better. She wanted to thank you again."

"Oh, great!"

"You act like you saw a ghost or something. You okay?"

"Yeah, of course. It's just, I don't know many people here other than you and the guys, so I was just wondering who could've been looking for me."

"No worries. You do great work, Hector. Sometimes, getting any type of acknowledgment goes a long way. You'll get used to it."

"Yeah, I guess I've gotta get used to it. I'm gonna fix that motor-cycle engine from yesterday."

"Cool. By the way, later this evening, a couple of us are going to the festival. You should come, get to see the town a little."

Ruben nods. "Yeah, okay, cool. I'm there."

LATER THAT EVENING, RITA PARKS OUTSIDE A BUILDING. SHE gets out and grabs a large bag from her trunk and walks inside the building with a sign on the brick façade that reads "Mary's Place." It's a halfway house for unwed mothers. A young woman is sitting at the desk as Rita walks inside.

"Hey, Lupe, you're early tonight. As a matter of fact, I thought you were off tonight."

"Yeah, I am. But I brought one of the new girls some stuff from home she could probably use."

"You know you're their saving grace."

"No, not really. I'm just somebody who knows the struggle. One day we'll talk, and I'll fill you in."

The phone rings.

"Yeah, I can hardly wait to hear your story." She picks up the phone and answers, "Mary's Place."

Rita walks toward the back as Mary continues with her conversation on the phone. She goes in one of the rooms, where a young woman, around eighteen years old and pregnant, is getting situated in her new surroundings. Rita taps on the door. The young woman seems excited to see Rita. She runs over to her and gives her a sincere hug.

"Hey, I got you some things that maybe you can use." Rita dumps the stuff out onto the bed.

"Wow, thank you!"

"It's really nothing. It's just stuff I figured it's time for me to get rid of."

As the young woman is looking through the stuff, Rita notices the young woman's nose starts to bleed profusely, dripping onto one of the pieces of clothing and the bed. Rita's nursing instincts quickly go into action.

"Oh no, I'm so sorry." The young woman gestures.

"It's okay. Just sit down, lean your head back. I'm going to pinch the top of your nose, closest to your sinuses."

Rita applies pressure for a few moments and the bleeding stops. She grabs a tissue from the dresser and hands it to her.

"You're okay, but I wanna check your pulse."

Rita places her hand on the young woman's wrist and times it with her watch.

"Have you eaten today?" she asks her.

"I had some oatmeal early this morning."

"Is that it?"

The young woman nods.

"Okay, well, we're going to get you something from the kitchen."

"Am I okay? Is the baby okay?"

"You're fine. You just have to remember to eat."

"Thank you. Where'd you learn that from?" the young woman inquires.

"What do you mean?"

"You know, pressure check and everything. The only people I've ever seen do that is the doctor and nurses at the clinic."

Rita shies away from the comment at first. "Let's just say some things you never forget."

With that, Rita gets up and heads out of the room and out the front door of the building. She gets in her car and thinks about what she did. She then starts her car and drives off.

Over in the corner of the building is Dante, watching the young girl through the window as she looks at herself in the mirror, admiring the clothing Rita gave her. Suddenly, something falls out of one of the pockets. She picks it up. It's a baby picture of Ruben, and on the back of the picture is his birth name and place of birth. She tucks in her dresser for safekeeping.

CHAPTER 23

Liberation

t's a late evening back in New York. Maggie is just finishing up in the bathroom, washing off the day after returning from her evening class at FIT. She wraps her wet hair up in a towel and heads into the living room. She sits on her couch and puts her feet up to relax. Her classes are really going well. These young students have truly ignited a spark in her that has been gone for a while. Maybe this is truly her turning point. The news of O'Connell's gruesome death still haunts her, especially after he stopped by to visit her just days before. Each time she thinks of him joking with her, she sadly smiles. She knows she needs to keep moving in the right direction and teaching is allowing her to do that, otherwise these events, which she can't control, will continue to destroy her emotionally. She knows it's time to quit the diner and leave the shooting behind once and for all. By focusing on teaching, she can begin to rebuild her life, and maybe get a new apartment on the West side, start fresh again.

Her thoughts are quickly interrupted when she hears her cell phone ringing on the kitchen counter. She jumps up and rushes over to answer it. It's Dennis Hatcher on the other line. She quickly picks up.

"Hey, Dennis, is everything okay?"

"We got 'em, Maggie! We got 'em!"

Maggie walks over to the couch and slumps down in shock. "What? You're kidding. How?"

Dennis excitedly responds, "We nailed Valerie setting up a drug sale in a club and she gave up Kara and Brad. I went to the DA and they'll both be in handcuffs shortly."

"I can't believe it. This is a miracle. How'd they do it? I mean, get my signature on a fund transfer document?"

"A little bit of the old sleight of hand. They distracted you in Kara's office and made you sign it as you were leaving. Valerie doctored the paper to make it look like the one you were going to sign earlier."

"I knew that bitch Kara set me up. Well, now they'll get what they deserve."

"You'll be asked to press charges. Bottom line, once your board of directors knows the truth, you'll get your company back."

Maggie sits back in amazement and a huge smile comes across her face. A tear falls down her cheek.

"I don't know how to thank you. I can't believe it. I just can't believe it. Finally."

"Well, it's nice when the good guys win. We'll be in touch with more details. If I were you, I'd go celebrate."

"That's exactly what I'm gonna do. I can't thank you and Mark enough. Thank you. Thank you!"

Maggie hangs up the phone and lets out a loud scream of joy as she runs around her small apartment. She calls her sister.

Kate answers with a concerned tone. "Maggie, you okay? Why are you screaming?"

"They caught 'em. The investigators caught Kara and Brad! They're getting arrested and I'm getting my company back!"

"Oh my God! How? This is amazing! I told you not to give up!"

Maggie sits back down on the couch, still in amazement, holding the towel securely around her body.

"Get dressed and meet me at Harrigan's Bar on Second Avenue in an hour and I'll give you the details. We're getting drunk tonight, girl!"

Kate screams on the other end of the line before hanging up. "Oh my God. Okay. I'll see you there. Love you! I'm so happy!"

Maggie quickly gets dressed and heads out to meet her sister.

———

BACK IN LA, BRAD IS SEEN COMING OUT OF AN EXPENSIVE FIVE-star restaurant with an unknown woman. The parking lot attendant takes both of their tickets to retrieve their cars. They're flirting with one another as they wait. He seems preoccupied with his late-night rendezvous. His cell phone rings, but he avoids answering it, continuing to engage his flirtatious date. His cell phone rings again; he declines to answer. The attendant drives up in the woman's dark green Range Rover. She proceeds to tip him. The unknown woman plants a seductive kiss on Brad's cheek, implying some sort of intimacy between the two.

She glides into the driver's side of her car and waves to Brad as she pulls off. Brad's cell phone rings again. This time he answers it, annoyed. The caller is John Greer, one of the sales associates at Text Styles Inc. that Brad is friends with.

"Hey, Brad. You're not going to believe this, but the police just arrested Kara! They just took her away. The word is they're looking for you."

"Wait, what? What're you talking about?"

"The police were just here at the office. We were headed out after our team meeting and they were waiting for Kara downstairs by the parking garage. They put her in handcuffs."

The attendant pulls up with Brad's Maserati. He jumps in without tipping the attendant. Still on the phone, Brad, visibly upset, continues to probe John.

"What the hell is this all about? Is anyone talking?"

"Someone overheard them say she was being arrested for embezzlement. Someone also overhead the detective asking if you were in the building. I don't know what's going on, buddy, but they're looking for you for questioning."

Brad abruptly hangs up and jumps onto the highway. He makes a quick call to his attorney, Paul Johnson.

"It's Brad, what the hell is going on? I heard the police just arrested Kara!"

"It's not good, Brad. Where are you?"

"I'm headed toward the office."

"I suggest you meet me down at the police station."

"Why?"

"As your attorney, it's not a conversation we should be having over the phone."

Brad punches the steering wheel in anger. "You act like I killed somebody."

"I'm acting like your attorney, Brad. Like I said, it's best you meet me at the station if you want to avoid being humiliated here at the office in front of your employees."

"Humiliated! I don't get it."

"I'll be waiting for you out in front of the police station."

"Fine."

Brad gets off at the next exit, headed toward his fate at an LA police station. He parks his car and walks towards the entrance, where Paul Johnson is waiting for him.

"What's going on, Paul?"

"It's not good, Brad. Valerie cut a deal with the police. She gave them all the details of your scheme with Kara."

"Shit. That little bitch. I told Kara—"

Paul places his hand on Brad's shoulder.

"Just keep quiet. We're going in there and you are voluntarily surrendering."

"What are the charges?"

"Conspiracy to commit embezzlement, grand theft and whatever else they can throw at you. The board of directors is going after you and Kara hard. Do me a favor—say nothing. I'll have your bail posted right at the arraignment."

"I can't believe that little bitch Valerie ratted us out. I took good care of her financially, more than she ever made."

Paul nods and responds, "Yeah, except her and her stupid boyfriend, Alfonse, had a little ecstasy business going on the side. The cops set up a sting and got her to roll on you for immunity on the drug charges. What in the hell were you thinking, Brad?"

"Shit. Am I screwed?"

"Let's figure out your defense later. Just go in there and swallow your pride and keep your mouth shut."

Brad and his lawyer walk in and Brad surrenders to Detective Bill Stevens.

"Bradley Collins, you're under arrest for conspiracy to commit felony embezzlement, felony grand theft larceny and felony wire fraud, which is a federal offense. You have the right to remain silent. Anything you say can be used against you in a court of law. You have the right to talk to a lawyer for advice before we ask you any questions. You have the right to have a lawyer with you during questioning. If you cannot afford a lawyer, one will be appointed for you before any questioning if you wish. If you decide to answer questions now without a lawyer present, you have the right to stop answering at any time. Do you understand these rights?"

"Yeah, what do you think? My lawyer is standing next to me, isn't he?"

Paul Johnson shoots Brad a dirty look as if to tell him to shut up.

"You are being taken into custody, pending your arraignment tomorrow before the judge."

Brad frowns. "You mean I have to spend the night in this cesspool?"

Stevens glares at him. "Look at it this way—it'll give you a chance to get used to it. Take him away."

With that, two uniform officers escort Brad out of the room and to a cell on the lower level. Brad's attorney walks out of the precinct.

Bill Stevens turns to a fellow detective. "Every now and then, it's nice to see one of these assholes gets caught. What he and Kara did to Maggie Hargrove is pathetic. The felony wire fraud is enough to send him away for a while."

Stevens walks back to his office and dials Dennis Hatcher. "Yo, Dennis. The attorney got Collins to surrender. He's in custody."

"Nice. Text Styles Inc. wants him and Kara put behind bars. This embarrassment is hurting their reputation. It was bad enough they forced Maggie out. Now they have egg on their face for getting duped by Kara. They've got some damage control to deal with."

Stevens sits back in his chair, pleased. "For sure. I'm certain they'll welcome Maggie back with open arms to calm things down. Thanks again for the lead. The captain is really happy with this collar."

"No problem. Next time we're out, I'll remind you to pick up the tab."

"You got it. Talk to you later."

"Take care, Bill."

Stevens hangs up and puts his feet up on his desk.

BACK IN NEW YORK, MAGGIE'S CELEBRATING AT HARRIGAN'S Bar. She's sitting at the bar, waiting for Kate, doing shots and laughing it up with the bartender. Her sister walks in. Maggie waves her over.

"I see the party already started." Kate gestures.

"Hey, Kate. Just in time for the next shot of tequila! This is Chris, the best bartender in New York. At least he is tonight!"

"I'm sure he is."

Chris greets Kate. "Nice to meet you, Kate. Can I pour you a shot?"

"Hell yeah! We've got lots to celebrate."

Kate grabs the stool next to Maggie and hops up. She holds up her glass and offers a toast to Maggie.

"To Maggie. The bastards got their due!"

They toast and swallow down their shots.

"Yep, I hope one day I get to see that bitch in her orange jumpsuit. Maybe I'll design one for her. After all, Kara needs to be stylin' behind bars. Wouldn't want her looking like the rest of the common criminals."

"I see the tequila is kicking in. So, tell me what happened," Kate demands.

"Honestly, I listened to what you told me last time we met—you know, about getting my life back. So, I hired the Hatcher brothers, the private investigators. Turns out, Valerie, the intern, was in on it.

They caught her dealing ecstasy in a nightclub and got her to give up Kara and Brad to save her ass from getting busted."

"But how did they get the account under your name?"

"Can you believe they doctored a document they wanted me to sign, making me think it was something else? They created a diversion and asked me to sign it when I was heading out the door in a rush. Basically, it transferred company funds to an offshore account in my name, making it look like I was stealing money."

"Those bastards."

Chris pours them another shot. Kate lifts her glass, motioning Maggie to lift hers.

"Well, here's to the Hatcher brothers!"

They clink glasses and quickly down another shot.

Maggie smiles with enthusiasm. "I got a new lease on life, Kate. Things are going to be different. I'm going to open a small satellite office here in New York. I want to avoid that whole LA scene if I can. I'll go back and forth, but I'd rather be here. I'm also gonna keep that teaching job at FIT. I'm gonna make an apprentice/scholarship program to help some of those kids. They really lifted my spirits."

"That's great. I'm so happy for you. This whole thing took you to a depressing place. At one point, I thought I was losing you."

Maggie looks down at the bar, knowing she herself felt like she was losing it as well.

"Trust me, I doubted myself. I started losing my faith in humanity. But, hey, that's enough of that. We've got drinking to do."

"You're right. Chris, the best bartender in New York, another round, please!" shouts Kate.

After a few more shots, Maggie staggers to the ladies' room. She starts singing in the stall when someone walks in and hears her.

"Good night, huh?" a woman's voice utters.

"Yes, a great night," says Maggie from behind the stall.

"It will be, regardless of the situation—remember that."

Maggie opens the stall and looks out as the door to the bathroom closes. There's no one inside. In her tipsy state, she pays little attention to the woman's words. Instead, she washes her hands and walks back to the bar.

"Where's Kate?" she asks the bartender.

"She said she needed some air."

Maggie puts down a hundred-dollar bill for the shots and walks outside to find Kate standing in front of the bar. They're both feeling no pain from their multiple shots of tequila. Kate pulls a pack of cigarettes out of her pocket; she slips a cigarette in her mouth and lights it. Maggie's caught off guard as she's never seen Kate with a cigarette.

"Hey, when did you start smoking?"

"Shit, after that fifth shot of tequila. It's only when I drink."

They both laugh loudly.

"You want one?"

"Nah, believe it or not I'm trying to quit, at least for this week." Maggie looks over at Kate fondly. "You know I love you, sis?"

"I love you too."

They hug each other. Kate affirms, "So, don't forget tomorrow we're going to plan that trip, right?"

"Yes, a vacation of a lifetime! The beaches in Belize, with nothing but sun, sand, booze and tan men. Here we come!"

"Okay, I've got to get home. I do believe I'm drunk, really drunk. I have to be up by six to open my shop."

"Right, that and rushing home to be with that man of yours."

"That too," Kate laughs.

"Okay, okay. Talk to you tomorrow."

Kate grabs Maggie for another long hug and then starts to walk down the street. Maggie's just about to cross at the corner when a white Mercedes sedan pulls up to the light. A well-dressed woman is driving with a young child in a car seat in the back. Suddenly, out of the darkness, a man in a hoodie and ski mask pulls a gun and bangs on the driver's window.

"Get out of the car, bitch!"

He opens the car door and starts pulling the woman out, dragging her by her jacket. The woman screams at the top of her voice.

"Help! My baby's in the car! Help!"

Maggie hears the screaming and sees the commotion. She runs toward the man.

"Hey, leave her alone!" she shrieks at him.

Maggie jumps on his back as the woman is screaming. Kate hears Maggie's voice and quickly starts back toward the bar. She sees the disturbance.

"Maggie! Maggie!"

Kate runs over to the car and sees the little girl in the back. She opens the opposite-side back door and grabs the child out of the car seat. Maggie has her arm around the assailant's neck and can somehow pull him off the woman. The woman, still screaming, runs from the car to her child on the ground with Kate. The assailant breaks Maggie's hold and gets behind the wheel. A few people start running out of the bar to help. But it's too late. The assailant looks at Maggie intensely with rage, points his gun and fires twice. Kate looks up in shock as the attacker quickly speeds off. Maggie, full of adrenaline, tries to chase after the car, not realizing she's been shot. Suddenly, just a few feet away from the chaos that occurred, she drops to her knees as Kate watches in terror. Maggie falls over onto the ground. A pool of blood forms beneath her.

Kate runs to her, screaming at the top of her lungs as others look on.

"Maggie! No, no! Maggie! Somebody, help us!"

Kate clutches Maggie tight and caresses Maggie's lifeless body in her arms as her moans of anguish quiver in the night air.

CHAPTER 24

Afterlife

The night is somber, and the commotion is over. There's nothing left in the solitude of the moment. Maggie opens her eyes to see smoke and fire in the isolation of darkness. She's confused, although aware of the incident that transpired. She looks around and the street is still. Harrigan's Bar is unlit and looks desolate just as everything else within her view does. She slowly rises to her feet. She feels around on her body, looking for the gunshot wound or blood. But it is as though she was never shot. There's no wound or blood to be found on her, not even on the ground where she lay. In the stillness of the night, she hears what sounds like hissing. The sound frightens her. She quickly looks to her left and then to her right, but she sees no one.

She walks over to the unlit bar. The windows are covered in shabby pieces of wood. She pulls a piece of wood off to look inside beyond the broken glass. It's empty inside. There's no bar, no barstools or tables, no pool table, no alcohol behind where the bar once was and no people. Maggie thinks she's dreaming until she looks out of the corner of her eyes and sees a figure coming toward her. Its dark shadow rises from the ground and approaches her. It's Dante. She's terrified even more. As he speaks, the hissing sound is harsh.

"Come with me. See? There is no God to save you. Come with me and I'll help you get revenge on him and all the rest who've screwed with you in your life."

Maggie's fear of him disables her. She's frozen. She tries to run in the other direction, but her feet become wedged in her shoes

225

and her shoes stick to the ground like a rat's glue trap. He and his demons come closer. His fiery red eyes gaze at her.

Maggie screams, "No! No! Leave me alone. Help me, God! Help me, please!"

"Come now, Maggie. You didn't deserve this. Let's make this bastard and the others pay," Dante murmurs in the night air.

"Stay away from me! Leave me alone!"

"I'm the only one who will really help you. Come with me," Dante demands.

Maggie closes her eyes, not wanting to stare into his flaming red eyes. Suddenly through her closed eyes, she feels a sense of calm overtake her. She opens her eyes to a flood of light from above that illuminates the entire street, blinding Dante and his demons. The angel Matthias swoops down and carries Maggie's spirit upward, away from the demons and Dante. The angels that dive down with Matthias fend off the demons, who flee under the ground. The street rumbles and cracks, shifting its appearance and turning into solid gold, shimmering brightly and lighting up everything in sight. The bar shrinks beneath the ground and a huge bed of roses appears in its place. They are in the purest of colors.

The angel Matthias looks down over at Dante. "You've won nothing here, fool! This soul is not yours to take."

"Curse you and your God," Dante screams up at him.

Dante hurls a ball of fire towards them, but Matthias blocks it with a gust of wind he forces from his hand. Dante curses Matthias and plunges beneath the ground, enraged.

What seems like seconds later, Maggie now finds herself standing in the playground of her childhood school. Across the way, she sees herself and Kate as young girls, laughing and playing on the swing set. As they laugh and tease each other, joy overcomes Maggie. She smiles and suddenly hears a voice beside her.

"Remember those days with your sister? Remember how you used to play and just loved being together?"

Maggie looks over and sees a woman, an acquaintance from before.

"Wait, you're the lady from the church, Yolanda. I met you there when I was upset over the shooting. You spoke to me."

"Yes, that was me, child. I've always been around to watch you."

"To watch me? Who are you?" Maggie questions.

"I'm kind of an angel. You are someone I was assigned to help. Now I'm here to take you forward."

Maggie looks around. As she turns, there's a pleasant scent in the air and the playground vanishes. She sees nothing but beauty: rolling hills of wildflowers, mountains draped by a bright blue sky. She then starts to see everything in life she loved, like a View-Master toy with stereo images, flickering in slow motion. First is her dance school, next playing hide-and-go-seek with her friends and pillow-tossing sleepovers. Her house decorated for Christmas, and her friends' trick-or-treating on Halloween.

"What is this place, Yolanda?"

"This is the gateway to heaven. That's up ahead. Let's just say this is your road there. We all have one."

Maggie shakes her head. "I don't deserve to be here."

"Why would you think that, Maggie?"

"I'm divorced. I tried to kill Kara, my partner. I wanted revenge on her and Brad. I've done some dreadful things in my past, things I thought were unforgivable. I just don't belong here."

Maggie looks around.

"My dear, you do belong here. Fear and anger drive everyone to the brink of breaking. You were pushed into things that were beyond your control. These things almost broke you. But you didn't break, because deep down you had a faith that held them back. Trust me, the evil one tried to push you over the edge. He manipulated others to try and destroy you. But with everything you went through, you never gave up hope. Even at your darkest moments you cried out to God and asked Him to help you. Even though He sent me and others to help you, you helped yourself. The love you had deep in your heart made you trust your faith, and that trust in God spared you."

Maggie looks away. "You don't understand, I…I've done things, horrible things, things that are unforgivable, and not just to me but to innocent people to—"

"Your child?" Yolanda interrupts.

Maggie looks over at Yolanda in shock. A tear falls from her eye. Maggie remains silent for the moment, remembering one of the most difficult times in her life, a time where she felt so alone. She was in her second year of college, an exciting time in a young person's life. Everything seemed to be coming together for her and her future, not only in her academics but in a flourishing relationship. She was dating a young man, a science enthusiast. She met him during a science group meetup. Although she was never keen or interested in scientific facts, she thought she'd humor her roommate at the time and attend one of their assemblies. For years Maggie had placed the memory of him deep down in a black hole, never to bring up his name again. She considered it a serious relationship, one that would grow into a marriage proposal, a white picket fence in a place she would call home. But the fairy tale wasn't quite what he had in mind, and by the time Maggie was aware of this, she was already three months pregnant and hadn't told a soul.

She remembers the feeling of embarrassment and fear of what her family would've thought of her. And her young man, the one she had fallen head over heels for, his discontentment when she told him the secret she had kept. Instead of joy, Maggie was faced with displeasure. She'd have to make this decision alone—one that she felt would define her for the rest of her life. She confided in her roommate, who knew of a place that would accept Maggie's four-month pregnancy and rid her of a problem that existed in her life. Standing there with Yolanda, Maggie recalls how she showed up to this small clinic, two hours away from the college.

The embedded recollection of a medicinal smell when she walked into the clinic still exists in Maggie's subconscious. The dull blue walls covered in an amateurish art collection, something that a child would've created, always seemed to haunt her in her dreams.

She sat across from a doctor after her examination. He was young then, handsome yet detached. His name plate sat in front of her on his desk as he explained to her in graphic detail about the procedure, the one that would allow her to continue in her college journey, as he so simply stated. Dr. Kirkland was oblivious to Maggie's concerns, especially after seeing the sonogram.

Maggie looks at Yolanda, removing herself from the memory for that moment.

"No one knew," Maggie shrieks.

"He knows everything, Maggie," Yolanda gently voices.

"I didn't know what to do. I thought about abortion, I did, but I…"

Maggie lapses back, to her memory of Dr. Kirkland and his echoing thoughts of what was best for her. His cold and uncaring demeanor made Maggie feel uncomfortable and unsure of herself. Yes, she wanted to finish college to make her parents proud, she wanted to have a career, but how would she be able to do that as a single parent? She left Dr. Kirkland's office that afternoon, sat in her car and cried for a few hours. She remembered praying and it was then that she realized she could still have it all. Lots of women had done it, but what was most compelling for her was that she had a choice. With the help of her professors, she found a way finish her courses for the remaining six months of her pregnancy. It was hard, sometimes almost impossible, but she made it work in the best way possible. In the fall, she gave birth to a beautiful, healthy baby boy.

Yolanda grabs Maggie's hand, offering reassurance.

"You spared him and gave him life, Maggie, and you gave him a home. A loving family and a place of safety. You might have thought it was unforgivable, but you saved lives."

"I didn't want to give him up. Yolanda, I wanted him, I loved him. I just couldn't give him what he deserved."

Yolanda tenderly touches Maggie's shoulder. "Maggie, you gave him exactly what he needed, and he knows you loved him."

"How?"

"From the moment you touched his little hand and gave him to his adoptive mother and father. Trust me, your son knows, and soon enough you will too."

Maggie is mystified but trusts Yolanda's words.

"Through all the darkest moments of my life, I felt God just wasn't there. I selfishly felt like I didn't deserve what happened to me."

"God was always there, and He was listening. He never promised life would be easy, Maggie. In fact, sometimes it's very hard. Sometimes we feel like we're not going to make it. Yet, through it all, if you have faith, He will deliver you. You just don't understand the depths of His ways. But you will, shortly. His love for you is never-ending."

"But how can He forgive the things I've done? I don't deserve to be forgiven."

"Nonsense. You just don't understand God's compassion and mercy. Take your last day. You sacrificed yourself for that little girl and her mother. Those are the acts of unselfish love that have always defined the real you. Not the times when you stumbled. You see, the love that lies deep within your soul always rises to the occasion. That's who you really are. Through all the difficulty and the pain, the real you was always in your heart. Do you remember Alice Perez?"

Maggie thinks for a moment. "Yes, she was one of my students at FIT."

"Well, what you didn't know about was her troubled life. It wasn't just the drug addiction of her mother and father, and her father's overdose; she also contemplated suicide many times. Your designs inspired her to try and make something out of her life. It was no accident she was in your class. When you encouraged her as your student, you unknowingly healed the pains in her soul. Your kindness saved her life."

"I saved her life? Really?"

"Yes, Alice will go on to inspire hundreds of others throughout her life. She will follow in your footsteps as a great designer. Your simple act of kindness towards her did that."

"I never knew I could impact someone that way. I know I loved teaching and sharing my passion for design, but I never knew."

"People underestimate the power of kindness. It is the simplest form of love. Throughout your life you did that countless times."

"So, I really do belong here?"

"Yes, like I said, dear, you do. Remember this. God is merciful and forgiving. His compassion is immeasurable. He, unlike any person, knows the true intention of every heart."

Maggie begins to cry tears of joy. Yolanda gently embraces her, and Maggie faintly hears a voice from behind her. Yolanda whispers in her ear, "This is your road."

Maggie turns. "Hey, sugar smile!"

She looks out upon the face to the voice; it's her father, Bill, who affectionately called her 'sugar smile' as a child. Her father looks young and healthy, not at all like he did when he passed.

"Daddy!" Maggie yells in excitement and bewilderment.

She runs to hug him like a child missing their father. Tears of joy flow from her eyes. Bill's once-frail body has been returned to its original physique of strength. His once-gray complexion is now a glowing appearance. Even his voice, although easily recognizable to Maggie, is stronger and more boisterous, as it once was before throat cancer took it completely.

He hugs her tightly. "I've been waiting for you."

Maggie melts in his arms. She takes in a long, deep breath.

"I always watched over you from afar. I'm sorry I missed so much in your life, your dance recital and school plays. All those years before, I tried my best to keep a roof over our heads. I know at times you thought I didn't care. I just never wanted you girls and your mom to know I was dying of cancer. That was my deepest regret."

Maggie looks up at her father. "That's okay, Daddy. I know how hard you worked to take care of us."

"No, it wasn't okay. I remember so many times I disappointed you. I remember your dance recital when you had that red señorita costume. You know, with the castanets? You looked so beautiful. I was on my way there and I got called into work. I had a big fight with my boss, but he was going to fire me if I didn't show. Your mom told me how you cried when you saw I wasn't there. That broke my heart. Yet, no matter how many times I didn't come through for you, you always told me how much you loved me. You always melted my heart, sugar smile. I'm sorry I wasn't the dad I should have been."

"Mom always told us how you never meant to disappoint us. I understood later what you were suffering when you got sick. You tried so hard to take care of us. I always loved you. You're my dad and I'll always be your little girl."

Bill wipes away tears as Maggie continues to sob and cling to her father.

"I love you too, sweetheart."

A whistling wind chime is heard from afar. Bill looks away for a moment and then down at Maggie.

"I think it's time you and I get going. There is so much for you to know and see."

"If I'm going with you, Dad, I'm ready."

Yolanda is close by, listening. "My job is done here, Maggie. You're in good hands with your dad. I've got others I need to attend to down there."

"I love you, Yolanda. Thank you for watching over me."

"I love you too, dear."

With that, Yolanda fades into the backdrop of the paradise's beauty.

Bill takes Maggie's hand and they start walking down the beautiful tree-lined road. They talk along the way as the wind whistles behind them. Up ahead is a striking radiant light in the far distance. Maggie's soul lives on.

Back on earth, in the present moment, Maggie's body that night lies in the street, covered in a sheet. Police have blocked off the area and talk to witnesses at the scene. An ambulance waits to transport the body to the morgue. Kate, covered in blood, is sobbing and is being attended to by EMT personnel. Angels and demons begin to swirl around all the people on the street, anticipating whose souls will be taken next.

"In each of us, two natures are at war—the good and the evil. All our lives the fight goes on between them, and one of them must conquer. But in our own hands lies the power to choose—what we want most to be, we are."

—Robert Louis Stevenson

EPILOGUE

Years passed and seasons changed, but some things remained the same in the land of the breathing. Kara was arrested and received a class B felony for embezzlement and fraud, resulting in a five-to-twenty-year bid in jail and a fine of fifteen thousand dollars. Considering her fate, she struck a deal with the district attorney and her sentence was reduced to three years. She's now serving her time in a women's correctional facility in Chino, San Bernardino County, California, east of Los Angeles. For her, living life lavishly and hobnobbing with the rich and famous became a thing of the past. Instead she'd walk the corridors of a jail filled with woman who had committed white-collar crimes. Her attire would consist of a light blue button-up shirt and dark blue khaki pants, designed by the women's correctional facility and stitched by the convicts themselves.

Brad, on the other hand, once arrested, continued to maintain his innocence up until the day of his trial. It was quite the news story. A man of his stature in the LA community made for great headlines. Yet during his trial his innocence was put to rest once Kara and Valerie testified that he was the mastermind behind it all—taking Maggie down, money transfers, taking over the business and even muddying Maggie's name. His jail time resulted in twenty years. He would spend every waking hour behind bars in one of the oldest jails in Los Angeles considering the easy way out, suicide, and every day for him would be a never-ending nightmare. His once-extravagant existence, just like Kara's, would end up in shambles; we could only imagine how life for them would move on. Would they be compelled to make the right decisions once released? Or would they resort to their old ways and see their life, after death, altered?

Officer Benuti remained with the police force, after months of recovery and rehab. He's fighting crime and often makes a visit to the diner where Maggie once worked, always placing one white flower near the station she was assigned to. He often strikes up a conversation with a familiar face, a construction worker with a tag on his jacket that reads Matthias.

Often, we come across those whose lives were saved, like Claire the mercy nurse. Upon her imagining life without living, and the hell that awaited her, she repented and was given a way out, a chance to change her very being. But, sometimes, even when given the opportunity to make amends, some fade back into their old ways overlooking the departure that may await them in the afterlife.

Grace Williams continues to see the supernatural, a true gift from God. Unlike a medium, who talks in generalities in their readings, Grace's visions come with complete detail. Grace remains at the church, assisting the Reverend Pitts, although she has quite the following of people who want to talk with her. The congregation is growing to this day. An anonymous donor bought the property that was formerly the Rojos clubhouse. It was donated to the church and has been turned into the Franklin Watson Community Center. The center is a wonderful community outreach facility for children and adults with a wide array of programs and activities.

Cookie, after the revelation from Grace that her mother was reaching out to her in a vision, worked on changes in her life. She has stayed clean from drugs and is no longer a prostitute. She began taking computer classes and is working on finding a real job. She meets with a psychological counselor to help her deal with some deep emotions and issues with depression she still struggles with. She became active in the local LGBTQ community by helping youth who have been bullied. Cookie also started volunteering at the Watson Community Center, as a tribute to her late friend.

Maggie's sister, Kate, is the most tragic figure left behind. She was never the same after seeing Maggie killed.

Yet, in honor of her sister, she established the Maggie Hargrove Scholarship Fund at FIT, providing free tuition to countless students in need of assistance. Kate even arranged to pay off the remaining tuition of Maggie's entire class. She even got Alice both an internship and a job after graduation at Text Styles Inc. Kate is currently working on creating a new art design studio at Elgin High School in Illinois in memory of Maggie.

With the loss of both Maggie and Kara, the board of Text Styles Inc. appointed a new head of the company, a young Italian woman named Caterina Giosti. By coincidence, she was a huge fan of Maggie's and worked with Maggie extensively on a major project between Text Styles Inc. and her top Italian design firm in Rome.

Earl still runs the diner with Stavros. Stavros thought about leaving after his wife died, but Earl convinced him to stay. Lexi's moussaka recipe is the main special on Greek nights at the diner.

The Hatcher brothers are still doing their investigative work. After uncovering the scandal at the company, the board at Text Styles Inc. has given them a retainer contract to follow up on trademark infringement violations. Alfonse, Valerie's boyfriend, didn't take advantage of his good fortune from Valerie's confession and wound up getting busted on drug charges.

And although everyone's story remains to be told, those who are amongst the living, existing in a world full of choices and decisions, we often wonder about others whose lives were taken due to greed and evil intentions.

Like Manny Medina, for instance. What became of his soul?

Manny awoke to the front of a golden gate, and on the other side was a huge baseball field. It was crowded, filled to capacity with onlookers. As he stepped beyond the gate, it simply vanished into the background. He walked out onto the field as the crowd bellowed his name, loudly and energetically. For him, it was a dream come true.

As a young boy Manny always dreamt of playing professional baseball in the major leagues. He tried out a few times, but it never worked out for him. So, he did the next best thing and worked with the kids in his neighborhood every summer, teaching them the sport he loved. But now, in this place that was so familiar to him, he was the center of attention and it was the major leagues.

As he looked up into the stands, he could see his grandmother, Amelia. She was standing on her feet, clapping, cheering and yelling his name. Farther out in another section of the stands, he saw a young boy, about seventeen. He looked familiar. Manny remembered him from an incident that happened in his neighborhood. He was the boy killed one summer, a year after Manny started working with the kids, shot by a stray bullet through his parents' living room window. Manny recalled the impact his death had on his teammates and in the community. He, too, was cheering Manny on in the stadium. Every section of the stands had someone that Manny knew, somebody who, in one way or another, played an important role in Manny's life.

He stood on the pitcher's mound, holding a baseball in his hand. He looked down at the glistening dirt beneath his feet. It wasn't at all like the soil in the field near the church. The field itself was rolling green from every position you stood; the whiff of freshly cut grass overwhelmed the air. He looked over at all the field positions. First baseman, second baseman, shortstop, third baseman, left fielder, center fielder, right fielder and the catcher—all eyes were on him. His other teammates observed him with anticipation from inside the dugout. It was everything his heart desired and he felt an abundance of calm, even while standing before a cheering crowd. He locked eyes with the batter at home plate. Manny rubbed his fingers together, tossed the baseball from one hand to the other, rolled it in his pitching hand. He threw his arm back and shifted his standing position. He lifted his right leg and threw the baseball with everything he had in him. The ball traveled like lightning, once, then twice, then three times, striking out the hitters of the opposing team, one right after the other.

In a matter of what seemed like seconds, the game was over, and Manny was being carried off the field by his teammates, celebrating their win. He then found himself on a road, and just up ahead was that same gate; he was still holding a baseball in his hand. As he looked out further, he could see beyond the gate. The stands floated above the billowy clouds and they were covered in glimmering gold. Manny smiled with contentment as he slowly walked toward the gates once more and the angels welcomed him.

SOULS, sensations and thoughts, desires and beliefs that perform intentional actions—they are essential parts of who we are. When we pass from this life to another, our SOULS will be judged by God and it will be determined whether our journey leads to a place written of songs of praise, streets of gold, of gates of pearls, stone as clear as crystal and He who sits at the throne. Yet, as we wait our fate and judgment, there is told of another place where our SOULS can or may reside, written as eternal suffering, darkness, a torment of wickedness and an eternal separation.

In the end, we must consider and acknowledge the existence and the relevance of internal judgments and decisions of the external choices we make in this life. It is a never-ending battle; which will you choose?

BOB TODARO

———

Bob Todaro was born and raised in New York City on Staten Island and now resides on Long Island in the town of Floral Park. A life-long Catholic, he is a product of the parochial school system and is a graduate of Monsignor Farrell High School. Bob holds a bachelor's degree in business administration from Bryant University in Rhode Island and a master's degree in theology from the Seminary of the Immaculate Conception in Huntington, New York.

Bob spent his career in the beverage industry, working in sales, marketing, and brand development.

After completing his degree in theology, Bob continued to study the Christian faith. The topic of spiritual warfare and its effect on our everyday lives is one of the driving forces leading Bob to collaborate on writing this series.

For more information, visit
BOOKSBYBOBTODARO.COM

HOPE HOLLINSWORTH COAXUM

Hope Hollinsworth Coaxum is a long-time resident of Yonkers, New York, and a member of Community Baptist Church. She is a novelist, a playwright, screenwriter, producer, and director of various theatrical works and short films significant to social cause. Hope is the wife of Antonio Coaxum and a mother of two, her earthly child, Nicole, and her heavenly child, Courtney, KIA 09/09/07, and a proud grandmother. Hope has been instrumental in organizing and creating various programs, writing workshops, and events related to homelessness, domestic abuse, and child abuse. Her third published novel, *A Gift of Sunshine*, which was also developed into a theatrical production, won the Betterment of Community Award. Her other novels are *A Juicy Story*, *Delusional*, *Everything Necessary*, and *Once Upon a Place in Time, The Rebirth*. Her documentary, *The Diary of a Mother*, explored losing a child and was also written and produced for the stage. Her other theatrical work and films include *Never Judge a Book by its Cover* and a short film, a psychological thriller, *The Smile of a Monster*, which won the audience choice award at YOFI Film Festival and debuted on Cablevision. Hope is a community advocate, establishing and co-founding two community-based organizations, Hope Healing and Growth and The Mothers' 2016. She is devoted to her military family of veterans as president of the Gold Star Mothers of Yonkers and Westchester County and launched a County Tie Drive appropriately named after her son.

For more information, visit

BOOKSBYHHC.COM